The Last Husband
Forever Love #2

J. S. Cooper

www.jscooperauthor.com

JMC Creations

Copyediting by Carolyn Pinard-
Carolynpinardconsults@gmail.com
Editing and proofreading by Editing Queen-
Editingqueen@outlook.com

CONTENTS

Acknowledgments 6
Chapter 1.. 7
Chapter 2.. 25
Chapter 3.. 62
Chapter 4.. 83
Chapter 5.. 116
Chapter 6.. 143
Chapter 7.. 194
Chapter 8.. 217
Chapter 9.. 232
Chapter 10.. 252
Chapter 11.. 291
Chapter 12.. 321
Chapter 13.. 348
Epilogue... 358
OTHER BOOKS 363
Connect With J. S. Cooper 364

Acknowledgments

Thanks goes out to: The Cooper Gang aka The Zane Fan Club, for all the love and support they have given me, my favorite Wakefield for all her late nights with my novel, my family and friends who have supported my writing and read my very first pieces of work, my dog Oliver for sitting faithfully by my side as I type away and God, for without him nothing is possible.

Chapter 1
ZANE

"Zane, I want you to look after your little brother, Noah, okay?" She looked at me with an intense look in her sky blue eyes. Tears were threatening to fall and ruin her mascara, and I could tell something wasn't quite right.

"Yes, Momma." I sucked on my strawberry lollipop with relish, as only a 6-year-old could do, anxious for her to let me go and ride my bicycle outside with my friends.

"You're the bigger brother, so you're in charge." Her grip tightened on my hand and I winced. "I love you, Zane. Take care of Noah while I'm gone."

"Can we go for McDonald's fries later?" I asked hopefully, not appreciating the gravity of the situation. "And get milkshakes, too?"

"You know McDonald's is only for a treat, my love." She half-smiled, but the turn of her lips didn't quite match the sorrow in her eyes.

"But, Momma," I pouted with big, wide eyes. "Please."

"I have to go, Zane. Your father will be back soon." She kissed me quickly and held me close to her. "Remember I love you."

"I love you, too, Momma." I continued sucking on my lollipop, unaware that was

going to be the last time I'd see my mother. But her words always stuck with me. "Take care of Noah." That had been the only request she had for me. And I had failed. Love meant nothing if you couldn't be there for the ones you loved. My mother had failed me and I had failed Noah. I didn't want to fail anyone else.

Blinding bright yellow rays of light shone through the uncurtained windowpanes, and as I opened my dry, heavy eyes, an unfamiliar feeling of well-being filled my soul. For a moment, I wasn't sure why the dream hadn't awoken me with a heavy heart, but then I remembered that I was with Lucky, and she always made me feel all right. I grinned to myself as I thought about the almost bed-breaking sensual seduction of the passionate night before. I turned around carefully in the bed so I wouldn't wake Lucky, and a feeling unlike any I had known before consumed me. It wound its way up from the tip of my toes, through the tendons in my legs, shuffled in my belly for a few seconds, and then exploded in my heart as I watched Lucky sleep. She slept as peacefully as I imagined an angel would, and I wondered at how this captivating and beautiful woman had given me a chance. There was something about the way she smiled in her sleep that comforted me and made me smile back, even though I knew she couldn't see the grin on my face. She smiled as if she was content, and somehow that made me feel happy. It delighted me that I could make her feel that way because she filled an emptiness in me that I never knew existed before.

I thought about how miserable I had been the few nights before without her in my bed. How my head had pounded when I had thought she was with that dog, Braydon. I had wanted to break something so badly just thinking about it. I had barely been able to sleep. In fact, I had nearly banged down Lucky's door, and was ready to kill Braydon. Just thinking about him made my blood boil. I wanted to beat him up so badly. Braydon had consumed my thoughts for the last year and I was ready to see him locked away. When I thought Lucky was interested in him, I felt like I was going to explode. I'd been beside myself with jealousy and anger.

I watched Lucky sleep and I wondered what I would have done if she had slept with him. As a dart of pain pierced through me at the thought, I shook my head. A part of me knew that Lucky wasn't that kind of girl. She wouldn't have me in her bed one night and Braydon the next. She just wouldn't do that. I knew I had to learn to let go of my fears and trust her.

I stroked her back slowly, tracing my finger from her neck and down her spine, and then ran it over her hips. Her skin was soft and delicate, and I grinned as she moaned and rolled over towards me. Her eyes opened slowly and her brown eyes squinted their anger at me for awakening her.

"Good morning." I leaned forward and kissed her nose, unable to stop myself from touching her with my lips. She was like a drug to me, intoxicating me with her mere presence.

"I'm not awake yet," she moaned, but a shy smile spread across her face as she closed her eyes again.

"What do you want to do today?" I whispered in her ear and she giggled as my breath tickled her eardrum. The sound of her giggles brought a smile to my face and I blew in her ear so I could hear them again.

"Sleep." She brought her arms around me and pulled me down towards her and then buried her face into my shoulder and kept her arms wrapped tightly around me. "I just want to sleep."

"But why are you so tired, my dear?" I grinned, relishing the feel of her naked body up against mine. Her skin was warm, silky,

soft, and lush, and it was teasing me delicately as it caressed my hard exterior, making me think all sorts of naughty thoughts.
"You know why," she said coyly.
"Hmmm." My hands cupped her butt cheeks and brought her in closer to me so that she could feel my morning erection against her. "Are you saying you're too tired for another round?" I wanted to take her then and there. I wanted to feel myself inside of her, moving with abandonment until she screamed out and moaned my name in pleasure.
"Yes, I am."
"What if I tell you I'm taking you to London?" I said impulsively, not even sure what I was saying. The thought popped into my mind that maybe I could get her to join the mile high club.
"London?" She pulled away and looked at me with shocked eyes. "What are you talking about?" She looked bewildered, her expression reminding me of a lost baby bear, and I laughed.
"Would you like to go?" My voice was soft and I considered making my statement a real possibility. After the week that we'd had, maybe a trip was needed.
"I'd love to go one day." She yawned as she nodded and I laughed before caressing her

face. I ran my finger down the pink tinge of her cheek, and then took in her full appearance. I started laughing hard, unable to contain my gut-wrenching chortles.

"What's so funny?" She frowned. "Is this some sort of bad joke? Are you punking me?"

"No, sorry. I just think you're in need of some of your chia." I laughed as I looked again at her frizzy mass of hair.

"Chia?" She looked confused for a moment and then realization dawned. "You mean Chi? Ass." She hit my shoulder and ran her hands through her hair. "Welcome to the realities of dating a girl with curly hair."

"So we're dating then?" I asked lightly, watching her face intently and trying to ignore the pounding in my head. I felt exhilarated yet scared at her words.

"Well, I …." She paused and looked up at me with a slightly worried expression. "I thought after last night that—"

"Lucky, I'm joking." I shook my head in chagrin and forced a smile. "I suppose it wasn't a funny one." I chuckled and Lucky rolled her eyes.

I didn't know how to tell Lucky that I was still trying to figure out my feelings. How could I explain that a part of me wanted to be with her and never let her go, but another part of me wanted to run and hide and pretend we had never met. That part of me wanted to close my heart again so I could protect it from the unknown. I so badly wanted her to know how I felt inside, but I knew that she wouldn't and couldn't really understand.

"No, not really." Her eyes held a question that I ignored.

"I'm sorry." I ran my hands down her hair and kissed her on the lips. "Let me take you to London to celebrate." I brought up London again, hoping we could focus on something else. I wasn't ready to get into another conversation about feelings.

"Celebrate what? And what about the documentary?" She frowned. "Sidney Johnson is expecting us to come back with a video camera soon."

"You're such a dedicated worker, aren't you?" I laughed and brought her face closer to mine. "I don't know that I've ever met such a hard worker before." I kissed her lips lightly again, enjoying the sweet taste of her and wanting to lose myself in her essence.

"Zane," she groaned, her eyes twinkling at me. They reminded me of liquid chocolate, so warm and silky. I loved her eyes, they seemed to pull me into her world and never let me go. Sometimes I daydreamed that I could jump into her irises and just remain there, surrounded and warmed by her soul.

"Okay, okay." I pulled away reluctantly, loathe to leave her heady heat. "I thought we could go to London because you know so much about British history. I'm sorry I don't have a time machine or I would have taken us back to the '60s and we could have gone all out during the Civil Rights years."

"Actually, I would have wanted to go back to 1954, that way I could have asked Thurgood Marshall what he was thinking when he won *Brown vs. Board of Education* and then seen what we could have done to make sure it was implemented a bit better."

"Sorry, you lost me," I admitted wryly. "I barely understand and remember King Henry VIII and his, 'Off with their head!'"

"You would remember that." She laughed and I resisted the urge to kiss her tenderly.

"So, would you like to go?" I wasn't sure why I was pushing the issue. Maybe I felt like a trip abroad would cement what we had quicker than just letting everything run its course. Though, I wasn't sure if I needed to cement the relationship to myself or to Lucky. I wanted her to be mine. Yet, I didn't want to think about what that meant too deeply. There

was still too much I had to take care of in the other areas of my life.
"I've always wanted to go to London," she responded thoughtfully. I stared at her breasts as she stretched, though it was hard for me to concentrate when all I wanted to do was caress and bite them.
"But?"
"I don't know." She sighed. "I just don't want you to spend the money on me. It's too much."
"I have it and I want to spend it." I sighed as well, annoyed that she was using money to prevent me from spoiling her. "We may be parents soon, Lucky. Then I'll be spending lots of money on you and our baby." I ignored the jump in my heart as I spoke.
"Zane, I doubt I'm pregnant." She looked at me with worried eyes. "I can't afford to be pregnant right now."
"I just told you I have the money," I retorted, my face twisting with displeasure and disappointment. I wasn't sure if I was mad because she was talking about money again, or not being pregnant. And I wasn't sure why I couldn't stop picturing a little Lucky in my arms.
"I don't mean money, Zane. I mean, I still have to finish school and we barely know

each other," she mumbled, and I watched as the tip of her tongue ran along her lower lip, teasing and tantalizing me.
"I don't know what you just said." I jumped out of bed. "All I know is that I want you again very badly, and I better get in the shower before I ravish you and leave you sore for the whole day." I walked away quickly, confused at the gamut of emotions coursing through me.
"I think I'm already going to be sore." She jumped out of bed and walked towards me slowly, her arms reaching out to me. Her long, brown hair flowed down her back in a frizzy mess, but she looked absolutely gorgeous to me. More perfect than any magazine model could ever hope to be. I walked towards her and pulled her into my arms so that she was pressed against me tightly. Her breasts were crushed against my chest, and I placed my hands at the small of her back and put my nose in her hair so I could breathe her in. Her very essence was like heaven to me.
"I love this moment." She peeked up at me and smiled. "This is a perfect moment."
"All of our moments from here on out are going to be perfect." I grinned at her and ignored the hollow feeling in my stomach.

"Just promise me you won't continue doing stupid things." I frowned at her and stared into her eyes, trying to convey to her the seriousness of what I was saying. I needed to be sure I could protect her from everything. And I wouldn't be able to protect her if she did stupid things.

"Can I tell you something, Zane?" She pulled away from me with a sheepish grin and I ran my fingers along her collarbone, tracing the delicate lines carefully.

"You want me to tie you up?" I grinned and tried not to picture her tied up against the bed, begging me to take her.

"No thanks, Robert Grey." She laughed.

"If my name was Christian, you'd say yes."

"I think you're obsessed with that book."

"I do own the book *Kama Sutra*." Our eyes locked and I continued running my hands along the side of her body. "We could learn some new moves and make our own book."

"*Fifty Shades of Zane*?"

"*The Wonderful and Mysterious Sex Life of Lucky*."

"*Tying Up Beaumont*."

"*Morgan's Sex Tips For the Inexperienced*."

"*How to* …." She laughed. "You got me, I can't think of anything else."

"We can start on any of those books as soon as you want." I brought her towards me again so she could feel my hardness against her leg. "And," I continued, "if you want, we can get some handcuffs so you can do kinky things to me."
"You wish." She laughed and rolled her eyes. "Actually, I wanted to tell you that I hate your duvet cover."
"What?" I chortled as I saw the look of humor on her face. "That's random."
"I hate your duvet cover. Can we change it?" She laughed at my expression and I joined her in her mirth. I fell back on the bed as I laughed heartily. Lucky was so unpredictable and I hadn't seen that coming. *So much for the handcuffs and whipped cream*, I thought to myself.
"Of course. Do you want to go shopping today?" I stroked her curls and wound my fingers through them.
"We can go after we work."
"Who's the boss here?" I faked a growl and she poked me in the arm. I jumped up, walked to the wardrobe and grabbed a T-shirt, and flung it to her. "Put this on, I can't keep staring at your naked body and keep my hands to myself."

"Thanks." She blushed and I saw a small smile cross her face.
I could hardly believe that I was here in this room with Lucky. Just a few months ago, I had been trying to stop myself from going to Lou's Burger Joint because I had enjoyed seeing her there every Friday, and now, well now she was here with me. It didn't feel real. I couldn't believe how light and happy I was. It was as if a missing piece of me had been plugged in and now I was operating at 100 percent. I was feeling and seeing emotions and colors that had been in darkness for most of my life. I just hoped nobody pulled the plug again.
"So, we'll go shopping after we do a little bit of work," I told her firmly. Then I shook my head. "I can't believe you don't like my duvet cover."
"It looks ugly and cheap." She cringed. "And dirty."
"Okay, okay. I get it. You don't like it. Anything else you'd like to change?" I looked around the room. "The paint color? The wood of my wardrobes?"
"Well, if you're asking." She grinned and I reached over to tickle her, but she ran away from me, giggling. "I'm going in the shower now, by myself."

I groaned at her words, I'd already pictured us making love again under the cascade of warm water.
"Oh yeah," I spoke casually, straightening out the sheets as the words came out of my mouth. "My best friend, Leonardo, will be joining us for dinner." I made a mental note to call Leo as soon as Lucky went into the shower. I ignored the warning bells in my head. I needed to do this. I needed to make sure that all I had to worry about was getting Braydon imprisoned.
"Oh." Her voice sounded surprised and I turned around to see a look of shock on her face.
"What's so shocking?" I frowned, my stomach churning slightly. Did she know what I was planning? Did she have some sort of ESP?
"I don't know. I didn't think you had a best friend, aside from Noah, of course." Her eyes were wide and begging for understanding. It saddened me that she would never know Noah, and that he would always be mentioned in a whispered and lowered voice.
"Noah was my best friend and brother. I was his protector. A failed protector," I sighed, remembering the dream. "I won't ever be a failure like that again."

"You can't watch someone's every step, Zane." She grabbed my hands earnestly. "You can't protect people from themselves."

"I can try though." I shook my head and changed the subject. "Would you like to cook dinner or take Leonardo out to eat tonight?"

"What do you mean, would *I* like to cook dinner? What about us cooking dinner together?" She rolled her eyes.

"Well, if you're going to be the mother of my child and my companion—" For some reason I couldn't bring myself to say "wife." It seemed too permanent and constrained. Too real. I ignored Lucky's hurt expression at my words. I knew she had noticed my use of the word *companion*. "Shouldn't you learn how to throw a good dinner party?"

"I'm going to pretend you didn't just say that." She grimaced and a flash of worry pricked me. "If I am carrying your child, it doesn't mean I'm going to become some sort of domestic goddess."

"I don't expect that, I'm not Charlie Sheen," I joked and she frowned again.

"What are you talking about? What does Charlie Sheen have to do with it?"

"Sorry, poor joke." I grabbed her hands and caressed them softly, bending down to kiss each finger. "Let's not start the day off with

an argument. We'll go to dinner instead then, okay?"
"No. I want to cook." She laughed and I looked at her in bewilderment. I shook my head in exasperation. Lucky was a typical female, so very hard to understand. "I just don't want that to be an expectation that I'm going to be barefoot and pregnant in the kitchen, cooking for you all the time."
"I don't think I have ever pictured that." I laughed heartily, happy that we were back on track and joking again. "What's wrong?" I looked at her nervous expression and worry filled me. Did she already know she was pregnant?
"This guy, Leonardo, he's not like your other friends, is he? The ones that came to the party?" She grimaced.
I laughed. "I'm guessing you weren't fond of them?"
She shook her head and made a face, and I wanted to kiss her and take away her obvious unease. "I'm sorry my friends weren't very nice to you at the party. In my defense, I don't really like most of those people. I just know them."
"Why did you invite them over then?"

"I wanted you to think I had a lot of friends and that I wasn't some sort of weirdo whose only friend was his brother."
"But you have Leonardo?"
"Yeah." I looked away quickly and I wondered if I was doing the right thing.
"Now, get in the shower and get ready, and I'll make breakfast and we can get to work."
"Are we going to go interview someone else?" she asked excitedly.
I shook my head. I watched as her long, brown hair swung back and forth. Her curly locks were bouncing up and down as she moved, and I wanted to reach over to pull a ringlet down to see if it would coil back up.
"So what are we going to do then?" she questioned, cutting me off.
"All shall be revealed soon." I laughed and pulled on a pair of boxer shorts. "Now hurry and go shower."
"Aye-aye, Captain." She rolled her eyes and saluted me as she finally went into the bathroom.
I grinned as I heard the water running and then looked at the duvet cover. *It was a pretty ugly color,* I thought as I stared at it. But I certainly wasn't going to allow her to get me to purchase anything pink or frilly. No way, Jose. The pink could be saved for a little girl's

room. If we had a girl, of course. If Lucky was pregnant. Oh shit, what if she was pregnant! The enormity of that thought hit me like a ton of bricks. What if I had a baby? How would I be able to ensure that Lucky and the baby were protected and safe—that they wouldn't leave me? The thought of losing Lucky and our child was too hard for me to imagine. A churning sensation gripped me and I felt my head pounding with worry. I could not let anything happen to either of them. I couldn't mess this up. I grabbed my phone, and any last-minute concerns left my mind as I called Leonardo. Love meant having to make hard decisions. And sometimes it meant knowing when to let go and let another guy take over. In my heart of hearts, I had already accepted what I knew to be true. Leo was a better man than I, and it was he I would entrust my Lucky to. Because sometimes love meant letting go when you knew you couldn't provide everything your loved one needed. Even if they didn't know what those things were.

Chapter 2
Lucky

I held my stomach as I showered. I wasn't sure how I felt about the possibility that I may be pregnant. I was a fool for getting myself into a situation like this. After everything I had planned for my future, the fact that I had unprotected sex with Zane without even a thought of using protection made me cringe with embarrassment. I knew better than that. "Have I told you that you're beautiful..." I heard Zane singing in the bedroom and I smiled to myself. He had a nice, deep voice, it was melodic and he was able to hold a tune pretty well. I wondered if he played the guitar as well. I felt like I had asked him if he played a musical instrument, but I couldn't remember what his answer had been. Musical men held a certain attraction for me, and I'd love it if he serenaded me. I laughed at my romantic notions and continued soaping up my body. As I shampooed my hair, I thought about the last 24 hours and Zane's revelation about Braydon and his brother. I couldn't believe that Braydon was a drug dealer. He was a big-time movie star; why would he be dealing drugs? I scrubbed away and thought about everything that had been said the night before.

It seemed to me that everything was happening so quickly between us. Just a few weeks ago, he was still the gorgeous but *shady* guy that I talked to every Friday night. He was the guy who brought in a different girl to the diner and made me scoff about him with Shayla and Maria. I understood why he did that now, and my heart went out to him, but there was still a layer of worry that seemed to enclose me. I think it was because of the pregnancy, or possible pregnancy. There was a part of me that believed that Zane was only interested in a relationship because he thought it was the right thing to do. Maybe he felt obligated to take care of our child and me. A chill ran through me. What if he only wanted to date me because he thought I was pregnant? Did I want to be with a man who was only with me out of obligation and a sense of propriety? And what would happen if it turned out that I wasn't pregnant?

"Lucky, are you okay?" Zane knocked on the door, interrupting my depressing thoughts, and I smiled.

"I'm fine," I called out to him.

"Should I come in and get the parts of your back you can't reach?"

"No thanks, Zane." I laughed and scrubbed myself, half-hoping he'd come in and join me.

I don't know what it was about him, but I felt lonely when he wasn't by my side.
"You don't know how hard it is for me to stand outside the door and not come in, Lucky."
"Well, at least I can think you want me for more than my body if you don't come in." I spoke lightly, but I was only half-joking.
"Don't be silly, my dear." Zane growled at me through the door. "So, I called Leo and he'll be over at about 6 p.m."
"Are we going to go to the grocery store first then?" I turned off the shower and stepped out carefully, grabbing one of the plush towels from the rack and wrapping it around my body tightly.
"If that's what you want," he called through the door and groaned. "If anyone is looking through the window right now, they will think I'm an idiot." He laughed, a wry tone in his voice.
"Why?" I asked suspiciously.
"Because I'm leaning against the door with my ear pressed against it closely so I can hear what you're saying clearly."
"Oh, Zane." I walked quickly to the door and opened it. He was standing there in his boxer shorts, just staring at me. His eyes were serious as he studied me in my big, fluffy

towel and he half-smiled before turning away from me. He had a small package in his hands and he held it towards me with a sheepish smile. "I got you something."
"What?" I looked up at him in shock and surprise. "Oh, Zane, you didn't have to get my anything."
"Open it." His lopsided, eager smile stopped my protestations and I took the package from his hands.
"I can't believe you got me a gift." My voice was emotional. I was touched by his gesture as I unwrapped it carefully.
"You're so much more patient than me." He laughed. "I would have ripped that paper off so quickly."
"We can reuse the paper if there are no rips."
"Reuse?" He looked at me in amusement and I laughed.
"When you grow up poor, you learn how to be thrifty."
"There's nothing wrong with that." I looked up into his eyes and I smiled gratefully at him, happy that he understood what money meant to me.
I peeled the wrapping paper off of a small box and opened it slowly. My heart was beating rapidly and I was excited to see what he had gotten me.

“Wait.” Zane held up a hand. “Don’t open it yet.”
“What? Why?” I frowned. “Please tell me there are no bugs in here.” I shuddered. “I hate bugs with a passion.”
“Lucky, I would never get you bugs.” He laughed. “Hold on a second.” He walked quickly to the night table and came back with his phone.
“Can I open it before or after you check your text messages?” I asked sarcastically.
“Don’t be silly.” He laughed. “I want to take a photo.”
“A photo?” I blushed and pulled my towel up. “You do not want to take a photo of me in my towel and wet hair.”
“No, silly. I want to take a photo of your expression when you open your first gift from me.”
“Oh?” I laughed. “That’s a bit sentimental.”
“I wanted a photo of you on my phone.” He grinned. “And don’t say a word.”
“I won’t.” I looked down, trying to hide my grin. His words had made me happier than I had ever thought possible. *Oh, Lucky,* I thought to myself. *You’re so easy to please.* I laughed and opened the box slowly.
“Look up, Lucky.” Zane’s voice was soft as I lifted the necklace out of the box. I stared into

his eyes and I felt tears building up in mine as I glanced at it.

"Oh, Zane. It's beautiful. I love it. I love it so much." I smiled widely at him and blinked as the camera flashed. "I can't believe you bought this for me." The light flashed again and I laughed. "Enough, you're going to blind me."

"Do you really like it?" He looked at me with an uncertain expression. "I know it's not diamonds or anything, but I thought you would like it."

"I love it, Zane." I stared at the necklace in my hand. The actual necklace was made of small, dark blue pieces and there were several turquoise stones that made up the band. "This is beautiful."

"I remembered one day in the diner you had told me you loved the color blue." He looked embarrassed. "I thought you would like this. Most women like necklaces, right?"

"I love it, Zane. Thank you so much. I held it carefully in my hand and reached over to kiss him on the cheek. I held his gaze and touched his cheek. "This really means a lot to me, Zane. More than you'll ever know. Thank you." I looked down at the necklace again and grinned. "Will you help me put it on? I want to wear it now." I handed him the necklace and he tied it around my neck carefully. I twirled around once it was on and touched it with happiness, allowing the moment to carry me away.

"Are you okay, Zane?" I touched his shoulder and he glanced at me with emotion-filled eyes.

"You look beautiful, Lucky. Really beautiful." He paused. "I just can't quite believe you're here." He frowned. "Guys like me don't get girls like you …"

"Girls like me?"

"The good ones, the special ones. I don't even know if this moment is real. It doesn't feel real. It doesn't feel like my life. I'm so scared that someone is going to wake me from a dream and you won't be here."

"I feel the same way," I whispered. "It just seems to all have happened so quickly." I chewed on my lower lip and looked up at his handsome face from under my lashes. "I'm scared that something will go wrong."

"So am I." He cleared his throat and looked away. "I don't know that I can be exactly what you need."

"What do you mean?" My breath caught in my throat and I stared at him in fear. Was he breaking up with me already? Was the necklace a goodbye gift?

"I had a dream about my mother this morning." He tried to keep his tone light, but I could tell he was masking a deeper emotion.
"What did you dream?" We walked back to the bedroom and sat on the bed, my hand enclosed in his.
"I just remembered the day she left." His voice cracked slightly.
"I didn't realize you remembered that."
"I try not to think about it." He forced a laugh and my heart filled with sympathy for him. "I was so young, I didn't even realize what was happening."
"You couldn't have known."
"She asked me to look after Noah. I was too busy sulking about not getting to go to McDonald's."
"You were just a kid, Zane."
"Why didn't she take us? Why didn't she love us enough to make sure she could be the one to take care of us?"
"I don't know how she could have left you." My heart ached for him and the pain and rejection he was remembering and feeling. I wished that I could say something to make him understand and feel better. But frankly, I couldn't comprehend his mother's actions either.

"Noah never spoke about her. Well, he tried and I wouldn't engage, and then he just stopped trying." He looked at me searchingly. "I sometimes wondered if that was healthy. Maybe we should have really talked about it. Maybe we should have confronted our dad."
"How did your dad react when your mom left and Noah died?" I asked curiously, wondering what sort of man Zane's dad was.
"He had another woman, so he didn't really care when my mom left. He said she was a whore and we were all better off without her." Zane's voice was bitter. "And when Noah died, he got free publicity for his new movie."
"Oh." My voice was hollow and I grieved for the man sitting next to me—the man who had never felt the unequivocal and whole-consuming love that I had gotten from my parents.
"Let's talk about something else." He shook his head and jumped up. "I'll get in the shower while you change, and then we can get this party started."
"What party?" I half-smiled at him, understanding why he wanted to change the subject. I hated it when people asked me about my parents and the conversation lagged on. I loved my memories of my mom and dad, but I didn't want to think about their deaths

constantly. And I had happy memories. I could only imagine the crushing heartache and unresolved pain that he felt.
"The party that will be our day today." He grinned. "Even if we can't have sex to get it started."
"Zane," I admonished him. "We are about more than sex." I shook my head. Men were so predictable sometimes.
"We are?"
"Shut up and get in the shower." I laughed and stood up to push him towards the door.
"Leave your hair curly today." He smiled at me as he lifted a finger to my curls.
"It'll get too frizzy." I shook my head. "I don't want to look like Frankenstein."
"But you'll be my Frankenstein."
"I'd rather be no one's Frankenstein."
"Well, I think we can fix that. I think you'd be more like Worzel Gummidge than Frankenstein." He burst out laughing and I frowned at him.
"Who's Worzel Gummidge?"
"I'll let you figure it out." He laughed and walked to the bathroom. "And think about what you want to eat for breakfast or lunch."
I hurried to grab my phone and brought up Google so I could type in that name. I plugged

in Worzel Gummidge and some hideous photos of an unkempt man popped up.
"Zane Beaumont, just wait until you get out of the shower!" I shouted, trying to stop myself from laughing. "That was not funny."
I looked once again at the photos of the dirty scarecrow and dropped my phone on the bed.
"I'm definitely not staying curly now!" I shouted again and quickly put my clothes on.
I was just applying some lip gloss when Zane exited the bathroom, all wet and dripping. I stared at his naked chest in awe and lust. I watched as a drop of water held on to a chest hair for dear life, and as he moved, it danced down his body and onto the floor. I looked back up at his chest and saw another drop about to make the same journey and I felt an overwhelming urge to rush up to him and lick it off. I groaned inwardly; I was starting to become as horny as Zane. I blamed it on the fact that I hadn't had sex in ages before Zane and, of course because Zane was dynamite in bed. I giggled at the thought and Zane raised an eyebrow at me.
"Are you laughing at my body, Lucky?" He put a hand on his hip and cocked his head.
"Do I not meet your approval?"

"Well, you know… you could do a couple of pushups." My tone was serious as I looked him over. "And maybe some bicep curls."
"Oh really?" His voice was light with humor and his blue eyes sparkled. "Is that all?"
"Your abs look a little flabby." I pretended to look embarrassed for him. "So maybe some sit-ups as well."
"I promise I'll still love you if you get fat." He grinned at me and I stuck my tongue out at him.
"Uh huh."
"It could happen soon if you're pregnant."
"Oh," I groaned. "My body." I clutched my stomach and twirled around. "My modeling days will be over."
"You can model for me any day of the week, baby."
"Don't you mean night?"
"Day or night. I'm always ready to be wowed by your beauty."
"Liar! Way to try and butter me up, flabby chest." I giggled and reached over to run my hands down his chest. "Now get ready so we can go eat. I'm hungry."
"I'm guessing that's not for me?" He looked at me hopefully and I walked away from him, laughing.
"I'm going downstairs, Don Juan. Hurry."

"I used to be the one who said that." He grabbed his towel and started drying off his body, and I felt my face flush as I thought about all the things I could be doing to him right now.
"Don't be long." I ran out of the room and down the stairs. I walked to the kitchen slowly, stopping to look outside into the backyard. There were a lot of pretty flowers in bloom, and I stared as they swayed in the light wind. The pinks and the yellows against the deep green of the grass made me feel warm and cozy inside. I decided to make some coffee and come back and sit outside while I waited for Zane.
As I sat drinking my coffee, a sudden panic rose up in me. What if I was pregnant? Was I allowed to drink coffee? I knew I wasn't supposed to drink alcohol, but I had no idea about coffee. I had no idea about anything that had to do with pregnancies and babies. I'd never really been around any pregnant women. A wave of sadness crashed down on my heart as I realized I couldn't even ask my mom for help. I pictured my mother's smiling face and I thought about what she would say if she knew the situation I was in and how irresponsible I had been. I groaned as the enormity of everything I had done came

crashing down on me. I had basically quit my job and had withdrawn from school—all for a guy. A guy I barely knew. A guy who had more issues than I did. A guy I wasn't sure would ever be able to fully give me his heart, no matter how much he wanted to. A man who may have gotten me pregnant. How was I going to go back to school with a baby? Would I now be a college dropout? I knew my mother would have admonished me. She and my father would have been upset at my choices. I should have asked Zane to let me finish college first. I should have held on to my rules a little longer.

A noise behind me distracted me from my thoughts and I looked behind me. I saw Zane walking through the living room and into the kitchen, and my heart lit up. It literally felt as if someone had lit a match and the warmth was heating up my entire body. I felt light and happy, and as I watched him, I knew that I wouldn't have done anything differently if I had to do it all over again. This was my moment. He was my Zane and this was how it was meant to be. I just hoped that everything worked out the way that I wanted it to. I wasn't sure if I would be able to cope if it all went wrong.

***

"Where do you want to go for breakfast?" Zane joined me outside in the garden and drank his coffee.
"I don't know. Maybe we can grab something and go eat in the park?"
"Like a picnic?"
"I guess."
"I suppose I should get some flowers and champagne as well?" He grinned at me.
"Well, I don't know if I can drink." I bit my lip and blushed as he realized what he had said.
"Shit! I didn't even think about that." His face turned serious. "I don't really know much about babies."
"Neither do I." I put my mug down and picked some of the flowers next to me. "In fact, I know nothing."
"What a fine pair we make." Zane chuckled and I looked up to see his eyes were shining with mirth. "We'll have to take some classes. And read some books. Yes, let's go to the bookstore and get some books."
"Before or after we shop for new sheets and groceries?"
"I guess we can go and get the books tomorrow."

"Let's wait to see if I'm pregnant first." I heard the words coming out of my mouth, but they seemed so surreal. Everything seemed surreal. I pressed my hand to my forehead and closed my eyes.

"What's wrong?" Zane rushed towards me with concern in his voice. "Are you okay?"

I opened my eyes and saw him staring at me with worry. I smiled at him shyly, not sure how to feel about him being so protective. On the one hand, it made me feel like he really cared, but then it also made me feel like he thought I was weak. And I never wanted to be that weak girl. Not again. I'd matured past that.

"Do you need to go lie down?" He reached over to pick me up, and I pushed him away.

"No, I want to go and eat. Preferably pancakes."

"Pancakes on a picnic?" Zane gave me his special 'I like you, but you're kind of kooky' look, and I had a vision of him at the diner a few months ago, sitting at his special booth, waiting for his date to decide between a garden salad and a veggie burger. I had stood there waiting patiently, trying not to tap my foot and sigh, and he had given me a special look while his date had taken her sweet time thinking about what to order. I can still

remember the special feeling that had caressed me and I laughed now as I had then: uncontrollably and hysterically. I was laughing so hard that I had to bend over to catch my breath. "You okay, Lucky?"
"Yes," I gasped. "Just don't make that look again." I hiccupped and Zane wiggled his eyebrows at me. "Or do that," I glared at him and he contorted his face.
"Would you rather me look like a scary monster?"
"You're still a handsome scary monster."
"She thinks I'm handsome, she thinks I'm handsome." He jumped up and ran around the garden, pumping his fist in the air, and I laughed again. This time I was able to control it and I watched him running around like a man with no worries or concerns. For that brief moment, everything was all right and was going to be fine. There was nothing that was weighing our minds down.
"Zane, are you done yet? I'm hungry." I jumped up and looked at the flowers still in my hand. "And what flowers are these? I love them."
He walked over to me, still smiling, and looked down at the stems in my hand. He picked up the flower with the huge white

petals and a green center and smiled. "This is my favorite; it's a Pom Daisy."
"A Pom Daisy? Like a pom-pom?" I questioned, secretly happy that his favorite flower was my favorite of all the flowers in his garden as well.
"Well, you can't do a cheer with it, but yes," he laughed.
"I bet you dated all the cheerleaders in high school, didn't you?" A flash of jealousy hit me as I asked the question and I surveyed his face intently. I wanted to ask him what sort of girls he usually dated, but I knew that would be opening Pandora's Box and I didn't really want to go there.
"Not all." He stared back at me. "Just some."
"Oh, sounds like me, I only dated some of the football players," I retorted instinctively. I groaned inside at my words. *How immature was I?*
"I'm sure they all wanted to date you," he said lightly, his eyes piercing into mine. "Now, this flower here," he continued and picked up another flower from my hand. "This flower is an Amaryllis. It's a native plant of South America. Do you see how the petals are red on the outside and white on the inside? Well, I always call these petals blood-soaked."

"Blood-soaked?" My voice rose. "Well, that's morbid."
"I know." He grinned and handed the two flowers back to me. "I wish I had some roses to give you, then I could recite Shakespeare or make up my own ditty: Lucky, let me count the ways that …"
"You want to eat me," I interrupted laughing.
"Well, among other things."
"Zane!" I grabbed his hand and pulled him inside with me. "Let's go out. And no more sexual innuendos for the rest of the day."
"That I can't promise."

***

I licked the last drops of syrup from the corners of my mouth and grinned at Zane. "I can't believe I've never noticed the way you eat before." I watched as he put his cutlery down on the plate. "You're so prim and proper, Miss Emily would be so proud."
"Who's Miss Emily?" He looked at me in confusion.
"The etiquette queen, duh."
"Oh you mean Emily Post?"
"Yes!"
"I've never heard her called Miss Emily before. It must be a southern thing."

"I'm not southern," I growled.
"You're from the South."
"I'm from Florida."
"Florida's in the south." He grinned. "Or do you need a geography lesson?"
"I know it's in the south, but it's not *the* South like South Carolina and Arkansas. Now they are the South."
"What about Alabama and Mississippi?"
"Well, they are as well." I rolled my eyes at him as if to say, *duh*.
"So all the states in the south are the South aside from Florida?"
"That's not what I mean."
"So are you telling me I'm not dating a Southern Belle?"
"I'm telling you that if you're looking for Scarlett O'Hara, you're dating the wrong girl."
"Did your grandparents live on a plantation? Did they have slaves? Did your mother have a mammy?" Zane cocked his head at me and I reached over and slapped his hand.
"You're an idiot, you know that?"
"Tell me, Lucky, what do you think of the Civil War? Do you wish the South had won?"
"Zane Beaumont," I growled. "I do declare that you're trying to upset my righteous mind, but I will not let you do that to me this fine

morning." I spoke in my best Southern accent and we both laughed.
"It's fascinating though." Zane looked up at me seriously. "Our country has such a rich and deep history. Our grandparents lived such different lives, had such different views. I sometimes wonder what life would be like if certain things didn't change."
"I sometimes wonder what it would have been like to have lived in the 1940s." I paused and looked up to make sure I wasn't boring him. "And in the Middle Ages."
"The Middle Ages?"
"Yes, I've always wanted to witness what society was like during that time. There was an expansion of population of about 35 million to 80 million people in Europe between 1000 and 1347. Can you believe that? That's incredible! And then there were the religious crusades and the system of feudalism was introduced. It's all so fascinating."
"Wow, you really do love history."
"I do. My heart is with modern history, as you know, and the Civil Rights Movement, but I'm a bit of a European history buff as well. I've often thought about doing my dissertation on the parallels between the Middle Ages and the Civil Rights Movement."

"There are parallels?" Zane looked surprised and I laughed.
"Well, I'd have to research. That's the point." I laughed and then looked down as I remembered that I may never get to do that research. I'm not sure how I would be able to do it if I were pregnant and had a baby. How would I be able to go to grad school then?
"What's wrong?" Zane frowned as he saw my expression change.
"Nothing." I smiled brightly, not wanting to share my thoughts with him. "Are you done? We still have to go shopping." I changed the subject quickly.
"Did you know that when I was in school, we learned about William the Conqueror and Harold of Hastings, and Noah and I would always play a game called The Battle of Hastings comes to Los Angeles?" Zane smiled at the memory. "And we used Star Wars light sabers that my dad got us. And we would run around, zapping each other." He laughed. "I just remembered that, that was a fun game."
"I'm impressed that you remember what happened in 1066." I smiled at him gently and leaned forward. "You're more of a history buff than I thought."

“I should note that William had R2D2 on his side and Harold had C-3PO and we weren’t fighting for England, but for the moon,” Zane laughed.
“Well, as long as it was for the moon.” I reached over and grabbed his hand. “I wish I would have gotten to meet Noah.” I spoke gently, not wanting to upset him.
“So do I.” He laid some money on the table and stood up. “Now, let’s go shopping.”

***

“I can’t believe you wanted to come to Ikea.” Zane looked lost in the sea of people. “I can’t say that I’ve ever been here before, but I’ve never heard it was the place to get bedding.”
“I don’t know that it’s the place to get bedding, but it is the place to get affordable bedding.” I made a face at him.
“I don’t want to push the fact that I have money in your face. But I don’t need to go to the Costco of bed sheets.”
“This isn’t the Costco of bed sheets, you snob.” I shook my head. “In fact, I don’t even know what that means. How can this be the Costco of bed sheets? Do you think we’re going to get a big pack of 10 sheets and

duvets?" I laughed. "To go with our 100 pack of toilet paper."
"You can get a 100 pack of toilet paper rolls?" Zane looked like a light bulb had gone off in his head. "You mean I could buy a lifetime's supply of toilet paper on one trip?"
"Zane! Focus, we're here to buy sheets and a duvet cover."
"I'd still like to know why we're in an Ikea, and not some swanky store in Beverly Hills."
"I can't afford to buy sheets in Beverly Hills." I sighed. "I wanted this to be my treat to you because you're changing them for me."
"Lucky, no." Zane looked at me in shock. "You can't afford that."
"I want to," I said obstinately. It was true that I didn't really have the money to buy him sheets, but I also needed to feel that I wasn't just getting a free ride. "Besides, I'll be getting a paycheck soon, right?"
"I don't really want you spending your hard-earned money on me." He frowned. "But if you insist. And if you will actually accept and cash my paycheck."
"I …" my voice trailed off. He was right. I did feel funny about cashing the checks. It just didn't seem right to take money from my boyfriend, no matter if I was working for him or not. It was okay when we were just friends,

but to be sleeping with him and taking money made it all seem a bit sleazy.

"Lucky, you have to take the money." Zane folded his arms across the chest. "You still have to send Leeza your rent money every month."

"I know, I know." I crinkled my nose and grabbed his arm. "Let's go look at sheets, we can talk about this later." We finally moved away from the couches and I saw a little girl staring at us curiously. She was bouncing up and down on a beanbag chair while her parents measured the dimensions of one of white couches to the right of them. I was surprised that they were considering a white couch with a kid; frankly I wouldn't get a white couch if it were just me, not with how messy I was. I smiled at the little girl as we walked and she stuck her tongue out at me and turned her face away. I giggled to myself at her precociousness and I saw Zane giving me a side-long glance. I was sure he was likely wondering if I was crazy or not, but I just smiled and continued walking. Let him think what he wants. The crazy part might be right; I wouldn't doubt it if someone said that I was.

"No pink sheets, Lucky." Zane squeezed my hand. "Please no pink sheets."

"I'm not a little princess, you know."
"You're my princess." He purred and I punched his arm. He grabbed me around the waist and pulled me towards him, and I squealed as I pushed him backwards. He held onto me as he fell back and we both landed on the queen-sized display bed that was behind him. "Lucky, I know you want me, but we're in public." He grinned at me as we lay on our backs.
"You wish." I shook my head and tried to sit up. He pulled me back down towards him and kissed me hard and I melted against him, enjoying the warm sweetness of his lips on mine.
He smiled as he pulled away from me and licked my lips. "You taste like honey."
"It's maple syrup."
"Well, it's good." He leaned towards me again and ran his tongue over my bottom lip slowly. I stared into his eyes, and we laid there for a moment, just gazing at each other.
"Excuse me, excuse me! You guys can't be on the bed doing that." I looked up, embarrassed, and saw an elderly lady staring at us with a shocked expression. "You two need to get up off the bed. This is a reputable business, not a brothel." She glared at us and I

jumped up off of the bed quickly. Zane stood up slowly and smiled at the lady.
"Sorry, ma'am, my whore and I got a little carried away."
"Zane!" I gasped and noticed the lady's face turn red. She turned away from us mumbling something about how rude this generation was.
I turned on him and hissed, "Zane, how could you say that?" My face was still flushing a deep red and I wanted to sink into the ground.
"You know you're not my whore, but what did that busybody expect after saying we thought this was a brothel?" He grinned and grabbed my hand. "Now let's get these sheets and get out of here. I don't think I'm made for Ikea."
"You don't even know Ikea." I shook my head. "I didn't know you were an elitist about where your sheets came from."
"I'm not. I just want to be somewhere a little less crowded with you." He ran his hand down to my ass and I swatted it away.
"Zane," I protested quickly. "Let's not get kicked out."
"I don't mind if we do." He looked sheepish.
"You're bored, aren't you?" I laughed. "Let me choose something and we can leave." I spotted a green duvet cover with circles on it

and rushed over. "Oh, look at this. I love it. Don't you love it?" I grabbed the package and stared at it before eagerly showing it to Zane.

"Not really," he grimaced.

"What do you like?" I put the package down and walked over to a plain sky-blue cover. "Something like this?"

"No." He shook his head and walked over to a black striped set.

"No way." My voice rose, and this time it was me shaking my head. "There is no way I'm sleeping in a death bed."

"A death bed?" He looked amused.

"The color black in a home is not for me," I said. "It's too gloomy. I prefer bright colors. Don't get me wrong, though, I'll wear black clothes." I laughed loudly. "I do like the slimming look."

"You don't need any help looking slim." He purred and I hit him in the arm.

"You're such a suck-up, Zane."

"And you love it." He paused. "I mean, I'm sure you loved it when I gave you super big tips."

"You did that on purpose?" I turned around and gasped. "I mean, of course you did it on purpose, but did you do it to suck up to me?" I laughed at his 'you-got-me' expression. "I

guess I should say thanks. You saved me from getting evicted many times."
"You were that broke?" He frowned.
"Yes," I sighed, remembering all the stress from the last year. "My parents didn't have an insurance policy when they died. I had to use my student loans and credit cards to pay for the funeral expenses."
"Couldn't you use money from the estate?" He looked upset and I shook my head.
"There was no estate. My parents were in pre-foreclosure." I sighed as I remembered the stress they had been in before they died. "They were fighting just to keep the house."
"I'm sorry." His voice was tight. "I don't want you to worry about money with me, Lucky."
"I don't want your money, Zane. This can't be about money." My throat constricted as I looked up at his face, which was growing increasingly angrier. "Please understand that."
"I don't understand why you won't let me help you."
"A relationship built unevenly isn't solid, Zane, and money makes things uneven." I stared into his eyes, hoping he would understand where I was coming from. "I don't want to be dependent on you."

"I want you to be dependent on me. I want to be your provider." His words came out hoarsely. "I would do anything for you, Lucky. Money means nothing to me. I just want you to be happy and safe. And you're not going to be safe if you're on the streets."

"Well, right now I'm in Los Feliz." I smiled weakly.

"Yes." He stared at me for a few seconds and turned away. "What about this one?" He walked over and picked up a cream duvet cover with a shiny silver pattern running across it. I was glad for the change of subject and looked at it.

"I love it," I beamed. "I really love it."

"Should we get the matching sheet set, as well?"

"I … uh, sure."

"I'll pay." Zane's voice was firm.

"No," I sighed. "I'll buy the duvet cover. You can buy the sheets."

"I don't want you spending your money on me, Lucky."

"Please, Zane." I looked at him with pleading eyes, hoping he would understand how important it was for me to do this.

"Fine." He took my hand and kissed it. "You're one in a million, Lucky Starr Morgan."

I blushed as I noticed the stares of those all around us, and my heart stilled at the tenderness in his voice. Everything was going to work out. We'd figure it out. No matter what happened, we'd get over it. Some of the worry in my gut left me and I sidled up to him, cherishing the warmth of his body next to mine.

"Shall we go to the bookstore next?" He kissed my cheek and a flow of electricity passed between us.

"Maybe tomorrow?" I didn't want to go and look at pregnancy books today. Everything was still so fresh and new between us. I didn't want that additional pressure and worry to hit us so quickly. "Let's go grocery shop, so I can make a great dinner for Leonardo."

"Oh, yes." He pulled away from me. "You know, Lucky, sometimes we have to do things we think are for the best."

"Uh huh." I looked at him suspiciously. "And you're telling me this because…?"

"I'd do anything for you, Lucky. You are more important to me than I am to myself. Even if that means you being with someone else."

"What are you talking about?" It was my turn to frown and look at him. "I don't want to be

with anyone else, and I can look after myself."
"Well, I beg to differ." He smirked. "I do remember having to rescue you on a certain dark night in Florida."
"I didn't need you to rescue me." I glared at him and pulled away. Sometimes Zane was so obnoxious and annoying that he made my blood boil. I knew he had issues, but there was no way I was going to let him treat me like some 50s housewife who depended on her husband for everything. Even though he wasn't my husband. I could just imagine if I brought up the word *husband* to him. I bet he'd freak out. I giggled to myself, imagining what his face would look like. Maybe it would stop him from thinking crazy thoughts and talking even crazier.

***

"Hi, I'm Leonardo. Yes, like DiCaprio, and no, I'm not him." Leonardo shook my hand and smiled warmly at me. "I had to give you that disclaimer, as I knew you were wondering."
I laughed at his joke and felt myself relaxing at his warmness. I had been silently worried all night that Zane's best friend was going to

be as cold and as fake as the people at his party.
"Zane didn't tell me you could read minds." I grinned back at him and studied his face. He may not have been the real deal, but Leonardo was possibly even better looking than his namesake. He had short, dark blond hair and sparkling blue eyes. His skin was a golden tan and it positively glowed against his white shirt. But it wasn't his looks that drew me in, it was the warmth and honesty in his eyes. Implicitly, I trusted and liked Leonardo. There was something about him that made me feel special and warm.
"Zane never tells people of all my positive qualities." He laughed. "He just wants everyone to think I'm just a pretty face."
"You wish, Leo." Zane came up behind me and slid his arm around my waist. "I don't think anyone's ever said you had a pretty face."
"Well, the girl last night did," Leo began and then glanced at me. "Oops, sorry. I forgot I was in the company of a lady and not just a Neanderthal."
"No problem." I giggled and ushered him into the dining room. "Please, have a seat. Dinner's almost ready. I hope you like lamb."

"I love lamb." Leo smiled at me warmly. "In fact, it's my favorite meat."
"It's mine, as well."
"Okay, guys." Zane grabbed my hand. "Lucky, let me help you finish up in the kitchen."
"No, no. Stay with your guest." I pushed him away and walked to the kitchen. I looked back and saw Zane frowning at Leonardo and whispering something hastily at him. Zane looked slightly upset and I stared at him in bewilderment. What was his problem? Leo just stood there smiling, and eventually Zane shook his head and backed away from him. I turned back around quickly and went to check on my herb roasted potatoes. As I checked to make sure they were cooked to a nice crisp, I frowned at what I had just seen. Why had Zane been so upset? He couldn't have been mad just because we had been lightly flirting, could he?
As I went to pull the salad out of the fridge, my phone beeped and I picked it up from the table. When I saw Leeza's name, I smiled and opened her text message eagerly. I felt the blood drain from my face as I stared at the words on the screen:

Lucky call me NOW! I'm really worried about you. I have some new information. Zane is not who he seems. Call me now.
I dropped the phone on the table in shock and it slammed down, making a loud noise.
"Everything okay, Lucky?" Zane's voice sounded concerned as he walked into the kitchen. His eyes looked at me with a worried expression, and I attempted to smile back at him without showing him how anxious I was feeling.
"I'm … it's fine." I nodded my head and stood there for a moment, trying to ignore the urge to ask him if there was something he wanted to tell me. "I just need to make a call. Can you pour the wine for me?"
"Sure." He stood there for a moment as if he wanted to say something else. "Let me know if anything is wrong, please."
"Sure." I hurried out of the kitchen with my phone and ran up the stairs and went into my room. I locked the door and called Leeza.
"Lucky?" She answered on the first ring. "Thank God, you're okay."
"What's going on, Leeza?" I whispered into the phone.
"Lucky, do you remember that guy Evan from the party?"
"Who?"

"The guy I tried to set you up with?"
"Not really?" I frowned. "Can you hurry it up please? I'm in the middle of a dinner party."
"I saw Evan last night, Lucky, and …"
"Lucky, everything okay?" Zane banged on the door, his voice loud and concerned.
"Yes, I'll be right out," I called out. "Leeza, please hurry, I have to go," I whispered into the phone.
"Lucky, Evan told me that Zane knew …" Leeza's phone crackled.
"Zane knew what? I can't hear you," I hissed.
"My phone has bad reception, Lucky," Leeza said hurriedly. "But be careful … Zane… Evan said … stalking … blackmailed him …" And then the phone disconnected.
I stood there with my heart pounding. I had no idea what Leeza had been trying to tell me, but from the words I had heard, it didn't sound like anything good. I felt my blood chill and I wondered at just what I had gotten myself into. I loved Zane, but I wasn't sure that I really knew him at all. I stood there uncertainly, wondering what to do. I wanted to ask Zane what was going on but it didn't feel right to question him without knowing the full story. What had Leeza meant? She couldn't have been trying to say that Zane

was a stalker, could she? I just didn't believe that could be true. It just couldn't be true.

Chapter 3
Zane

I took a deep breath before going back down the stairs. I wasn't sure what was wrong with Lucky, but I figured she was having mood swings like most women seemed to have. I took two more deep breaths as I walked down and I tried to calm my nerves as I was still fuming mad at Leonardo. Who did he think he was to flirt with Lucky so blatantly in front of me? I was starting to think that it wasn't such a good idea to bring him into her life, no matter how close he was to me, or how worried I was. I couldn't stand to think of her with him, without me. What if she fell for him? How would I feel if they got together? I didn't even want to think about it. A part me thought that maybe she'd be happier with someone like Leo. He was the epitome of a happy-go-lucky guy. He had money. He was decent. He would treat her well. And maybe he would even love her. Not as much as I loved her, of course, but who said my love was special? Who said my love was what she needed?

Shut up already, Zane, a voice in my head was screaming at me. *Stop being such a defeatist and a pussy. If you love her, make it work.* I was scared even thinking the love word. I didn't even really know if I knew what true love was. I didn't know if I would ever feel the way Lucky felt. I don't know if I could love and lose and be okay with it. I didn't want to be okay with it. I didn't want to put that out into the universe. I didn't want anyone or anything to think that Zane Beaumont was okay if you screwed with him—'cause I'm not. I'm not okay with being fucked over. I'm not okay with it. I had already lost my mother and my brother. I wasn't going to allow myself to get to a point where I'd lose Lucky … I wasn't even going to continue with that thought.

Leonardo was staring at me as I walked across the room. He had a concerned look on his face and I knew he wanted to ask me a personal question. A personal question I wasn't interested in answering.

"Everything okay?" he finally spoke and I nodded.

"It's fine." I walked to the kitchen. "You want some wine?"

"I'd prefer a beer."

"I know, man." I attempted to be cool and laughed. "But Lucky wants to serve wine, let's go with that for now, yeah?"

"Sure." He walked up to join me in the kitchen. "She's nice."
"Yeah, she is."
"She's living with you?" he continued.
"You could say that." I nodded.
"That was a bit fast, eh? I never heard you talk about her before your call." His voice was unsure and he looked at me as if he was scared I was going to deck him.
"Why would I tell you about her?"
"I guess no reason." He sighed. "How's the case going?"
"We're close to getting him." This time my voice was animated as I poured the wine. "We're so close to getting that son-of-a-bitch."
"Do you think Noah would have wanted this?" His voice was light and questioning.
"Braydon killed my brother. He's going to jail." I was angry at Leo's question. "He's a drug dealer and he will kill others."
"He didn't make Noah jump."
"He gave him, I mean, sold him the drugs. Illegal drugs. He has to pay for that."
"Dude, we've all done some drugs."
"I don't want to talk about this." I looked him in the eyes evenly. "I know you're a good guy, Leo—you're one of the best. And I trust you. I love you like a brother. You wouldn't

be here if I didn't think you were one of the best men I knew, but don't ever talk to me about my brother's death or Braydon again. I will not stop until Braydon is behind bars."

"I don't want it to make you crazy, Zane." Leo touched my arm. "But I support you, man, whatever you want."

"Yeah, thanks." I handed him his glass and took a big gulp of the Cabernet Sauvignon that Lucky had selected. I swallowed it quickly, trying not to grimace. It was a cheap bottle and had a cheap taste. "Pretend you enjoy the wine." I looked at Leo and grinned. "I don't want Lucky to feel bad. And she already seems like she's in a bit of a mood. I just can't keep up with these women."

"I don't have to pretend to a beautiful lady like that. And let me know if you need some help, I can always keep up." Leo winked and I wanted to punch him.

"Funny," I said instead and turned away. "Let me go and check on Lucky again and make sure she's okay."

I walked out of the kitchen quickly and back up the stairs. I frowned as I walked to Lucky's bedroom door. It was always a bad sign when Lucky went into her own room as opposed to mine. I wasn't even sure what was wrong.

"Lucky!" I banged on the door. "What's going on? Can you let me in?"
"I'm coming." Her voice sounded a little too cheerful and she opened the door.
"What's going on?" I tried to look into her normally warm and happy brown eyes, but she avoided my gaze.
"Nothing." She paused and I saw her lick her lips quickly, while furtively checking her phone.
"It doesn't look like nothing to me."
"I was on a call and they said some things about you and I don't want to bring it up right now because we have a guest and I'm not even really sure what they were saying exactly." She looked up at me and her brown eyes were wide and slightly worried.
"Who were you on the phone with?" Suspicions grew in my mind. "You weren't talking with Braydon, were you?" I didn't hold back the anger in my voice. I knew we hadn't heard the last of that asshole. "What did he say that's got you so upset?"
"I wasn't on the phone with Braydon!" she snapped back at me. "And let's talk about this later, okay?"
"Why are you mad at me, Lucky?" I grabbed a hold of her hand and pulled her towards me

at the top of the stairs. "What did I do to you to get you upset? I don't even know."
"Nothing." She sighed and finally looked up at me with woeful eyes. "I just don't know, okay? I'm just confused. Everything that is happening is confusing me. I'm worried and scared and I'm mad at myself and I just don't know what this is, what we are. Who you are."
"Why are you mad at yourself?" I held my breath. "Do you regret being with me? Do you regret coming here? And what do you mean you don't know who I am?"
"No." She bit her lip and I tried to ignore the yearning to reach forward and bite it for her. This was not the time to be having thoughts of sex. "Kind of. I don't know. You have to admit everything has been moving quickly, Zane. We don't really know each other that well. Sometimes I just worry that what we are feeling is …"
"Oh," I interrupted, then hesitated, trying to cull the feelings of panic swelling in me. "You don't love me?"
"Oh, Zane." Her eyes grew huge. "That's not the issue. One thing I know is that I love you."
"Okay." My heart didn't stop thumping. "But that's not enough for you, is it?" I ignored the

voices in my head that were screaming at me. They had warned me that it was a bad idea to get involved with her. It had always been a bad idea, and now I was going to pay the ultimate price. If she decided to leave me, I would never be all right again.

"I don't know." She shook her head, looking worried. "There are just so many things I'm unsure about. What if I'm pregnant? Will I finish school? Will I ever go to grad school? Will we get married? Should I even want to marry you? I barely know you. Am I crazy?" She rambled on and then paused and gave me a small smile. "I sound crazy right now, don't I?"

"If you're crazy, you're the most wonderful crazy person I've ever known." I couldn't resist the urge to grab a hold of her hand and trace the lines in her palm. I loved the feeling of her skin next to mine, even when it wasn't in an intimate way.

"And you're the most wonderful crazy person I've ever known, too."

"Wait a minute. Who said I'm crazy?" I laughed, happy to see the smile on her face. "I know most men wouldn't date Worzel Gummidge's twin sister, but I don't know if that makes me crazy."

"Zane." She laughed and hit me in the arm. "Is my hair looking crazy again?" She looked at me self-consciously.

"No." I tilted her face up to mine and kissed her forehead as I ran my hands through her long, cascading locks. "Your curls look like you."

"So it does look crazy?" She smiled at me and pushed her arms around my waist before placing her head against my chest. "You're so warm."

I brought her closer to me and wrapped my arms around her as I held her warm body tightly against me. The feel of her so close to me made me feel whole. It made me feel complete. Lucky fit me in a way no other woman ever would.

"Are you still mad at me for reasons unknown?" I whispered into her ear.

"I'm not mad at you, Zane. I'm just confused. The call confused me." She looked up at me, with a glint in her brown eyes, and all of a sudden, I felt extremely uneasy. "But I would be lying if I told you I didn't love this, didn't love you. Your warmth soothes my soul." She giggled. "Shit, I sound corny."

"I was going to say you sound like a sweet, innocent farm girl." I grinned back at her, letting my words mask my concern and

worry. "So, Lucky, please tell me, what farm did you come from?"
"The tobacco farm, duh."
"What, not the cotton farm?"
"My family grew tobacco and cotton, I'll have you know."
"Oh, on the plantation?"
"Why, yes, I do miss the plantation." She reached up and ran her fingers across my lips and I nibbled on the tip of her index finger.
"Ow." She pulled it back quickly.
"There's more where that came from, ma'am."
"I bet there is."
"Hey, guys, any chance of dinner anytime soon?" Leo shouted up the stairs and Lucky pulled away from me with a guilty look.
"Oh no, I forgot Leonardo was here." She looked at me with anxiously. "I'm such a bad host."
"No worries, love." I grinned. She hadn't even remembered Leo was there. I guess he hadn't made a huge impression on her after all. I tried to stop myself from gloating. I needed Lucky to like Leo if I was going to follow my plan. I just wasn't sure if I was making the right decision. One part of me—the part in my brain that was focused on emotions and my worry—told me it was what

I needed to do. But the sane part of me—the part that was here with Lucky—told me that I was making a mistake. That I should just appreciate what we had and live life. And I wanted to do that so badly. But I couldn't stop the voice in my head that told me that I was not enough.

"We're coming, Leo. Don't get your panties in a bunch."

"I'll pretend I didn't hear that." He laughed and looked past me to talk to Lucky. "I've been waiting patiently for your lamb. I hope it's nearly ready."

"Oh, my lamb!" Lucky cried out and ran down the stairs. "My lamb's going to be dried out. Nooo!" I watched as she ran into the kitchen, and a warm, domestic feeling overwhelmed me. Maybe I was old-fashioned, but I wanted to see Lucky in the kitchen, with a bunch of kids around her. I wanted to watch her grimace when she burnt the cookies and delight when her soufflés rose perfectly. I wanted to make s'mores in the fireplace and I wanted to enjoy late night ….

"Zane, can you come and help me, please?" Lucky called out to me and interrupted my daydream.

"Want more wine?" I asked Leo before hurrying to the kitchen.

“I never thought I’d see the day where Zane Beaumont was domesticized.” Leo laughed as he shook his head.
“Shh.” I frowned at him and hurried into the kitchen. “What’s wrong?”
“The potatoes are cold and the lamb has cooked too long.” She looked at me with wide eyes. “The dinner’s going to be awful.”
“It smells and looks good,” I said gently, ignoring the fact that the lamb chop looked like a dried up piece of charcoal.
“Liar,” she mumbled and sighed. “I just don’t believe this.”
“It’s okay, Lucky.”
“Argh.”
“Are you okay?” I was starting to think that Lucky was having pregnancy wiles. Maybe that was why she was so emotional? I wasn’t even sure if that was a real symptom, and if it was, I didn’t know if it would be showing up so quickly.
“No, my dinner is ruined.” She opened the fridge and pulled out a glass bowl that I vaguely recognized. “At least the salad is still good.” She lifted up the plastic wrap from the top of the bowl. “Maybe we can do salad and …”
“Did someone say that we were having a salad for dinner?” Leo sauntered in. I gave

him a look and nodded my head quickly to the counter where the burnt lamb chops sat. I saw him glance over and he winked at me. "Salad sounds great. I didn't want to tell you before, but I'm trying to avoid meat right now."
"You are?" Lucky looked at him suspiciously.
"Yes, I'm trying to stick to only veggies on my new diet." He paused. "It's a Hollywood thing."
"Hmm." Lucky frowned and shrugged her shoulders. "Oh well, let's have salad for dinner then." I looked at Leo gratefully and smiled. There was a reason why we were friends. He winked at me again as Lucky got the plates assembled and I laughed and walked to the fridge. "Thanks for that. I owe you. Do you want a Blue Moon, Beck's, or a Corona?"
"Corona with lime, please." Leo grinned and I took two bottles from the fridge.
"What about my wine?" Lucky frowned and then just shook her head. "Have your beers, you Neanderthals." She smiled at me. "Typical men."
"Hey," I cried out, pretending to be offended.
"I'm joking. My dad would always drink beer, no matter what the occasion was." She laughed. "Even on their anniversary when my

mom wanted to do a champagne toast, he'd be drinking Bud."
"You can't fault good American beer," Leo laughed.
"Even at nice dinners," she continued. "Even at my birthday parties at McDonald's."
"You can get beer at McDonald's now?" I looked at her in surprise.
"No." She laughed. "No, you can't."
"I used to love McDonald's as a kid." I smiled at the memory. "But we only got to go on special occasions."
"Me too!" Lucky exclaimed. "My parents said I could only go as a treat for doing a good job in school or birthdays."
"Noah and I were only allowed to go for a treat as well." I stared at Lucky in amazement. It seemed like the universe was trying to tell me that this beautiful woman was made for me.
"I hate to break up the McDonald's love-fest, guys. And I'm not going to tell you that their burgers are made with horsemeat, and that they have worms in their milkshakes." Leo laughed.
"What?" Lucky exclaimed and stared at him.
"I said I'm not going to tell you that." He grinned. "But can we please eat? I'm starving."

"It's coming, Leonardo." I rolled my eyes at him.
"It's all right for you, Beaumont. You're full of love in your stomach, but my stomach is crying out for a juicy steak." Leo realized his mistake as soon as the words were out of his mouth and I froze, worried that Lucky was going to start crying or start reacting in some other overly-emotional way.
It was silent for a few seconds before Lucky burst out laughing. "You should see your faces, guys. Like someone's about to die. I am not that sensitive." Lucky walked over to me and punched me in the arm. "I'm not a little kid." She looked up at me with laughter in her eyes and I felt myself floating in the endless pools of her love. "Let's eat the salad while we wait for the pizza."
"What pizza?" I frowned and looked at the oven.
"The one you're about to order." She grinned and kissed me on the cheek before sauntering into the dining room with the plates and salad bowl.

***

"That was some great pizza, Lucky." Leo licked his lips and I watched as Lucky

blushed and giggled. I kept a smile on my face, but I was annoyed. Lucky and Leo had been joking around all evening and I didn't appreciate it.
"Well, I tried hard."
"That pepperoni, ooh la la."
"I made it by hand."
"Talented, I tell ya."
"Well, you know, I'm the next Julia Child."
Lucky laughed and threw her head back.
"Next thing you know I'll be on Chopped or Top Chef."
"You can come cook for me anytime."
"Unfortunately, Lucky has a job, so she won't be able to cook for you anytime soon." I interrupted, snarky. Lucky looked at me in surprise with a frown on her face and Leo just smiled at me with his boy-is-he-gone look.
"Are you single, Leo?" Lucky turned away from me and smiled at Leo once again, and I knew my face reflected my anger and jealousy. Was Lucky interested in Leo? Was that why she was confused? Was she developing feelings for Leo? I knew it was an irrational thought and that they had just met, but maybe she had felt an instant spark? They certainly seemed to be getting along well together—too well. I was not happy about their camaraderie and was seriously

considering not hiring Leo as her bodyguard anymore. I wanted someone to be there to protect her, but not someone she may fall for. I trusted Leo with my life, he had always been a good friend, but why would I put temptation in his way? Lucky was a beautiful, vibrant woman and I knew there was no way that Leo was immune to that. I watched her as she spoke, her face was animated and glowing, and even her crazy curls weren't enough to detract anyone from her charm. There was a bustle of energy and an innate joy that surrounded Lucky. It was what had attracted me to her back when I first started going into Lou's Diner. Her energy was captivating, and you couldn't help but be swept away by her charm.

I remembered one Friday night when I had taken a particularly bitchy girl to dinner, and she had complained about there only being two tomato slices in her salad. Lucky had smiled widely and asked her how many more tomatoes she wanted, listing the different types available. "We have Heirloom, Roma, Cherry, and Pear. Which ones would you like more of?" And then she had turned to me and winked—a sexy, innocent, knowing wink and I couldn't stop myself from grinning back at her. Something my date had not appreciated. I laughed at the memory.

"I didn't know you found my dating life so amusing." Leo's voice interrupted my flashback and I saw the concern in his eyes.

"Hey, you know. An ugly guy like you has it hard."

"Well, you know." He shrugged his shoulders and we laughed. Leonardo had always been the guy who had women hanging on to him wherever we went. It didn't hurt that he was handsome and well-built. It seemed that women had a thing for strong men. Even when he was a doorman at a club, he had more women outside in the streets flirting with him than in the bar.

"Do you have any friends you could hook me up with, Lucky?" He smiled at her easily and I felt my breath release slowly, and some of my pent up tension disappeared.

"My best friend, Leeza, would love you." She smiled and then looked at me with a clouded look.

I tried to make eye contact with her and she looked down. Something was still wrong. I could sense it. Was Leeza the one she had been on the phone with? What was going on? A dull ache filled my heart as I wondered if Lucky and I would ever fully be on the same page. I didn't want to go through these feelings of panic and worry anymore. I didn't want my head to pound constantly in confusion and concern, and I didn't want to drive myself crazy every time something felt off. I wanted Lucky to come to me when she was worried or upset. I took another deep breath as I knew I was getting upset.

"So any dessert, Lucky?" Leo licked his lips and leaned towards her. "After that delicious meal, I'm feeling like some brownies."

"Are you sure you want to ruin your perfect body?" She cocked her head and surveyed him. "How will you get all the girls if you stuff your face with brownies?"

"That's why he spends so many hours in the gym," I interjected with a smile. "If I spent five hours a day, I'd be buff as well."

"Now you're only half as buff." Leo grinned at me, not sensing the tension between Lucky and me. Or if he was sensing it, he was being very careful not to make it worse.

"Let me go and see what we have for dessert." Lucky gave me a hooded look and jumped up.

"I'll help you check." I jumped up behind her and followed her to the kitchen.

"What's going on? Did you speak to Leeza?"

"How did you know?" She looked at me in shock. "Are you tapping my phone?"

"What?" My jaw dropped. "Am I tapping your phone? What sort of question is that?"
"How did you know Leeza contacted me?"
"I didn't know. I was just guessing." I looked at her in confusion. "Why do you think I'm tapping your phone?"
"Because you always seem to know what's going on, and I think Leeza was trying to tell me that you've been stalking me."
"What?" I laughed. "What are you talking about?"
"Leeza called me and said that she was worried." Lucky's brown eyes were huge and accusing. "I don't really think you've been stalking me or anything. But you know, I couldn't help but be worried ..." Her voice trailed off.
"Worried about what?" I frowned, fearing the worst. Did Leeza think we were moving too fast? Was she going to try and convince Lucky to leave me?
"I'm not sure exactly. She had a bad connection."
"Call her back," I commanded her angrily. "I want to know what she's talking about."
"I'll call her later." Lucky turned away from me and I heard her mumble something under her breath.

"What's that?" I walked towards her and it took everything in me to not pull her towards me and ask her what was going through her mind.
"Nothing," she sighed. "Let's please finish dinner and talk later?"
"Fine." I left the kitchen and walked back to join Leo at the dining room table. He sat there with an amused expression on his face and I scowled at him. "What's so funny?"
"You're so sprung on this girl. I never imagined I'd see the day."
"Whatever." I sat down and gulped down the rest of my beer. "So are you free to do the work?"
"You sure you want me to do this?" Leo frowned.
"I'm sure."
"And you haven't talked to Lucky about this?"
"She'll say no." I shook my head. "I need to make sure she's protected."
"I really think you should tell her what's going on, Zane." He leaned forward and stared at me. "She has a right to know."
"Not now." I was firm. "You don't know her like I do. She needs to be protected and I can't do it by myself. I need you to look after her for me. You need to protect her."

"Zane, I don't want to be dishonest." Leo shook his head. "I really think she's a good person. I don't want to fool her. As a bodyguard, I need the person to know they can count and depend on me."

"You need to be her friend first. You can't tell her, understand?" My voice was low. "Do not tell her that I've hired you to be her bodyguard. All she has to know is that we're friends."

"I don't feel good about this, Zane." Leonardo frowned and I could see the tension in his shoulders. I was tense, waiting for him to make a decision. He was the only one I trusted with Lucky. I had to make sure that she was protected at all times, I couldn't stand it if anything happened to her. I had to hire the best.

"I'll do it because I like her, Zane. I'll do it because you're my best friend. But I must tell you, you're going to lose her if you keep lying to her. I hope that one day soon, you'll tell Lucky what's going on. And I hope you do it before it's too late."

Chapter 4
Lucky

I felt awful eavesdropping on Zane and Leo, but something just didn't feel right. Zane was acting crazy and possessive and I wasn't quite sure if Leo was flirting with me or just being nice. Not that I wanted him to be flirting with me seriously, of course. That would make him a really shady friend to Zane, and I would hate for his best friend to be shady, seeing as his family wasn't exactly the strongest. So I stood there and listened discreetly.

Unfortunately, I couldn't hear their whole conversation. The only words I had heard were, "Tell Lucky what's going on" and my heart started beating like crazy. And then I started to feel angry; Zane was still shutting me out. After everything that had happened with Braydon, he still didn't trust me. And I still didn't know what the stalking thing was all about. I'd been very surprised when he asked me call Leeza. But maybe it had been a trick. Maybe he was tapping her phone as well, and knew what she was doing too. Maybe he knew she couldn't answer.

I shook my head at my own thoughts. *Stop being crazy, Lucky*. I told myself over and over again. He's not tapping your phone, and

he's certainly not tapping Leeza's phone. I felt like I was going crazy and wondered if I wasn't just plain crazy. I was crazy for all of it. I mean, really, what sane woman would up and leave college and move to another state with a guy she barely knew? *But you knew him for three months*, a voice whispered. *Maybe you weren't dating him and maybe you weren't bosom buddies, but you got to know him. Three months is a long time. People get married after three months. You just moved for a job. Don't be so hard on yourself.*
I stood there debating in my head for another couple of minutes before I realized that I still had no clue what to serve for dessert. I quickly opened the freezer and saw a frozen apple pie and some ice cream. Bingo! I pulled the pie out and preheated the oven quickly. Who could say no to apple pie and ice cream? As I stood there waiting for the oven to preheat, I realized that this couldn't go on any longer. Zane and I needed to talk. Everything was all over the place—we were both all over the place. It wasn't healthy and it wasn't a great way for a relationship to begin. Not if it was going to be a relationship that lasts the long haul. We were like two birds with broken wings that couldn't fly, living in the same nest. We trusted each other a little bit,

but not enough to leave the nest to go and get food. And if we continued in this vein of not leaving the nest, one of us was going to starve. And I didn't want to starve, and I knew Zane didn't want to starve either. And now I had another concern: What if I was pregnant? I couldn't bring a baby into a situation like this. But I also knew I couldn't do it by myself. There were so many unanswered questions, and I knew it was time to be a grown-up and start asking them.

I peeked into the dining room again and saw that Zane and Leo were still talking animatedly. I was surprised to see that it was Leo who looked upset and angry and not Zane. Why was Leo upset? Maybe Zane had accused him of trying to flirt with me and he was sticking up for himself? Who knew? I couldn't keep up with Zane and his moods. I wanted to go into the dining room and ask him what they had been talking about, but I decided to call Leeza first. I grabbed my phone and tried calling her again. I was really hoping to find out what she had been trying to tell me before I had a conversation with Zane.

"Lucky?" Leeza's voice was airy and I frowned. How could she sound so happy and carefree when she had just been trying to tell me that my boyfriend was a stalker?

"Yes," I whispered.
"Why are you whispering?" Leeza asked, confused.
"Because I don't want Zane to know I'm on the phone." My voice was exasperated. Sometimes Leeza just didn't have a clue. "Now hurry up and tell me what you were trying to say before. I don't have all day."
"Before?" Leeza giggled and I heard a guy in the background. "I'm kind of busy, Lucky, can we talk later?"
"No," I hissed, my face growing red with anger. "You made it sound really important, so I want to know exactly what you were talking about."
"Oh." She sighed and I heard her whispering. "I'll be right back, Evan." I heard what sounded like kissing and then she came back to the phone with a sigh. "Sorry, I was kinda busy."
"Are you with Evan, the guy from the party you tried to hook me up with?" I asked, surprised.
"Yeah." Her voice sounded happy. "He's great and I just love being with him."
"How do you even know him?"
"I met him months ago at a frat party."
"You did?" I frowned. "You never told me."

"Well, you know," she sighed. "I didn't think he was into me."
"Okay, and …?"
"I met your Zane before as well." Her voice was light and my heart skipped a beat. "I didn't have time to tell you before."
"Oh?"
"Yeah, a few weeks before the party. He was with Evan and that DJ guy, hanging out with some guys I know."
"And …?" Please God, don't let her say that she slept with him. Please God no.
"And nothing much." She paused. "Look, it might not be a big deal, and I wasn't going to tell you, but he was the reason why I pushed so hard for you to go to that party that night."
"What?" I frowned into the phone, feeling confused and overwhelmed. "What do you mean?"
"I don't really remember exactly. But I was telling Evan how crazy you were and how you had left school to go to LA with some guy named Zane, and Evan was like, 'Wow, stalking really works.' And he reminded me of what had happened before."
"What are you talking about?"
"Well, Evan had asked if I had any hot friends to bring to the party and I'd been a bit upset because I thought he had been into me and

then I thought he really wasn't, because if he was, why would he ask me to bring a friend? Well, who knows, I mean I—"

"Leeza." My voice was sharp. "Get on with it please."

"Oh, sorry. Well, he asked if I had any friends to bring and I guess I said something like I could bring my friend Lucky."

"And?"

"And that creepy guy, Zane. Sorry, you know, *your* Zane? Well he looked at me hard and was like, 'Lucky?' Or something like that. And I was like, 'Yeah, that's her name.' I was like, 'I can ask her to come, but she's a waitress and works late nights, so I don't know.'"

"Ok."

"And then Zane was like, 'Does she work at Lou's Diner?' And I was like, 'Yeah, yeah.' At the time, I didn't think about it. But that's just weird that he knew that."

"And?"

"And nothing. The conversation ended. But a couple of days later, Evan called me and he was like, 'Can you try really hard to bring your friend Lucky? I'd like to meet her.' And of course I was upset, but then he said he'd hook me up with some concert tickets, and so you know, I invited you."

"I thought you wanted to hang out as roommates." My voice was cold and dry as I tried to process all the information she was giving me.
"I did, I did." She paused. "But, you know. Anyways, I saw Evan a couple of days ago and he was all like, 'Hey what's up?' But I was like, 'You wanted to date my friend.' And he was like, 'No, no, no. My friend, Zane asked me to call you and to make sure Lucky came to the party, but to leave his name out of it.' I was like, 'Why would you do that? You didn't seem like great friends.' And he was like, "Well, Zane's dad is huge in Hollywood" and you know Evan is trying to be an actor.'"
"I see."
"Yeah, he's hoping to make it as big as Braydon Eagle."
"Uh huh." Mentally, I was no longer paying attention to her.
"You know him, right? Handsome blond, I think I saw you talking to him at the party."
"Look, I have to go, Leeza," I sighed, frustrated. I needed to think about the information she had just given me. Zane had wanted me to be at that party? But he didn't even really know me, aside from the diner. And he'd never let on, not for one minute,

that he had orchestrated that whole event. What else had he done? I felt cold as I thought about him helping me when my car had broken down. Had he done something to my car so he could rescue me? I froze and took a deep breath. No, he hadn't done anything to my car. I had known my head gasket was about to go. There was no way he could have made that happen. But maybe he had been following me. Because how was it that he just happened to pull up behind me? How long had he been following me? My hands felt clammy and I realized that I still had the phone next to my ear.

"Lucky, are you there?" Leeza sounded concerned.

"Yes," I whispered.

"Be careful, okay? I'm worried about Zane. I know he's cute, and you've been a bit desperate, but I don't trust him."

"I have not been desperate!"

"Well, it's been over a year."

"I had my rules, Leeza, you know that."

"Yeah, but you dropped that pretty quickly once a man came along."

"No, I didn't. And he wasn't the first guy who tried to get with me." I was angry now.

"I'm just saying be careful." She paused. "I was thinking that maybe I could come visit you. Make sure he's not a stalker."
"He's not a stalker, Leeza!" I sighed. "And when did you want to come?"
"Next weekend?" Her voice was hopeful.
"I'll let you know." And then I hung up, not caring that I was being rude.
My head was spinning and I knew that I needed to sit down and think about everything. I felt like I was lost in a maze of people I didn't know and everything I thought I knew about was wrong. I was angry and upset, and if I was honest, I was a little bit scared. What else had Zane lied to me about?

***

We ate the apple pie in silence. There was a cold air between Leo and Zane, and I was also giving Zane the silent treatment. I wanted very badly to ask him why he hadn't told me he had arranged to have me at the party. I wasn't even that mad. In a way, it was endearing, and I felt a warm glow. He'd had his eyes on me, just like I'd had my eyes on him. However, I kept my mouth shut because I didn't want to bring Leo into our drama.
I could see Zane's surreptitious glances and I just avoided all eye contact with him. I felt

like I was in a spy movie or something—only I was the oddball that didn't realize that she was in it. I had no clue what was going on anymore and I was annoyed. Really annoyed. I liked being in control and knowing exactly what was going on. Zane had my head spinning.

"This is delicious, Lucky. Thank you." Leo smiled at me and I smiled back at him.

"Thanks to Sara Lee."

"Well thank you, Sara Lee." Leo licked his lips and dropped his spoon back down into his bowl. "That was really good."

"I'm sorry that nothing was homemade." I frowned.

"The salad was to-die-for." Leo made some noises that reminded me of sex, and I blushed.

"Really, Leo?" Zane muttered at him.

"He's just showing me that he liked the pie," I snapped at Zane. "At least he can express his feelings."

"What's that supposed to mean?" Zane looked at me with a question in his clouded, blue eyes. "I don't tell you how I feel enough?"

I remained mute and looked away from him. I didn't want to start an argument with him in front of Leo. I wasn't that angry. And it wasn't even about expressing feelings.

“Do you want me to sing you a love song in front of Leo, Lucky? So he knows how I feel?”
“No.” My face burned with humiliation.
“How’s about some Frank Sinatra?” He cleared his throat. “Let me see, I could sing ‘Lady Luck’ or … wait, ‘Strangers in the Night.’”
“You’re an ass.” I glared at him.
“You’re a woman.”
“Excuse me?” I jumped up. “What does that mean?”
“You’re so moody. I don’t even know what your problem is.” He glared back at me.
“You stalked me!” I spat out.
“Here we go again,” he sighed. “I have no idea what you’re talking about. I’m sorry to burst your bubble, but I’ve never stalked you, Lucky.”
“I know about the party and Evan.” I stared him down, and if it wasn’t for the slightest flinch, I would have thought I was wrong. Zane looked at me calmly and didn’t say a word.
“Hey, guys, I think that is my invitation to leave.” Leo jumped up and walked over to me and gave me a hug. “It was great meeting you. Thank you for a lovely dinner, and maybe we can hang out again soon?”

"Thanks." I smiled at him weakly, slightly embarrassed. "And sure."
"Awesome." He kissed my cheek and then turned to Zane. "Remember what I said, man."
"I'll call you tomorrow." Zane spoke to him, but his eyes never left mine.
"Bye, guys." Leo walked to the front door and let himself out. I heard the door close behind him, but still we both remained silent.
"That was rude of you." I couldn't help myself. "You should have seen Leo to the door."
"He'll live." Zane didn't blink.
"Typical response." I rolled my eyes. "What do you have to say about the fact that you were stalking me?"
"I didn't stalk you," Zane sighed and I watched as he swallowed.
"Explain it to me then. I'm extremely curious." My cheeks were heated and I stood there staring at him with wide eyes. Tears were threatening to fall and I wanted to turn away from him, because I didn't want him to see how he had affected me.
"Lucky, I …" He sighed again and stood up and walked over to me. He made a gesture to bring me into his arms and I pushed him away.

"No."
"I don't understand why you're mad at me." He pursed his lips.
"Because you're a creeper!" I shouted at him and his eyes darkened. "Are you going to explain to me what happened or not?"
"I didn't stalk you." He sighed. "I was hanging out with some friends and your roommate was there."
"Are you sure you didn't plan that?"
"I didn't even know she was your roommate." He looked at me pleadingly. "But she made some comment about having a roommate named Lucky who worked in a diner, and I figured out that it was you. She said she didn't think you'd go to the party. And I wanted you to go."
"I see." I continued frowning at him, but I was starting to relax inside.
"So I asked Evan to convince her to invite you and bring you to the party."
"How did you know Evan could convince her?"
"He has powers of persuasion." He laughed.
I shook my head. "So what was in it for Evan?"
"An audition for a movie if you made it to the party." He smiled.

"I did wonder why Evan didn't seem that interested when Leeza dragged me up there." I frowned. "But you never said much to me. Not really."

"Evan texted me when you got to the room, but two things happened." Zane sighed. "Angelique wouldn't leave my side, and you ended up talking to Braydon."

"So you just left me?" For some reason I felt sad.

"I watched you like a hawk the whole night." His voice was hard. "I wanted to punch Braydon so hard, but I didn't want to do anything that would make him suspicious and think that I liked you. So I just watched to make sure nothing bad happened."

"So you followed me home?" I already knew the answer.

"I wanted to make sure Braydon wasn't following you." He frowned. "I had no idea your car was going to break down. I was so angry at you. I kept thinking, what if Braydon had been there? What if it was him you had to depend on? I wanted to throttle you."

"Yeah, I could tell you were pissed." I laughed at him, and I saw him smile back at me.

"I was more than pissed." He replied. "I was angry that you had spent the whole night

dancing with Braydon and then you gave him your phone number. It should have been me."
"But we were talking when I first got there, you had your chance."
"But then your friend Leeza came and dragged you away." He sighed. "And I had to play along so it didn't look so obvious. I didn't want you to know just what lengths I had gone to, to try and spend some time with you, outside of the diner."
"And then you came to the room too late," I continued understandingly.
"Exactly, my perfect plan was foiled."
"What was the plan for?" I smiled at him, wondering what he had expected.
"I wanted us to talk and dance and get to know each other, outside of the diner." He looked a little embarrassed.
"Why?" I continued.
"Because I liked you and wanted to get to know you better," he muttered.
"You liked me?" I grinned.
"Yes, Lucky." He pulled me towards him, and this time I didn't protest. "I thought you were beautiful, engaging, delightful, and someone I very much wanted to get to know better."
"So you really liked me, huh?" I couldn't stop smiling and I felt his hands wrap around my waist and bring me in closer to him.

"Yes, I really liked you." He grinned at me. "I guess I didn't know how to approach you in the restaurant and not get shot down."
"Why would I shoot you down?"
"Uh, let me think … because I was on a different date every week."
"You could have asked me out."
"And you would have said yes?" He looked at me in surprise.
"No." I laughed. "I don't think I would have. Well, I don't know. You did have me intrigued."
"Not as intrigued as you had me." He smiled at me and bit my nose. "I used to live for Fridays and your smile and witty comments."
"I used to live for Fridays so I could see you and make fun of you with Maria and Shayla."
"I know." He laughed.
"What?"
"I used to see the three of you peeking at my table from the kitchen."
"Oops." I laughed.
"I love your laugh." His voice was emotional. "It makes me feel all warm and happy inside. Your smile and your laugh make me feel like life is worth living. All I want is to see you happy. You know that, right?" He looked at me and I nodded back at him silently. "Please be patient with me, Lucky. I'm rough around

the edges when it comes to love and how to treat a lady. I know that sometimes I don't give you what you need, but I'm trying. I'm really trying. I want to be worthy of your heart."
"You are," I protested, and he leaned forward and kissed me.
"I want to feel like I'm worthy of your love." He smiled awkwardly. "You deserve the best. And sometimes I know it's hard for me to let other people in. I don't want you to ever feel like you can't talk to me or come to me."
"I feel the same, Zane. I want you to trust me and come to me as well."
"I will." His eyes flashed with an emotion I didn't recognize and I was about to say something when he pulled me against him hard.
"Tell me you're not aroused right now?"
I looked up at him in amazement as I felt his erection press against my belly.
"I'm always aroused when I am with you, Lucky." He kissed my forehead and slid his hands to my ass, cupping my buttocks. "I want to make sweet love to you all day and night."
"All day and night, huh?" I grinned and pushed my breasts into his chest, relishing in his hardness against my body. "You smell so

good." I leaned my nose into his chest and breathed him in.
"How good?" I could hear the smile in his voice.
"Really good." I sighed and lay my head against his chest, loving the warmth of his embrace.
"Good enough to eat?"
"I'd eat you in a second," I giggled, running my hand down his chest to his pants and grabbing hold. "In fact, I'm feeling quite hungry right now."
"Do I turn you on then?"
"Hmm, I'll have to think about that." I fiddled with the button at the top of his jeans and then yanked the zipper down before pushing my hand down his pants and grabbing a hold of him. I slid my fingers up and down the length of him, amazed at how hard he was already.
"I think you know you turn me on."
"Isn't that what all the stalkers say?" I giggled again and I felt Zane's hand on my chin bringing my face up to his.
"I wasn't stalking you, Lucky." He looked at me seriously. "Stalking is a serious thing. I don't want you to think I'm that crazy guy. I did do everything in my power to get you to that party, and I did follow you because I was scared of what Braydon may do, but I would

never stalk you, or tap your phone, or anything like that."
"Okay." I nodded. "Good."
"I'll do everything I can to protect you, Lucky. You're the best thing that's ever happened to me." I watched as he cringed and I pouted up at him.
"Why do you look like I'm the worst thing that's ever happened to you then?"
"I just heard myself say those words and I wondered how I became the cliché king." He laughed. "I never thought I'd say a statement like that."
"You never thought you'd be in love?" I knew the answer but I wanted to hear him say the words that warmed my heart. I loved the fact that I was Zane's first real love.
"No. Never. I never wanted it." He sighed. "Sometimes I wonder if my life was easier before you came into it."
"So you wish you never met me?" I pulled away from him, slightly hurt.
"No. No." His eyes pierced into mine. "Never that. I just care about you so much that sometimes I don't even know where I am or what I'm doing. I'm consumed with thoughts of you and your well-being."
"That's not so bad." I smiled up at him. "I think about you a lot as well, you know."

"I need to know you're safe at all times." He paused. "And that you'll never leave me."
"I'll never leave you, Zane." I reached up and kissed him slowly, increasing the pressure of my lips on his before pushing my tongue into his mouth. He grabbed a hold of it eagerly and I felt him nibble on my tongue before sucking it. I reached my hands up to run my fingers through his hair and he cupped my ass and brought me in against him hard. I felt his hands run up my back and under my top. He unclasped my bra and I lifted my arms up so he could pull my top off. He yanked it off and my bra was tossed to the side right after it. I grabbed his shirt and undid the buttons quickly, pulling it off of him and crushing my breasts against his naked chest. I giggled as his chest hair rubbed against my nipples and he growled as he reached up to cup my right breast, squeezing and molding it to his hand. I sighed against his lips and ran my hands up and down his back. Zane broke away from me and kissed down my neck lightly and across my collarbone. Within seconds, I felt his lips sucking on my breasts and his teeth nibbled on my nipple.
"Oh, Zane," I moaned as he set my body on fire with desire. "Ooh." I cried out as his mouth left my breast, but all was right again

when I felt his lips move over to focus on the other one. "Stop," I whispered as I felt his hands on my pants. "We should go upstairs."
"Why?" He growled, and he grinned as he pulled my pants down. I stepped out of them quickly, only slightly self-conscious of the fact that I was standing there in just my underwear.
"Because we're about to, you know." I smiled at him, blushing.
"We don't have to have sex in only the bedroom, you know."
"But this is the dining room." I looked up at him in shock.
"So?" He laughed and I felt his fingers slide between my legs. "It seems to me that you're ready now."
"Oh, ah." I closed my eyes as he explored me with his fingers, delighting in the roughness against my inner skin. The tips of his fingers caressed my throbbing blossom and I felt a wanton need fill my whole body. He removed his fingers from my wetness and I cried out, wanting and needing to feel him there and inside of me. "Zane." I moaned his name and he looked down at me with desire-filled eyes and a satisfied smile.
I grabbed a hold of his jeans and pulled them down so that I could release him from the

cage. His penis leaped out at me and I took hold of it and delighted in its warmth and girth. I played with it in my fingers before slowly going down onto my knees. I stared up at his surprised eyes and maintained eye contact as I took him into my mouth. He tasted salty and warm and I slid my tongue along his girth as I sucked him. Zane grunted and leaned back against the table. His hands reached down to my head and he played with my hair as I pleasured him. I felt him grow harder in my mouth and I was excited to feel him inside of me.

"Stop," he groaned and pulled me away from him. "I'm going to come."

"I don't mind." I tried to put him back in my mouth, but he shook his head and pulled me up towards him. He lifted me up onto the dining room table and slid my panties down to my ankles before lifting my legs up. He reached into his pocket and pulled out a condom wrapper before sliding it on and giving me a small wink. My heart was pounding as I stared at him up above me and then I felt him slide his length into me. All I could think about was how good he felt inside me, and how I never wanted this feeling to end. He slid back and forth slowly and I

grabbed him towards me, urging him to go faster.
“Not yet, my love.” He shook his head and grinned, and pulled himself out of me completely. I groaned at his withdrawal and tried to sit up, but he pushed me back on the table and leaned down. Before I knew it, his tongue was on me, and then in me, and I cried out to the heavens above as he lapped me up and sucked on my sweet spot. I couldn’t contain myself and I felt my body shudder as I came furiously, all while Zane was still there licking and teasing and sucking. I lay there, overcome with emotion, and Zane looked up at me with hooded eyes. I stared at him and smiled, a sweet sleepy smile and he lifted his face up and pulled me towards him again. Within seconds I felt him push himself into me again, only this time, there was nothing slow about his movements. He slammed into me furiously and I felt him in places I never knew existed. A second orgasm built up in me and he reached his fingers down to play with me as he made passionate love to me. I screamed as his intensity increased, along with the pressure of his fingertips against me. My body started trembling as I came for a second time, and I saw Zane grinning before I felt his body tremble. I then heard his deep

grunts of satisfaction before he pulled out of me.
I saw him pull the full condom off of his penis and drop it somewhere before pulling me up against him. He kissed me eagerly and I wrapped my arms around him, kissing him back.
“Next time, we’ll try and come at the same time,” he whispered in my ear and lifted me up. “And now, we can go to bed.”
“Shouldn’t we clean up first?” I looked around at the mess.
“No.” And with that he carried me up the stairs slowly and to his bedroom before laying me down on the bed. He stood there and watched me as I stretched and he smiled down at me sweetly. “I think I could watch you naked in my bed for hours.”
“I’d rather you didn’t.” I smiled and squirmed. “I’d rather you lay down in the bed beside me.”
“Oh?” He raised an eyebrow.
“I need someone to keep me warm.” I grinned up at him.
“To keep you warm, huh?” He fell on the bed next to me and reached over and ran his hands across my breasts. “Is that all?”

“Yup.” I grinned and moaned as I felt the excitement build up in me again at his touch. “I want to feel warm and toasty.”
“I’ll give you warm and toasty.” He laughed and sat on top of me, straddling his legs across mine. He reached down to his penis and I felt him rubbing the tip of it against my opening.
“Zane,” I groaned as I felt myself growing wet again.
“Yes, my dear?” He grinned as he caressed me with his member. He was now hard again and he brushed it up against me with intensity, allowing it to rest at my entrance for a second before pulling away.
“Nothing.” I pulled him down on top of me and kissed him before running my hands across his firm butt.
“Nothing?” He pushed himself into me halfway and I groaned as he pulled back out of me. He then rolled over and faked a yawn. “I think I’ll take a little nap.”
“You suck.” I rolled over to stare at him, my body still a quivering mess.
“Oh yeah?” He rolled over so he was facing me and his eyes sparkled. “I thought you liked it when I sucked?”
“Pervert.”

"You wish." He reached over and kissed my nose. "You've got such a cute button nose, did you know that?"
"No." I smiled back at him, staring into his eyes.
"I want to bite it, it's so cute."
"You want to bite everything." I laughed.
"I do?" He smirked at me. "If you say so."
"You love to bite."
"I'd love to bite your butt."
"What?" I looked at him curiously. "My butt?"
"Yeah." He laughed. "Does that shock you?"
"You'd have to want to do a bit more than that to shock me." I laughed. "A lot more."
"What if I told you I wanted to take you in the ass?" he whispered, staring at me intently.
"What?" My voice was loud and shocked, and he laughed.
"You should see your expression right now." He ran a finger across my cheek. "I'm guessing that means you've never done it?"
"Done what?" I could barely get the words out.
"Made love in the backdoor?"
"Made love in the backdoor?" I laughed. "I think it's generally known as anal, and no I haven't."

"Hmm." He licked his lips. "So I guess I can still take your virginity."
"Zane." I hit him lightly in the chest. "You're gross."
"It's not gross." He laughed and his eyes teased me.
"Have you done it?" I looked at him, with a slightly sad feeling.
"Uh oh." He looked at me with uncertainty. "We're not going to have the sex talk, are we?"
"The sex talk?" I was confused.
"The how many partners, how many different places, how many positions talk?"
"I wasn't planning on it." I paused. "But I suppose if you want to."
"I don't know. I've never found these conversations to be very helpful in relationships."
"I thought you haven't been in relationships before." I frowned.
"I've never been in love. Of course I've dated. I'm not a monk."
"Okay." I felt jealousy stirring in my stomach. "So have you made love in the backdoor before?"
"Uh oh, what have I done?" He sighed. "Lucky, don't be jealous."

"I'm not jealous." I protested. "I just want to know."
"Then yes, yes I have."
"I see." I looked away from him, trying to ignore the gnawing at my heart. "And was it everything you had hoped it to be?"
"What?" He looked bemused. "Anal sex?"
"Yes."
"It wasn't all that." He laughed. "I could take it or leave it."
"I see." I looked down and he grabbed my chin so that I would look at him.
"I've never made love to someone with a pussy as sweet as yours, my dear."
"Zane." I blushed furiously at his words.
"Well, it's the truth." He grinned at me and leaned forward. "Your pussy was made for my cock."
"Zane!" I shook my head at the crudeness of his words, while delighted inside that he had said them.
"I fit in you perfectly. Your body was made to welcome me. It was made to pleasure me. It was made to turn me on." He growled. "I can barely look at you without wanting you."
"Liar." I happily blushed again.
"It's true. I want you like no woman I've ever wanted before in my life."

“And I guess there have been plenty of them?”
“We’re definitely not having this conversation, Lucky.” He licked my lips and stared into my eyes. “I’m with you and the past doesn’t matter, okay?”
“I guess.”
“Okay?”
“Okay,” I sighed, wondering just how many women he had been with. He was gorgeous and rich; he must have been with plenty of women. And I bet they were all beautiful, a lot prettier than me, with perfect bodies. Zane could have any woman he wanted. I felt insecure as I lay there in his arms. Why would he want me when he could have any of those women?
“Lucky, look at me,” Zane sighed. “Please believe me when I say that I don’t want to be with anyone but you.”
I stared at him in amazement, wondering if he had a wiretap on my mind and was now able to read my thoughts as well. As I gazed into his blue eyes, I could see the love he had for me shining through his irises.
“You’re a goof.” I kissed him.
“I want to make love to you again so badly,” he growled in my ear. “I want to feel my skin on your skin.”

"You feel it now."
"I want my cock to feel the heat of your pussy as it slides up in you and makes you quiver and tremble," he whispered again and I blushed.
"Zane!"
"Maybe soon." He smiled wickedly. "If you're pregnant, we can have all the unprotected sex we want."
"Oh." My eyes widened at his words. "I guess we can."
"And if you're not, will you go on birth control?" His voice was hesitant.
"Birth control?" I frowned.
"Well, if you're not pregnant, then we want to make sure you don't get pregnant." He laughed.
"Oh, yeah."
"I'm all for safe sex and condoms, but when I make love to you, I want to feel all of you. I want to smell, taste, hear, and feel every emotion in your body as I make love to you."
"What if I'm already pregnant?" I looked at him with an anxious expression. It seemed to me that he was hoping I wasn't. It seemed to me that he didn't really want me to have a baby—his baby.
"If you're pregnant, we'll do the right thing." He smiled tightly. "We'll go to the classes

and get the books and get ready to welcome a baby into the world."
"Okay." So nothing about marriage then, I was disappointed in myself and in him. How could I expect him to want to marry me? He barely knew me. *He knows you well enough to let you sleep in his bed and stay in his house though*, a voice whispered in me. *Shut up*, the other voice shouted. Marriage is a big step. *Just shut up*. I plastered a wide smile on my face so Zane couldn't see how let down I felt.
"We should go to the doctor tomorrow and check." He stared into my eyes. "If you're okay with that."
"That's fine." I smiled tightly and pressed my face into his chest.
"We'd be a regular little family then," he whispered into my hair. "We'd be connected for life."
"Yes, yes we would," I whispered against his chest, and at that moment I knew. I knew that despite all my worries and concerns, I wanted to be pregnant. I wanted to spend the rest of my life with this man in it, it didn't matter to me how he was in it, he just needed to be in it in some way. I wanted to love and hold onto Zane Beaumont forever, and at times like these, when I was cuddled against his warm

chest and could feel his breath on my skin, I felt like it was a possibility. I felt like we had a real shot.

Finding out that he had had a crush on me as well when he had been going to the diner made my heart soar. I knew that to some people, it may have been creepy that he had tried so hard to get me to that party to get to know him better, but that just made me love him more. It showed me that what we had wasn't just a spur of the moment thing. He had been noticing me for all those months as well. We'd had a real connection in the diner. It wasn't just on my side. What I dreamt about for myself and for him could be a real possibility. I knew that if we had a baby, it would bring us even closer together. A baby would bond us for life. That's what I hoped at least. I just wanted to hold onto Zane forever.

"Penny for them." Zane pulled me back slightly so he could look at me.

"I was just thinking that you do a great job at keeping me warm." I smiled at him sweetly. "You're like my personal blanket."

"I see." He grinned at me. "Do you need some inner heat as well?"

I cocked my head and pretended to think. "Well, I do feel a slight empty coldness."

"I see. Well I can't let that continue, can I?"

"I hope not," I grinned back at him and then pushed him back onto the bed before straddling him. "Though sometimes I like to make myself warm."
"Oh?" His eyes clouded with desire as I rubbed myself back and forth on him.
"Yes, sometimes I like to take control." I grinned and watched his face as I slid down on him and started rocking back and forth.
"I have to say, I like it when you take control." Zane grinned and reached up to bring me down for a kiss, and as I rode him, I felt myself losing control. I felt the heat rising through me quickly and as I felt my first climax trembling through my body, I knew I was in for another wild night.

Chapter 5
Zane

It was still dark outside and I laid as still as possible so I wouldn't wake up Lucky. I laid staring out the window and imagined that the stars I saw twinkling were those of my mother and Noah. Though, I didn't really know where my mother was or what had happened to her. It was as if a whole part of my life was unknown to me. I continued watching the stars and held Lucky close to me as she slept in my arms.

"Everything okay?" she whispered sleepily, and I froze.

"Yes, sorry for waking you."

"You didn't wake me." She turned over and stared at me. "I've been awake for a while."

"Oh?"

"I didn't want to disturb you." She smiled sweetly and my heart stirred with an emotion I had never felt before.

"I didn't want to wake you either."

"Well, we did a good job of that." She laughed and stretched against me. "What were you thinking about? You look so serious in the moonlight."

"I was thinking about my mom." I kept my voice light.

“You think about her a lot, don’t you?”
“Yeah, her and Noah.” I attempted a smile. “I have memories that sometimes flash in my mind as if someone was putting a photograph in front of my eyes.”
“Oh?” I could tell that Lucky wanted to know me, so I continued.
“I was only six when my mom left, you know. And Noah was four.” I frowned. “We didn’t really understand what was going on. Every morning I would take my blanket and sit at the top of the stairs, waiting for her to come home.”
“Oh, Zane.”
“I waited patiently every morning, sometimes Noah would come out and join me and bring his little rubber duck.”
“Rubber duck?”
“It was a yellow plastic duck that my mother had bought for us. We both hated having baths and so she made it into this game. We would get to swim with the duck if we had a bath.”
“Oh.” She smiled at me gently. “Smart lady.”
“Noah loved that duck.” I laughed. “He kept it all these years. I used to wonder why. Now I suppose it’s because he wanted to keep it to show her when she came back. Wanted to show he never forgot her.”

"I'm sorry." Lucky's eyes were filled with tears and I squeezed her hands.
"It's not your fault." I shook my head. "We must have waited at the top of the stairs for months, and then one morning, my dad came out and saw us, and he just went crazy."
"Oh no." A tear slid from her eye and I reached over and kissed it.
"Don't cry for me, my love." My heart surged with love for this woman who was broken by my story.
"I just feel so bad for you and Noah." She bit her lip and for a moment, all I could think about was the pinkness of her lips and their taste.
"We never went back to the landing again after that. It was as if all hope was gone that she was ever going to come back."
"But you were so young."
"It may seem cruel, but my dad did us a favor. Who knows how long we would have been holding out hope." I sighed. "And for what? She never came back."
"She still loves you, Zane; she's your mom." Lucky looked at me in earnest and I kept my thoughts to myself. "The maternal instinct never dies. She's probably somewhere wishing she knew where you were."
"I doubt it."

"I bet she is, who knows what your father said, Zane?" She paused. "Maybe he blackmailed her or drove her away or did something to her."

"You watch too many movies."

"Will I meet your dad, by the way?"

"One day." I sighed. I didn't really want Lucky to meet my dad. I didn't want her to be caught up in his charm. He wasn't a good guy, but he knew how to fool a lot of people. I didn't want Lucky to be one of the people he fooled. Not my Lucky.

"Do you remember when you told me you didn't believe in love?" Lucky looked at me seriously. "And that you weren't looking for a serious relationship?"

"Yes." I kept my voice low, but I was scared where she was taking the conversation.

"Do you ever still feel that way?" Her eyes were questioning and I tried to ignore the nerves and panic in my stomach.

"No," I lied, not wanting her to know that every day I questioned if being with her and loving her was the right thing to do.

"So I changed your mind, just like that?"

"Yes." I sighed and avoided her piercing gaze. "No. Do we have to talk about this?"

"No to what?" Her voice was sharp and I could hear the distress in it.

"My natural reaction is to rebel from love, Lucky," I sighed. Sometimes I don't know if I can handle loving someone. Loving you. I don't know if I can live my life with this burden and this worry constantly encroaching on my heart."

"Do you want to be in a relationship with me?" Lucky continued, and I sighed.

"I can't keep having this conversation." I looked up at the ceiling for a moment. "I'm here, we're here. We're making it work. I'm trying to make this work. To give you what you want."

"You're the one that wanted to be my last boyfriend."

"Because I know that's what you need. I don't need labels."

"I thought you loved me."

"Of course I love you," I retorted angrily. I didn't understand how Lucky couldn't see that. "How many times do I have to tell you?"

"I want to hear you say it and know that you mean it." Her voice cracked. "I worry sometimes that …"

"Lucky, I love you. I don't know love like you do. I've never really felt it much before. But I know that what I feel for you is deep and strong and I can't guarantee you a forever

relationship, or a forever love, but what I fee now is deep and strong."
"I see." She closed her eyes and yawned. "I'm feeling tired." I watched her face and I wanted to shake her for cutting me out. I didn't understand how a conversation about my mother turned into a conversation about me loving her. What did I have to do to show her that she was the one I wanted to be with?
"You're mad at me?" I sighed, frustrated and aware that I hadn't given her the answer that she wanted. She opened her eyes slowly and smiled weakly at me.
"I'm not mad. This is just harder than I thought it would be."
"Oh?"
"I thought when you told me you loved me, it would be all roses and cupcakes from that point on, but it's not." She laughed to herself. "I guess that's not how life works."
"I'm trying." I pursed my lips. "Please just give me a chance."
Lucky sat up and I stared at her breasts, unable to stop myself from licking my lips. I felt a yearning in my loins as I stared at her naked body. How I loved her body. I groaned as she pulled the sheet up to cover herself and she shook her head at me with a smile. "Zane, listen to me carefully. I'm not going to leave

›ve you. I want you. I need you. We'll
ıgh this. We'll make it work. It's just
ːairytale I thought it was going to be."
My heart hurt at her words. I wanted to be her Prince Charming. I wanted to be the one to sweep her off her feet into the sunset and live happily ever after. I just didn't think I was ever that man. I was the Huntsman, not the Prince. I don't think I was ever going to be the Prince. "You deserve the fairytale."
"I don't need the fairytale."
"I want you to have the fairytale."
"Well, you're my Grumpy so I guess I do." She laughed.
"Funny." I leaned forward and kissed her. "Who knew I was dating such a funny girl?"
"Do you ever want to find out what happened to your mom?" Lucky looked at me with a thoughtful look.
"Not really." I shook my head. "What's the point?"
"To reconnect?"
"Reconnect? I don't know if we ever had a real connection in the first place."
"Does she know about Noah?"
"I don't know." My throat constricted and I took a deep breath. "My heart hurts, Lucky. I don't know if this pain will ever go away."

"Can I see a photo of him?" she asked softly. I jumped out of the bed and walked to my wardrobe. I opened it up and took out a box. I walked back to the bed and opened the box and took out a framed photograph of Noah and me when he graduated from college.

"He was really handsome." Lucky studied the photo and smiled at me. "He looked happy."

"He was happy," I sighed. "Ironic, right? He was one of the happiest guys I knew."

"I guess he hid his pain?"

"Yeah. He did try and talk about finding Mom, but I always blew him off. I didn't want to know." I sighed and looked at the wall, remembering the last conversation Noah and I had about Mom. He'd tried to convince me that we should try and find her so we could learn about our family's medical background on her side. But I'd dismissed his concerns and changed the subject. He didn't hold the same bitterness towards her that I did. I hated her. Every time I thought of her playing with us and laughing, it made me want to punch the wall. She had fucked me up emotionally. She had fucked me up so badly that I never wanted to give my whole heart. I never wanted to feel that pain and rejection again.

I loved Lucky, but there was still a part of me that didn't want to fully give in to her. I didn't want her to have my whole heart because if she left me, I would be crushed. I wouldn't be able to go on. When I thought of Noah and Angelique and how she had crushed him, I wanted to break someone. I lost my brother because he gave his whole heart to someone. I wasn't going to let that happen to me. I couldn't let it happen to me. I was scared that Lucky would see the real me. The dark me. The me who was consumed by revenge on Braydon. The me who couldn't sleep for more than a few hours at a time because memories consumed my thoughts, even in my dreams.

"We could try and find her," Lucky continued and bit her lip. "It may give you closure."

"I don't want to talk about her." I pulled Lucky towards me. "Tell me a memory you have of your parents, something happy."

"Are you sure?" She looked at me uncertainly.

"Yes. I need to know that there are happy families out there."

"We were really happy when I was growing up." Lucky's eyes glazed over. "The last few years it was hard because my dad lost his job for a bit and they nearly lost the house, but growing up, I had the perfect childhood." She

smiled. "I remember one Christmas, I woke up really early and I ran downstairs to the tree to look for my presents, and I was so disappointed because there were no presents there. And I just stood there crying."
"How old were you?" I frowned, not wanting to think of her as unhappy at any point.
"I was eight." She laughed. "All I wanted was a Barbie house, and a Barbie car, and a Ken Doll, and three more Barbies."
"I take it you were into Barbies?" I grinned.
"Yes." She smiled at me widely. "I cried so much that I made myself tired again and fell asleep next to the tree. I woke up a few hours later and my parents were sitting there on the couch drinking hot chocolate and feeding each other toast and laughing with each other." She paused. "And I just laid there staring at them, marveling at the love they had for each other. And my dad kept sneaking kisses and my mom pretended to push him away, but she kept grinning. And then I got up, and my dad and mom rushed off the couch. They picked me up and gave me a big hug and a kiss, and we all sang a Christmas carol. I think it was 'Hark the Herald Angels Sing.'" She laughed. "And then I looked towards the tree, and what do you know? There were four huge boxes waiting for me."

"How had you missed them?" I looked at her in surprise.
"My dad had fallen asleep before putting them under the tree." She laughed. "He was going to wake up early and put them there in the morning. Only thing was, I woke up earlier than him."
"Oh." I laughed. "So you got all your Barbie stuff?"
"Actually, no." She giggled. "I got a desk. And some remote control cars and a bunch of books."
"Remote control cars?" I looked at her puzzled.
"My dad wanted to race them with me." She laughed. "It was totally a gift for himself. My mom was so mad and then they argued over whether Barbie gave young girls low self-esteem."
"Oh, that's funny." I looked at the light of happiness in her eyes and I smiled, happy that she was happy. "You really loved them a lot, didn't you?"
"Yes." She nodded. "They were the perfect parents."
"Do you think we'd make good parents?" I kept my tone deliberately light, not wanting her to see how panicked I felt when I thought about being a dad.

"I think so." She nodded and I saw her swallow. Her eyes looked slightly distressed and she looked away from me for a second.
"You're worried as well, aren't you?" I felt relief rushing through me. It wasn't just me that was feeling this way.
"What if I never get to graduate?" she gulped out. "I wanted to get a PhD. How's that going to happen?"
"You want to get a PhD?" I frowned. "I didn't know that."
"Well, one day." She smiled. "I need to get my Bachelor's degree first."
"You'll get it soon." My mind raced as I thought about her leaving me to go back to Miami to finish her degree. I didn't want her to go. I'd have to plan my schedule around living in Miami for six months to a year.
"I hope so. It'll be hard with a baby." Her voice was soft. "So yeah, I'm a little scared."
"I'll help and we can get a nanny if you want."
"I don't want a nanny." Her voice rose. "I want to take care of my baby by myself."
"Hopefully I can help." I grinned.
"Oh, yes, sorry." She yawned. "Sorry, I really am tired now."
"That's okay. So am I." I pulled her towards me and wrapped my arms around her waist.

"Let's sleep. We have plenty of time to address our concerns in the morning."
"You mean in a few hours?" She wiggled her ass against me and I groaned as I felt myself rising.
"Continue doing that and there will be no more sleep to be had." I growled into her ear and fondled her breasts. They felt soft against my hand and all I wanted was to hear her screaming out my name as I pleasured her. I adjusted myself between my legs and was about to make my thoughts a reality when she giggled and pushed me back slightly.
"Go to sleep, Zane." Her words were sleepy and I kissed her shoulder, while mentally telling myself to come back to earth. That was the problem with being a man. My mind was constantly thinking about sex. I couldn't look at Lucky without thinking of making her come or taking her. I grinned to myself as I thought of our dining room sex. Maybe if I played my cards right, it could be kitchen sex tomorrow and then pool sex. Lucky didn't know it, but I had a thing for public sex; not that I was a pervert, I didn't want anyone to see, but there was a thrill in the possibility. I yawned and smiled at my thoughts as I closed my eyes. I had a feeling the dreams I was

about to dream would have nothing to do with my mother or Noah.

***

"Wakey wakey, darling." Lucky was standing over me with a plate in her hand. I yawned as I sat up and looked out the window in surprise. The sun was shining brightly, and I looked at my watch. It was 11 a.m. I never slept this late.

"Morning." I smiled at her lazily, taking in her disheveled appearance. She was wearing my shirt and she looked sexy as hell with half the buttons open. I tried to be casual and stared down her shirt, trying to catch a glimpse of her naked breasts. Her hair hung across her shoulders in big curls, and the top of her head was a frizzy mess. She looked at me with a huge smile and her makeup-free face radiated pure love. This was a look I would never get tired of seeing. I was so used to dating women who had on a full face of makeup when I woke up. There was something so unnatural in waking up to a woman with perfect hair and makeup and minty fresh breath.

"Are you hungry?" She nodded to the plate in her hands and I laughed.

I was hungry all right, but I didn't think she was talking about the same thing I was. There was something to be said about dating a woman who was a bit innocent, well innocent compared to the women I usually dated. Most of the time, I woke up to a woman riding me or giving me a blow job, not serving me breakfast in bed.

"Very, thanks." I took the plate from her and my stomach grumbled at the sight of bacon, eggs, and toast. I guess I really was hungry.

"Do you want some?" I mumbled between mouthfuls.

She laughed and sat next to me on the bed. "I had some cereal already."

She stared at me and I tried not to watch as my shirt rose up her legs. Was she wearing panties under the shirt? My mind was once again off of the food in front of me and on her. I shook my head mentally and smiled to myself. Lucky would kill me if she knew I was thinking about the state of her underwear as opposed to the food on the plate.

"This is delicious." I finished the last of the toast and licked my lips.

"I don't burn everything." She smiled, looking at my empty plate in satisfaction.

"Did you sleep well?"

"Magnificently," I said truthfully. "Can you pass me my phone, please?"
"Sure." She grabbed my phone from the side table and passed it to me.
"I'm going to call the doctor."
"Oh?"
"To see if we're going to be parents." My heart skipped a beat as I realized just how real a possibility this was.
"We can just take a test."
"I want us to be sure." I dialed the numbers on the phone and waited for it to ring. "Hi, can I make an appointment for my girlfriend? We want to do a pregnancy test." I spoke as soon as the receptionist answered.
"There are no appointments available today, sir."
"I see," I sighed. "When's the next available? I'll pay any price."
"We have one the day after tomorrow at 9 a.m."
"We'll take it."
"And your name is?"
"It's for Zane and Lucky Beaumont." I spoke without thinking and I looked up to see Lucky staring at me in amusement. "We'll see you in a few days." I hung up and pulled Lucky towards me. "We'll know in a few days."

"Yes, Mr. Beaumont." She winked at me and I realized what I had said. I had called Lucky my wife—well, had given her my last name. "Sorry about that." *Don't get any ideas,* I thought to myself hurriedly. I wasn't sure how panicked I would feel if Lucky started pushing for marriage.

"No worries." She smiled and gazed up at me. "Try not to look like you just struck a deer though." She laughed and I kissed her hard.

"All I want to do is make love to you." I reached into the shirt and started to undo the buttons.

"Uh uh." She shook her head. "Let's go and see the Johnsons today."

"Can't we go after a quickie?" I winked at her.

"No." She laughed and jumped off of the bed.

"You're so mean to me." I laughed and watched her walk towards the door. "I hate to see you leave, but I love to watch you walk away, baby," I called out in an Italian accent.

"You're so cheesy, Zane." She paused at the door and grinned at me. "Now hurry."

***

I looked at the text messages and missed calls on my phone and quickly put it in my pocket

before Lucky saw the screen. I thought back to our earlier conversation and how Lucky wanted me to share everything with her, but I knew that there were certain things I couldn't share with her. Not if I wanted to keep her in my life. I wasn't sure she would understand just how complicated everything was. How complicated I was. I knocked on the door and smiled when Mr. Johnson opened the door.
"Good to see you again, Mr. Johnson." I shook Sidney Johnson's hand and accepted his wife's hug gratefully. "Thanks for having us back so soon. Lucky just had some questions for you before we shot the video."
"I hope you don't mind," Lucky interrupted me. "I had a new idea I wanted to pursue that I think will make the documentary even better."
"You can come over anytime you like, my dear." Sidney smiled. "Betty and I are happy for the company. Our children are still in the Midwest, you see."
"I've never been to the Midwest, though I'd love to go one day." Lucky smiled and we followed the couple back to their living room.
"Maybe your young man will take you." Sidney smiled at me and we all took a seat while Mrs. Johnson got the tea ready in the kitchen. "So what's this new idea of yours?"

"Well, it's mine and Zane's." She nodded at me and looked a bit guilty. "We both decided."
"My dear, I'm sure Mr. Beaumont won't mind you taking the credit for your own idea." Sidney laughed. "I mean, the first time he contacted me, he had no clue what was going on."
"Oh." Lucky looked at him in surprise and I stifled a groan. *Here we go again,* I thought. I debated speaking up now or waiting to see exactly what Sidney was going to say.
"When I asked Zane why he was interested in residential segregation, the phone went silent."
"I think he took on the project because it was his brother's." Lucky's voice was soft and she smiled at me sweetly.
"I see." Sidney looked at me and I knew that he knew there was more to the story. There was an awkward silence and I cleared my throat.
"So, Lucky, I uh, I kind of heard you talking about history and civil rights in the diner one day." I smiled at her, hoping she wasn't going to freak out. "So I decided to create this project with the hope that I could convince you to work on it."

"What?" Lucky's eyes popped open and Sidney laughed.
"I say that's the sign that a man really wants you." He grinned at me. "Good man, Zane. I always knew you were a man who went for what you wanted."
"Thanks." I smiled at him and looked at Lucky to make sure she wasn't too overwhelmed. Maybe I should have told her about the documentary when she found out about the party. I just didn't want her to think I was going to be a total creeper. Or the lengths I had gone to get to know her better. Or—if I was honest with myself—the lengths I had gone to get her into my bed. I'd never tell her that part, though. Women didn't understand that men thought with their small head first.
"I didn't know how to tell you, Lucky." I watched her face closely to try and figure out how she was feeling.
"We can talk about this later, Zane." She frowned at me and turned back to Mr. Johnson. "I'm sorry about this. I didn't realize that …"
"Lucky, I'll let you know that I'm happy you came into Zane's life. When Noah first contacted us, well, we were overjoyed. Betty and I couldn't believe that someone wanted to

tell our story. That people actually cared what happened to the kids that grew up in the 50s and went through the transition. I knew right away that there was a reason for Zane calling me."

"I didn't realize." Lucky's voice expressed the same surprise I felt.

"Noah used to talk about Zane all the time." Sidney looked at me. "He was real proud of you, son."

"Thank you." I smiled as best as I could, even though I felt emotional. I wanted to ask him what else he talked about with my brother.

"I was happy when I got to meet you. Even if you were only picking up the documentary because of a girl."

"I, uh …" I stammered, embarrassed at the situation.

"I wish you would have told me, Zane." Lucky shook her head at me. "It's sweet that you thought of me, but I just wish you would have told me that you lied."

"Lucky, I want to tell you a story," Sidney Johnson cut her off.

"Sure." She turned to face him.

"It's about me and my wife." He chuckled and winked at me. "It's about what I did for love."

"Oh, you don't have to tell me." Lucky looked embarrassed.
"I want to tell you so you're not too hard on your young man."
"Oh." She looked down and I saw a small smile on her face.
"So, when I first saw Betty walking them streets, I thought to myself, this is a young lady that has a purpose and she don't want no boy like me. She wants herself a fine, respectable man." He nodded to himself as he remembered the past. "So the first time I got to talk to her, I told her that I was getting a scholarship to study."
"Wow, that was great," Lucky interrupted him with a huge grin. "What was the scholarship for?"
"There was no scholarship and there was no school." He laughed.
"What?"
"I lied." He smiled. "I knew she would never talk to me if she knew I was hanging out with my friends on the streets."
"And she didn't know?"
"Not for many years." He laughed. "By the time she finally gave me the time of day, I was in school and, as they say, the rest is history."
"So you lied to her?"

"I don't know if you can quite say lie, I like to think that I weaved some words together so that I could win her heart. Like a wordsmith."
"I suppose so." Lucky smiled and looked at me with veiled eyes. My heart thumped as she stared at me, and I wondered if this was going to be the hurdle that destroyed our relationship. When she issued me a small smile, I felt the tension lift from my shoulders. "Is there anything else I should know about, Zane?"
"No." I shook my head and ignored the niggling feeling in me that told me I was lying. I felt like my phone was a ticking time bomb in my pants, but I couldn't risk her finding out about that. "That's all." I could tell that Lucky wanted to ask me more questions, but we were both cognizant of the fact that Sidney was in the room with us.
"Who's ready for tea and cookies?" Mrs. Johnson bustled into the room with a large tray and I jumped up to help her. I took the tray from her hands and placed it on the table carefully. She looked at me with a smile and handed me a cup and saucer. "Milk and sugar?"
"No milk, one sugar. Thanks."
"I'll have milk and three sugars, please." Lucky laughed. "I have a sweet tooth."

"I'll say."
"Zane." She glared at me.
"What can I say? You do." I grinned at her and Mr. Johnson chuckled before speaking.
"Now, Lucky, tell me about your new idea."
"When we first talked about this documentary," Lucky paused and looked at me, "Zane and I were talking about filming several people, but I thought it would be more powerful if we did a documentary that focused on you and your family." She took a breath and looked at Sidney again. "If that would be okay with you."
"Of course it would be okay, dear child," Betty answered for Sidney and Sidney laughed.
"She's the boss, so if she says yes." Sidney shrugged and Betty gave him a kiss on the forehead.
"I ain't never been your boss, Sidney Johnson." She shook her head and laughed. "Well, not that you've ever admitted it."
"I try not to tell a lie." Sidney winked at me and stood up. "Let me go and get my address book. I recently found one of my brothers. I think he can help. He has a good memory."
"Recently found?" Lucky looked at him curiously.

“He done been lost for about 40 years.” Sidney shook his head. “I thought he was dead. But Betty here went inline and she found him.”
“Online, Sidney,” Betty corrected him.
“What?” He frowned at her.
“I went online and found him.”
“Oh?” Lucky took out her notepad.
“Yeah, there’s a website that helps you find people,” Betty continued. “My son helped me. We did it as a present for Sidney’s birthday.”
“He works for the government.” Sidney smiled. “He done good for himself. Got a good job. Had some kids. He even got married. He married himself a white lady.”
“Sidney!” Betty admonished him and smiled at us shaking her head.
“What, Betty?” He looked at her with a frown and she nodded at Lucky and me. “They don’t care if he married a white lady.” He laughed and Lucky and I joined him.
Watching Sidney and his wife, teasing each other and helping each other gave me hope for my future with Lucky, and gave me a glimpse into what aging love looked like. I’d be over the moon to be so happy with Lucky when we were senior citizens. To have kids and grandkids and a home full of love. I could rewrite my history. I could be the man that

went from no love to an abundance of love. Sidney and Betty gave me hope for the future.
"Zane, are you okay?" Lucky walked over to me and touched my shoulder lightly. I looked up at the concern in her eyes and nodded. "Sorry, I must have spaced out."
"It's okay." She took hold of my hand. "I'm not mad about what you did. It's even kind of romantic and sweet in a way." She smiled. "Don't worry."
"Thanks," I beamed at her, letting her think that that was the reason I had spaced out. "You're the best."
"As long as you tell her that every day, you'll be okay," Sidney shouted from the corner. "Now, let's go and look at those papers."
"Yes, sir." I jumped up, and Lucky and I followed him out of the room.
"Just don't keep anything else from me, okay?" she whispered and I squeezed her hand.
"Of course I won't." I waited outside the room for a moment and took my phone out of my pocket. I looked up to make sure Lucky wasn't looking and replied to the text I had gotten on the drive over to the Johnsons'.
Hey Angelique, I can't call you back right now but I've been missing you as well. I'd

love to go to dinner. Are you free tomorrow night? xoxo.
I pressed 'send' and walked into the room quickly. I loved Lucky, but I couldn't let Angelique go, especially not at this moment.

Chapter 6
Lucky

There was a warmth in my heart that I couldn't shake. I couldn't quite believe that Zane had decided to take up this project because of me. I felt my mouth aching to grin like an idiot, but I kept the huge smile off of my face because I didn't want Sidney and Betty to think I was some sort of weirdo. *He really did like me*. All thoughts that this was just about sex left my mind. He had done everything he could to get me to a party, and then when that didn't work, he had gone forward with a documentary that he had no real interest in, just because of me. All because he had wanted to be with me and get to know me. He had been as attracted to me as I was to him. I felt giddy inside and I looked up to see Mr. Johnson staring at me with a knowing look. I looked down, slightly embarrassed, but I just couldn't wipe the wide smile off of my face.

As Zane walked into the room, I stared at him with a new perspective. All those months, I had just thought he was a handsome, cocky, and sometimes nice and interesting guy who came into the diner. I had grown to like him, but had always berated myself for falling for a guy I just *knew* had to be a player or wouldn't be interested in me. And while I had reasons for those concerns, the truth of the matter was that Zane, like most of us, was just a really complicated human being. And he had been through a lot of shit. A lot of shit that had made him the man he was today: loving, shy, uneasy, jealous, untrusting. Sometimes I wondered if I had done the right thing coming here. Sometimes I felt like love was the daydream that you wanted to exist but never really lived up to the glory. But I realized that once you get a taste, a good sample of the real deal, you can't let it go. The biggest issue I'd been worrying about was that Zane liked me, but had acted on it spur-of-the-moment. Knowing that he had been plotting and planning for ways to get me into his life cemented for me that this was real for Zane as well. This wasn't about a possible baby, or some sex for him. This was about real feelings. This was about a mutual attraction we had built up for three months and finally acted upon. This was about us finding our happily ever after.

"Do you want to tell him, Lucky, or should I?" Zane's voice cut into my thoughts, and as my eyes focused, I could see a concerned expression on his face.

"Sorry, what?" I blushed, embarrassed that I had zoned out and completely missed the conversation.
"Sidney was just asking if we knew what we wanted to focus on for the documentary. Any particular part of his life?"
"Oh, sorry." I turned to Sidney and smiled. "Well, I think the central theme will be you, but we will use your family members' stories and relate them back to you. If that's okay."
"It sounds good to me." Sidney grinned. "To think, someone's making a movie about my life."
"I still want to focus it on what your early life was like," I continued. "I think it's important for people to know exactly what happened when African Americans moved to the North from the South. You know there is this general sentiment and belief that the North was more welcoming to blacks than the South, but that isn't really true."
"The North had its own problems." Sidney nodded. "It wasn't just us blacks, though; the Irish had it bad, the Italians, the Jews. None of us really fit in."
"But they were able to assimilate a little bit better." I paused. "Actually, maybe assimilate isn't the right word, but they were able to fit into the norm a bit easier."

“Well you know that song about when you’re black?” Sidney laughed.
I shook my head. “I don’t know the song, but I think I know what you’re talking about.” I looked over at Zane and he looked baffled, so I tried to explain it to him. “You know, when the Irish immigrated in mass numbers to the States, they were staunch Catholics, so they weren’t really accepted by the traditional WASP-y types who were Protestant. This was the same issues with the Jews. Most of the groups remained pretty insular, and there was a lot of hatred and mistrust among them. I guess the unknown and the different always does that.” I shook my head sadly. “But eventually the groups were able to come together a bit better, and these groups were able to move up the chain. Unfortunately, the same circumstances made it a bit harder for black people, because they were different in a way that would always be visible.”
“Ah, I see.” Zane looked at me thoughtfully. “But many black people did well for themselves, right? And when segregation ended, they had the same opportunities as everyone else.”
“That’s what we’d like to think,” I sighed. “But that wasn’t really the case. Many cities and states were vehemently against the ending

of segregation and opposed it. There was one city, I think in Virginia, that basically stopped the school session for a pretty long period."

"What?" Zane looked shocked. "That's awful."

"Well, you know the stories of the Little Rock Nine, right?" I looked at him curiously. "And how they were treated when they integrated the high school?"

"Vaguely." Zane grimaced. "Sorry. I was never really a history person."

"That's okay, son," Sidney chuckled. "Neither was I."

"You're too kind, Sidney." Zane smiled at him. "And thank you for allowing me to take over this project from Noah."

"That boy was like a son to me." Sidney laughed. "I never met a white boy so concerned and incensed about race. He would get angry for me. I used to tell Betty that this was a boy we needed when we were growing up."

"Noah always wanted to see the right thing getting done." Zane smiled. "Even as a boy, he wanted to make sure that people were treated fair and kind."

"Oh yeah?" I smiled at Zane, encouraging him to continue.

"I don't want to interrupt the conversation." Zane laughed and I sighed inwardly. I really wanted Zane to feel comfortable discussing Noah. I wanted him to get to a point where it wouldn't hurt so much.
"That's okay, boy, I'm sure Lucky here don't mind if we get to hear a story about Noah. He's a fine boy." Sidney ushered us into some seats. "And then we can look through these papers and talk some more.
"If you're sure." Zane smiled warmly. "I remember one time, when we were in high school, I think I was a senior and he was a sophomore. There was this huge controversy because someone had taken a CD player from one of the teachers' classrooms. Well, supposedly the teacher made this huge stink and basically wanted to get the student responsible suspended or expelled. Well everyone was wondering who would have stolen this cheap little CD player. It couldn't have cost more than a hundred dollars."
"That's a lot of money for a high school student," I interrupted.
"Well, not in L.A." Zane laughed and I rolled my eyes as he continued. "So, then of course, all eyes turned to two students in the school. An Asian guy and a black guy. They were both on scholarship and lived on the south

side, so automatically people assumed it had to be one of them. The principal called them both to his office and said that if one of them didn't speak up and admit he had stolen it, then they would both be expelled from the school. So a few days pass, and both guys maintained they hadn't done it. The teacher bans them from his class and they get called to the principal's office again, and he tells them he is going to suspend them. So that day, Jerome Richards and Harry Wang were escorted out of the school and sent home. The next day, Noah gets some of his friends from the tennis team to join him in a protest outside the school. I didn't even know he was planning it. They had signs and a megaphone, and they accused the principal of being racist. Well, the principal got mad and he suspended all of them for disorderly conduct on school premises."

"Wow." I looked at him with wide eyes.

"Well, it gets better." Zane's eyes sparkled. "The next day, the teacher who had caused the fuss about his CD player in the first place had to go sheepishly to the principal's office and tell him that there had been a mistake. No one had stolen his CD player; he had taken it home over the weekend so he could listen to some music while he washed his car."

"No way."
"Yeah." Zane laughed. "The principal reinstated my brother and the rest of the tennis team and had to issue a public apology to Jerome and Harry, who got a settlement from the county."
"That's crazy and kind of sad."
"Yeah." Zane shook his head. "It was horrible, but it doesn't have a horrible ending. Harry and Jerome are both in med school right now at Stanford University."
"Good for them." Sidney smiled. "I like to hear those endings. Too many of those stories end up with the kids winding up on the streets or in jail."
"Yeah." I nodded my head. "The statistics are horrible for low income and minority families. Well, for the most part. The system is failing so many people."
"Don't tell me you believe in handouts?" Zane said, and I frowned.
"It's not about handouts." I shook my head. "It's about fixing a broken system, it's about righting wrongs. It's about being able to go to school and not being judged based on your race or gender, or even your social class. It's about poor people being able to go to college and not be in debt for the rest of their lives."

"I was just joking, Lucky." Zane looked at me in concern and I smiled at him.
"Sorry, I just get a little incensed at times." I smiled. "That's a side of me you didn't know."
"It's a side of you that I like." Zane stared at me. "The more I get to know the multi-facets of you, the more I love you."
"Oh, Zane." My heart melted at his words and I wanted to reach over and kiss him. "I love you, too."
"And on that note, kids, I think we should take a break," Sidney said. "Zane, will you go and help Betty in the kitchen while Lucky and I have a brief chat?"
"Sure." Zane jumped up, walked over to me, and kissed me quickly on the head before walking out of the room.
"You're good for him." Sidney's face was serious as he stared at me. "Noah would be happy."
"Oh?" I looked at him curiously.
"Noah was worried about his brother. He was worried that Zane would never know what it was like to feel love."
"He told you that?" I was surprised at just how close they seemed to have gotten.

"I told you he was like my son." He smiled. "He talked to me about everything. It was me who told him about the website, you know."
"The website?" I frowned, not understanding what he was saying.
"To find his mom."
"Oh?" My heart started pounding. "He found their mom?"
"I'm not sure." Sidney paused. "Other things came up."
"Oh." I was disappointed. "It would have been nice if he would have found her."
"Maybe." Sidney frowned. "Sometimes people are best left in the past."
"What do you mean?" I sat forward.
"Sometimes things are as they are meant to be," Sidney sighed. "But I see Zane still carries the pain."
"I think he's still really hurt, you know?" My voice broke. "His mom leaving and then Noah dying, it's too much heartbreak for one person to deal with."
"He has you now." Sidney looked away from me and I saw him clutching something on his desk. "You know, Lucky, I like you. I like you a lot. From that first time that I saw you, I could tell you have a kind heart and soul."
"Thank you." I felt touched by his words. "I really like you a lot as well, Sidney."

"You're good for Zane. He needs love. And he needs someone who is patient enough to love him. There are a lot of things that have made him the man that he is."
"I love him so much." I bit my lip. "But sometimes it's hard. Really hard."
"He loves you a lot." Sidney smiled. "Noah would be happy. That was his greatest wish for his brother, to find love."
"But look where love took him," I continued sadly. "It breaks my heart that he took his own life."
Sidney cleared his throat. "Life is what we make of it. Everything is not always as it seems. Sometimes we have to make decisions that are for the greater good."
"Killing yourself isn't for the greater good!" I cried out.
Sidney's eyes looked at me sorrowfully. "Lucky, I wish I could tell you that I knew what was right and wrong. What was good and bad. Hell, what makes people happy and what makes people sad? But I don't have those answers. I can just be the man I was meant to be, and do the job that God wants me to do. I'm just a simple man, but I'm good to those I love and I keep their secrets. It's the least I can do." He leaned towards me again.

"Lucky, you have a kind heart. I trust you will do what you think is best."
"Do you think I should continue the search for Zane's mom?" My brain was churning.
"Maybe that would give him the answers he needs. Maybe they can even reconnect?"
"Whatever you decide to do, just be there for him," Sidney sighed. "I've a feeling that there is going to be a couple more rollercoaster rides to come."
"What do you mean?" I peered at him wonderingly.
"Nothing." He smiled. "Let's talk about my movie."
"Okay," I sighed. I wanted to ask him more questions but I didn't want to be rude.
"I don't have the answers for you, Lucky." He smiled at me gently. "I can't tell you what you want to know, but I think you should do what your heart tells you to do. Follow your heart, my dear; it will never guide you in the wrong direction."
"What will never guide you in the wrong direction?" Zane walked back into the room. "Don't say a GPS. Those things take me to the wrong destination fifty percent of the time."

"Those things get me all confused." Sidney stood up and winked at me. "I swear they are made to confuse the old folks like me."
"You're not that old, Sidney." I laughed.
"Well, you sure do know what words to say to butter me up, dearie. Just don't let my Betty hear you; she's a jealous one." Sidney grinned at me and we burst out laughing with Zane just standing there shaking his head.
I walked over to him and took his hand and squeezed it. I wanted to let him know that we were okay. I was okay. I understood him now. Well, a little better than I had before. And I was going to finish what Noah had started. I was going to find Zane's mom. I was going to give Zane his happy ending. Maybe once he had his mom back in his life and he understood why she left, he would feel a little better, a little lighter, and a little more trusting and believing in love. I felt like she was the key to fixing the broken piece of his heart.

***

"Hey, that was a really good session." Zane grinned at me as we drove out of the Johnsons' driveway. "I think this documentary is going to be awesome."

"Really?" I hesitated. "I know you did this for me and I don't want you to be bored by everything."
"How could I be bored? It's fascinating." He looked at me and laughed. "Okay, maybe not fascinating fascinating, but eye-opening."
"I still can't believe you took over Noah's project just to get me to come to Los Angeles with you."
"I don't think I was thinking it through properly," he chortled. "I just needed a chance to get to know you better."
"Well, it worked."
"Better than I would have imagined." He winked at me and I blushed.
"Why didn't you tell me when I found out about the party?"
"Honestly, I didn't even think about it." He looked at me sideways. "Sorry."
"Is there anything else I should know?" I stared at him seriously. "As much as I love that you tried everything you could to get to know me better, I don't want to find out a new secret every week."
Zane swallowed and continued driving. He turned on the radio and a Mumford and Sons song reverberated through the car.
"Zane?" I held my breath and tried to control my nerves. I was slightly angry that Zane

wasn't answering me and I was fed up with always trying to get something out of him. It was frustrating and tiring trying to get him to open up.
"I don't want to tell you," he sighed. "I wasn't going to tell you and I think that you'll be mad, but …"
"What is it, Zane?" My face grew warm. "Oh my God, what is it?"
"Don't get upset, okay?" He didn't look at me and I could barely hear his words over the blaring of the song.
"Can you turn the radio back off please?" I reached over to turn it off without waiting for him to do it.
"Hold on, let's go somewhere first." He looked at me quickly. "I promise I'll tell you, okay? I just want to be able to look into your eyes when I do, so I can explain."
"You're scaring me, Zane." My mind was whirling with possibilities. What was it that he was hiding from me?
"Can we discuss it later?" His voice was pleading.
I sighed. "As long as we get wherever we're going soon."
"We will." He pulled onto the freeway and tapped his fingers against the steering wheel. The sound irritated me, so I turned the radio

back on. I pulled out my phone to see if I had any messages, and was surprised to see messages from both Leeza and Braydon. I read them quickly and then closed my phone.
"Leeza wants to come to visit us this weekend," I spoke aloud. "Is that okay?"
I wasn't sure if I wanted Leeza to come after our last call, but I didn't want to tell her no. She had been my best friend for a while, and she had been there for me when my parents had died. She and her long-term boyfriend had been on a break for a few months, and I don't think she had really gotten over the fact that the relationship wasn't going well. I couldn't believe she was now interested in that guy Evan. I hadn't liked him at the party, and sure didn't like the sound of him now.
"Sure, I'd love for your friends to visit."
"Well, just Leeza." I paused. "I think she's dating that guy Evan. What's he like?"
"He's scum." Zane's voice was angry. "He hangs with Braydon. I don't trust him."
"But it seems like you're part of that group? Isn't that how you met Leeza originally?"
"Do I hang out with them? Yes. Am I friends with them? No." He sighed. "This last year I've done a lot of things I wouldn't normally do. It's for Noah."

"Huh?" I looked at him in confusion. "You befriended his friends to stay close to him?"
"No," he replied. "I infiltrated the group to get as much dirt on Braydon as possible. He is responsible for my brother's death. I will do anything to bring him down."
"Oh." I looked at him hesitantly. "Is that safe?"
I was scared. I understood why he hated Braydon, and that was why I wasn't going to tell him that Braydon had texted me and asked me to go to lunch with him so he could apologize to me.
"I'm working with the FBI and the DEA." His voice was short. "I'm helping them with the case."
"Are you qualified to do that?" I reached over and grabbed his arm. "That sounds dangerous." FBI and DEA? I didn't know Zane terribly well, but he certainly didn't strike me as a government official sort of guy.
"I already had an in with the group, thanks to Noah." He sighed. "It was easier for me to get in closer with them."
"But Braydon knows you don't like him."
"He knows I blame him for my brother's death." Zane's voice was angry. "He thinks it's because he was there when my brother

jumped. He doesn't know that he is suspected of being a part of a drug trafficking ring."

"Oh." I paled. "You're scaring me." My skin ran cold thinking of the danger Zane was putting himself in. "This sounds a whole lot more serious than I thought before."

"Lucky, did I tell you that I wasn't even able to say goodbye to my brother properly? I wasn't even able to kiss his body goodbye one last time."

"What? Why?"

"They cremated him." His voice was angry. "I don't really know what happened. I guess my dad gave permission. But they cremated him and all I have left of him are his ashes."

"Oh. I'm sorry."

"I didn't even get to see his body one last time. I suppose it was because his body must have been splattered from jumping." His voice was cold. "Braydon did that, Lucky. I can't let him get away with it."

"I understand." My voice was tight and I looked out the window so he couldn't see the tears in my eyes. I couldn't imagine what he was going through. I knew the pain and heartache of losing someone, yes, but the gravity of his pain was so much deeper than mine.

"I'm sorry, Lucky." He sighed and touched my arm. I realized that he had parked the car as well.
"Where are we?" I looked around and saw a couple of girls wearing bathing suits, walking and giggling. "The beach?"
"I know it's not South Beach, but I love Santa Monica." He nodded. "I hope you don't mind."
"No." I got out of the car. "I actually like walking on the beach." I watched as Zane took his shoes off and he motioned to me to do the same. "The sand will be too hot," I protested, but he grinned and pulled a plastic bag out of the car. He pulled out some flip-flops and smiled.
"I bought these for us." He threw me a pair and I caught them, laughing. I looked down and saw that they were size 8, the exact same size as my feet.
"How did you know I was a size 8?"
"I checked your shoes." He grinned. "I was hoping we could go to the beach later this week. They were going to be a surprise."
"Another gift?" I giggled. "You're spoiling me."
"I want to spend my life spoiling you." He smiled at me tenderly. "Now take off your shoes."

“Yes, sir.” I laughed at him. “You should have been a Sergeant in the Army.”
“If you want me to order you around just say the words.”
“You wish.”
“Don’t you know it!” He winked at me and we both laughed.
“So tell me, Zane,” I couldn’t hold it in any longer, “what exactly did you want to tell me?”
“It’s about Leo.” He bit his bottom lip and looked at me seriously. “I want you to listen and not get mad.”
“Uh, I can’t promise that.” I frowned. “What about Leo?”
“Well, I want you to spend more time with him.” He paused and studied my face, a slight worry in his blue eyes.
“Why?” My heart was beating quickly as we walked along the beach. I was in such anticipation of what he was going to say that I didn’t notice the white sand of the beaches or the aquamarine of the ocean. I was so caught up in what he had to say that I almost got hit by a stray volleyball before he grabbed me out of the way.
“Lucky, pay attention.” Zane shook his head at me and mumbled something under his breath.

"What was that?" I spoke sharply. "I didn't quite hear you."
"I said, this is why you need Leo!"
"Why I need Leo?" I turned toward him. "Are you trying to hook me up with Leo? Are you crazy, Zane Beaumont? Are you fucking crazy?" I started shouting at him. I could feel the blood rushing to my ears as I got more and more angry. "You think it's a good idea to set me up with your best friend? What was last week? A meet-and-greet? Make sure that I was good enough for him? You're sick, Zane. Do you know that? You're sick."
"Are you done?" He looked at me and there was a slight smile on his face and I could tell that he was trying not to laugh.
"What's so funny?"
"You." He pulled me towards him and I struggled free from him as he kissed me on the lips. "You're so feisty, Worzel."
I glared at him, which caused him to laugh again before he continued talking. "Leo is one of my best friends, but he is also a bodyguard. I've asked him to be your bodyguard."
"What?" For a second, I was speechless. Bodyguard? What was he talking about? "Bodyguard for what?"
"For you, silly." He sighed. "I want to make sure you're safe, I don't know what Braydon

is capable of doing. I thought it was for the best. It's the only way I could think of to ensure your safety."

"And you weren't going to tell me?"

"No." He averted his gaze sheepishly. "I thought you would say no if you knew."

"This is what you were arguing about with Leo, isn't it?" I tried to contain my anger. "This is what you didn't want to tell me."

"Don't be mad, Lucky." He stared at me with puppy-dog eyes. "I just wanted to make sure that you were protected when I wasn't with you."

"How were you planning on getting away with that, Zane?" I shook my head. "Didn't you think I would notice Leo by my side every time I went out? Or was he going to follow me?"

"I just wanted you guys to become friends and hang out."

"Really?" I scoffed.

"He's going to call you tomorrow to go to dinner." He laughed. "I have a, uh, business meeting I have to go to tomorrow, so I figured you and him could go eat and get to know each other better."

"Oh, Zane," I sighed. "You're incorrigible."

"Please, Lucky. It will make me feel better to know that he is with you when I can't be."

"This is crazy." I shook my head. "I don't want to go everywhere with either you or him."
"Just until we get Braydon," he pleaded with me. "Please, Lucky. I need to make sure you're safe. I need to make sure I'm not worrying about you when I'm not with you. I've already lost two people I love in my life. I can't afford to lose another one. I don't even want to think about it."
"I …" I paused and stared into his eyes. The pain and worry that shone out of them made my heart stop. I was vehemently against having a bodyguard, but maybe I would acquiesce for now. "I'll see how it goes." I smiled at him weakly, Sidney's words ringing in my ears. *Love means following your heart*. Well, okay, Sidney, I hope you're right.
"So, you'll go to dinner with him tomorrow then?" He looked at me hopefully. "And you'll let him accompany you on days that I can't be with you?"
"Yes," I sighed. "There's nothing else I should know, right?" I looked at him carefully. I wasn't sure how much more I could take.
"There's nothing else." He leaned forward and kissed me hard. "I love you, Lucky. Thank you for trusting me and loving me."

"Zane," I squealed as I felt his hands on my ass. "We're in public."
"So?" His eyes twinkled back at me. "That's part of the fun."
"People are going to stare." I pushed him away, giggling as his hand crept up my shirt and cupped my breast. "Zane." I hit his hand away. "Stop."
"I want to make sweet love to you, Lucky," he whispered in my ear. "I want to throw you down on the sand and kiss you all over, and then take you from behind. I want to hear you crying out my name to the wind so that the birds can hear."
I listened to him and swallowed hard. He was turning me on and I was loath to admit it.
"Oh, Lucky. Can you feel what you do to me?" I felt him press into me and his erection was hard against my belly. I giggled as I stared up at him.
"Zane, you're so bad."
"Bad enough for you to throw caution to the wind?"
"Zane!" I rolled my eyes. "There is no way in hell I'm gonna to have sex with you for everyone to see. And I don't want sand in unspeakable places either."
"We can go in the ocean." His eyes bored into mine. "No sand there."

"Whatever." I shook my head, exasperated.
"Look." He pointed to a stretch of sand about 300 yards away. "There's no one on the sand there really, and no one in the ocean."
"Zane," I giggled, though I was slightly intrigued. I'd never really had crazy sex or outdoor sex, and I had to admit that it was slightly thrilling to me.
"What do you say?"
"We have all our clothes on."
"I can strip down to my boxers and you have on a skirt." He raised an eyebrow. "You could go into a restroom and take off your panties."
"I can't do that." I shook my head hesitantly and Zane grinned at me before taking my hand and pulling me.
"There's a restroom up there."
"Zane." My voice was soft and my heart was beating. "Oh, my gosh, are we really going to do this?"
"Yes." He wiggled his eyebrows at me. "Please say yes."
"As long as you promise that you don't intend for me to have a bodyguard forever." I grinned at him.
"I promise." He laughed. "I promise."
"Fine. But if we get caught I will hate you forever."
"Hey, it's a great story for the grandkids."

"You've got to be joking." I laughed.
"I'm excited for our doctor's appointment." He smiled into my eyes. "I can't wait to see if we're pregnant."
"Zane, way to ruin the mood," I groaned. "Isn't it me who's supposed to do that?"
"I'm excited." He laughed.
"You really want to have a kid, huh?" I looked at him in surprise.
"I shouldn't be so excited. I know!" He stroked my hair. "But when I think of having a family with you, I feel like I can finally have the happy family life that I've always wanted. I know you still have school and all that stuff, but I promise you, we can make it work."
"I know." And in my heart, I did. I knew that Zane and I were in this for the long haul. There was nothing that could tear us apart. We were made for each other.
"I don't have protection." He stared at me and bit his lip. "And frankly I'm not sure how it would work in the water."
"Oh." I stared into his eyes, my heart was thumping. "I guess it won't hurt this once."
"Are you sure?" He looked hopeful.
"No." I laughed. "You make me forget my own mind, Zane Beaumont."

"Let's go." He grinned and walked into the men's room to change. I quickly walked into a stall in the ladies room and pulled down my panties and decided at the last moment to take off my bra as well. I held them in my hand and shook my head at what we were about to do. I ran out quickly and my breath caught as I saw Zane standing there in his white Calvins.

"Zane, those are not boxer shorts!" I gasped as I stared at him standing there in his briefs half-naked.

"What can I say?" He grinned at me and grabbed me by the waist. "I have no shame when it comes to you."

"Why do I think we're making a huge mistake?" I laughed and we ran to the ocean hand-in-hand. We dropped our clothes on the sand and I raced ahead of Zane. "Catch me if you can!" I jumped into the water and gasped at how cold it was. I dove under and swam to warm myself up and as I bobbed back up, the cool air caressed my face while the sun kissed me. I lay on my back and floated in the water, enjoying the warmth on my face for a few seconds before Zane grabbed me from behind.

"Come here, you," he growled and wrapped his arms around me tightly. I felt his hands creep up under my top and his fingers

encircled my nipples and he squeezed them tightly.
“Zane,” I squealed while treading water, and I turned around to face him.
“Shh.” He grinned and lifted my skirt up. “Wrap your legs around my waist.” I obeyed his command dutifully and felt him press against me.
“You still have your briefs on.” I bobbed against him and his mouth came down onto mine, shutting me up. I felt his tongue dart into mouth and I reached my hands down and pulled his briefs off before grabbing him. His eyes popped open at my bold move, and I winked at him as I eased him into me. I closed my eyes and cried out as he pushed into me hard and I bit down on his shoulder. I cried out as we bobbed back and forth in the water and it was minutes before I realized that I had let go of his briefs in the water.
Zane grunted in my ear as he pummeled into me and we both came pretty quickly. I held onto him tightly and we were both gasping as we bobbed in the ocean.
“That was hot.” He grinned.
“Yes,” I gasped. “It was.”
“I want to take you home now so I can have my way with you slowly.”
“Uh, about that.” I grinned.

"What?"
"I let go of your briefs."
"What?" His eyes widened and he chortled as he realized what that meant. "You do realize there is a very good chance I could be arrested for flashing now."
"No." I shook my head. "Oh, man."
"We'll have to walk out slowly with you in front of me."
"Okay." I nodded.
"You planned this, didn't you?"
"No, no. I swear." I laughed. "It was a mistake."
"I guess I'm to blame." He winked.
"Why?"
"I made you lose your mind with my good loving."
"Yeah," I snorted. "That was it." At the same moment, a huge wave crashed over us and I swallowed a mouthful of saltwater. I started coughing and spitting and Zane grabbed a hold of me tightly.
"Are you okay?" He looked concerned and I nodded.
"I'm just a bit cold."
"I guess we need to get out now?" He paused and grimaced and I stuck my tongue out at him.
"It was your bright idea."

"I didn't expect you to drop my underwear in the ocean." He shook his head. "I bet you did it on purpose."
"Who me?" I shook my head in denial. "I promise I didn't, but I can't say it's not funny."
"You won't think it's funny if I get arrested." He laughed and we swam back to shore.
"Now what?" I looked at him as we got to the shore and he winked at me.
"Now we run." He grabbed a hold of me and we ran to our clothes with him pressed against me. He let go of me quickly and grabbed his pants and tried to drag them on. I laughed as I watched him wiggling and hopping around, trying to pull his pants up his wet body.
"What are you laughing at?" he growled as I watched him struggling and he shook his head. "Maybe this wasn't such a great idea."
"It would have been better if you had a towel."
"You're so helpful, Lucky."
"I try." I walked around and slapped his pale white ass before reaching down and helping him to pull his pants up. I had noticed a couple walking towards us and I knew we only had a few seconds left to cover his naked penis.

"Thanks." Zane buttoned up his pants and turned around to kiss me. "I'd do it over again if I had to."
"Sure you would." I winked at him and held onto my panties and bra tightly. "Let's go home. I need to shower."
"You need to shower?" he groaned. "I have sand in places that nothing should ever have access to."
"Ha ha. I'll have to guess where those places are."
"Perv." He reached over and grabbed my breast through my wet top and licked his lips. "Oh the things I want to do with you right now."
"You wish, Beaumont." I screamed and went running as quickly as I could across the sand and to his car. I heard him behind me and I increased my pace. I felt Zane grab hold of me and we fell to the sand, laughing and exhausted. "No fair." I studied his face and smiled up into his eyes and he gazed down at me.
"You know all's fair in love and war."
"Are you in love with me or are we at war?"
"I love you more than words can say, I'll love you for a million days, I love you in many different ways, I love you if you'll always let

me pay, I'd love you even if you were made of clay."
"You're a goof." My heart thudded at his short little ditty. "But thank you."
"I never told you before, but I like to write songs." He stared down at me carefully. "I'm not great, but I like to do it for fun."
"Ooh, write me a song." I grinned. "I love music and musicians."
"Oh, so now you love me because I'm a musician?"
"Well, of course."
"Let's make a deal." His eyes sparkled. "I'll write you a song, if you write me a song."
"I can't sing," I wailed. "There is no way."
"You don't have to sing it."
"You want me to write you a song?" I looked at him in amazement. "Why?"
"The same reason you want me to write you a song."
"But you have talent."
"I'm sure you do as well."
I thought about it for a moment, and while I didn't want to accept the challenge, I did very much want for him to write me a song.
"Okay, you're on. Get ready for a reggae masterpiece."
"Reggae, huh?"
"I am from Miami."

"No, you're from the South. I was expecting some country. A little something about me, your pickup truck, and your dog."
"That's messed up, Zane. All country songs are not about pickup trucks."
"Sorry, should I clarify it's a Ford?"
"Idiot." I swatted him in the arm. "I do like country. I just really like reggae as well."
"Like Bob Marley, mon." Zane spoke in a Jamaican accent and I burst out laughing.
"Don't ever do that again," I chortled. "Is Bob the only reggae artist you know?"
"No, I know his son, Ziggy, as well." Zane bent down and kissed me on the lips. "Okay, you do your reggae song and I'll do my creation."
"Please no heavy metal."
"Wait, you don't want me to scream about how I want to love and kill you? Lucckkkkkyyy, I want you to knoooowwww, that I love you sooooo. Don't ever goooooo," he started shouting in a rock voice and I covered my ears.
"Please, no."
"Come on." He pulled me up. "Let's go home and shower."

***

"I called Leo, he's going to come over tomorrow and pick you up for dinner." Zane looked up as I stepped out of the bathroom in shorts and a t-shirt.
"Okay."
"Thanks for doing this, Lucky."
"I don't even know why this is needed."
"I don't know what Braydon and his lot are capable of. I don't want to risk anything." His voice rose and I groaned.
"Okay, okay. I don't want to get into it again." I rolled my eyes and Zane sighed.
"I don't think you understand the seriousness of the situation, Lucky. These guys aren't going to care if they have to hurt you." He grabbed my face. "Please do not do anything stupid."
I shook him off of me, feeling annoyed again. "I'm not a little kid. I don't want to have to keep telling you that, Zane. Sometimes you can be so annoying."
"I'm just trying to be your protector."
"I don't need a protector." My voice rose.
"You're right; we don't need to go into this again." He turned away from me. "I'm going into my office to do some work. Will you be okay by yourself?"

"Yes." I nodded, annoyed at him. "I'll start making some notes for the documentary."
And looking up your mom online.
"That's good. I'm glad it's something you love." He smiled at me sweetly and came over and gave me a kiss on the head. "Be good, and I'll be in the study if you need to talk."
"Yes, papa," I whispered under my breath as I rolled my eyes at his retreating back.
"What was that?" He turned to look at me with a frown.
"Nothing, sir." I stood to attention and saluted him. "Nothing at all."
Zane shook his head at me and walked out through the door. I flopped down on the bed and checked my phone. I had another message from Leeza and I decided to call her.
"Lucky!" she answered on the first ring.
"Hey." My voice was hesitant and not super friendly as I was still upset at her from the previous call.
"Evan and I broke up," she sighed. "He's an asshole."
"I didn't even know you guys were dating." I shook my head and my words were angry.
"Well, we weren't dating dating. We just hung out a few times and had sex."
"You slept with him?"
"He was hot."

"You didn't even know him."
"I don't have your rules, Lucky. Anyway, did you ask Zane if I can come to Los Angeles?" I could hear her pout over the phone.
"I thought you said he was creepy."
"Oh, I just said that. Evan made me think that, but maybe he's just sweet. And not a stalker." She paused. "Sorry."
"It's okay," I sighed. "And you can come to L.A. whenever."
"This weekend?" she asked hopefully.
"I guess." I wasn't really too anxious to see Leeza.
"What about tomorrow?"
"Tomorrow? You can't afford that."
"I got a ticket already." Her voice was low.
"Why? You didn't even know if it was going to be okay."
"Well, Evan and I were going to take a trip, and …"
"And you broke up, so now you want to come and visit me instead?"
"Yeah." Her voice was low. "Don't be mad at me, Lucky, please," she pleaded. "I miss you. I want to see you and make sure you're okay. You just left Miami so quickly, and I know you don't really know Zane that well."
"You can come," I groaned.

"Thank you, Lucky," she squealed. "I'm so excited. I've never been to California before. Can we go to Beverly Hills tomorrow?"
"I already have dinner plans for tomorrow." I frowned. "I guess you'll have to come."
"Oh, I don't want to interrupt your dinner date with Zane."
"I'm actually having dinner with a different guy." I paused to think if I should fill Leeza in on all the drama.
"Oh me, oh my. Are you guys swingers, Lucky?" Leeza's voice sounded shocked. "I blame myself, like, I knew this would happen. It always does. You had no sex, for like, what two years?"
"A year."
"And now you've gone crazy. That's why I just let myself indulge when I feel like it."
"Yeah, that's why." My voice was sarcastic. "Anyway, I have to go. I'm getting another call. Email me your flight info and I'll see if we can pick you up." I didn't wait for her to reply, and clicked over to the other line.
"Hello?" I asked slowly and cautiously, praying to God that I wasn't about to hear Braydon's voice on the line.
"Lucky?" Sidney Johnson's warm voice filled the airwaves and I smiled.
"Yes, hi, Sidney. How's it going?"

"Good, good. Betty just made me some pound cake and tea. I think she's trying to fatten me up." He laughed into the phone.
"That must be nice."
"So, I was just thinking about our conversation the other day," Sidney continued and I heard Betty mumbling something in the background. "Well, I told Betty and she told me to give you some information."
"Oh?"
"I told her it wasn't our place to get involved, but she said she thinks Noah would have approved, had he been here." He cleared his throat. "Anyway, when we saw Noah for the last time, he gave me some files, and well, me and Betty never really went through them before. But today, we had a look and, well, there's some information on his mom."
"On Noah and Zane's mom?" My jaw dropped and I lowered my voice. "You mean he found her?"
"Well, it looks like he did." Sidney's voice was worried. "I don't really know, but there's a number and an address. I don't know if they are good. But yeah, Betty thought I should give you the information. Save you some time, if you were going to look for Zane's mom."

"Oh, Sidney, that would be great," I gushed with my heart beating fast. "Let me get a pen and paper so I can write the information down."

"So there's one thing," Sidney continued. "The address and number, well they're in Paris. Paris, France."

"Oh." My heart dropped momentarily. There went my images of a happy family reunion and a trip to Disney.

"But we figured you could still call her."

"Yes, yes. I'll call her." I grabbed a pen and paper and wrote the number and address down. "Sidney, thank you so much. You don't know just how much this means to me."

"I just hope it will help." His voice sounded unsure. "I don't like to be a busybody, or in anyone's business. I know most old people get a bad name for that."

"It's okay, Sidney. It's more than okay. Thank you."

"Don't go gushing, girl," he sighed. "And don't go getting your hopes up. It may lead to nothing."

"But it may lead to something." There was a wistful tone in my voice. If Zane was able to reconnect with his mother, if he was able to understand why she left, then he may be able to fully let go of that pain and rejection. He may be able to love me without being so worried all the time. It was something that could possibly make our relationship a whole lot better.

"Well, just let me know." He paused and I heard Betty talking to him. "Oh yeah, Betty told me to tell you that we're going to Chicago next week to visit family, so we won't be available for the next few weeks. But feel free to call our cellular phone if you need to talk. It's not connected to a wire so we can talk from anywhere."

"Awesome." I tried not to laugh.

"Technology, I tell ya," he chortled. "Well, my dear, I better go before Betty takes offense that I'm not eating her cake."

"Enjoy, Sidney, and have a good time in Chicago. I'll see you when you get back."

"We better see you, girl, Betty's already planning the outfit she wants to wear to the Oscars."

"Ha ha. You two are too funny." I hung up with a smile and looked down at the paper in my hands, my stomach churning with nerves. I wasn't sure what to do. I wanted to call the number, but I didn't want Zane to be upset with me or to think I was meddling. Without knowing what I was doing, I felt myself

pushing in all the numbers and waiting for the phone to ring with my heart in my mouth.
"Bonjour," a man's deep voice answered, and my breath caught.
"Ah, Bonjour. Is Mrs. Beaumont there?" I cursed inwardly at the fact that I didn't know her first name.
"Allo?" the man continued.
"Is Mrs. Beaumont there?"
"No English." I heard him put the phone down and I waited impatiently, hoping that this wasn't going to be a lost cause.
"Bonjour," a woman's voice spoke and my heart skipped a beat at the slight hint of an American accent I heard.
"Mrs. Beaumont?" I asked softly, praying that I had the right number. The phone line went silent and I could hear music playing in the background.
"Sorry, who is this?" her voice sounded strained.
"I'm a friend of your son Zane," I continued quickly. "Is this Mrs. Beaumont?"
"No, no. Sorry. I think you have the wrong number."
"Wait, please," I pleaded.
"I'm sorry, but I can't help you." The voice paused and I heard a voice in the background whispering something.

"It would help Zane if he knew why you left," I burst out. "I don't know why you did, but he's your son. You owe him an explanation. If you love him …"
"I can't talk to you." She sounded angry. "Do not call me again."
"Mrs. Beaumont," I cried out. "Please."
"I don't know how you got my number. I don't go by that name anymore. Please do not call me."
"Do you love your sons?" My voice cracked, not knowing or understanding why she wasn't even asking me if her sons were okay.
"My sons were my life." Her voice was low and I could tell she was walking. "Noah and Zane were my life. You will never understand what it took for me to walk away."
"Explain it to them," I pleaded. "I could go and get Zane right now and you could explain it to him."
"No!" she called out. "I can't. I won't."
"Mrs. Beaumont, he has never gotten over you leaving him."
"It was my life. I had to leave that life. I was suffocating." Her voice cracked. "I'm sorry I have to go." And with that, the line went dead.
I called her back right away, hoping it had been a bad connection, but the phone just kept

ringing and ringing. My emotions were shot and I lay on the bed with heavy eyes. The call hadn't gone as expected. In fact, I felt as if my heart had broken just a little bit more for Zane. How could a mother be like that? I clasped my belly and vowed that no matter what happened, if I had a baby, I would always put them first.

"You still in here, lazy butt?" Zane entered the room and stared at me on the bed.

"I'm tired. It's late."

"Too tired for some loving?"

"I'm never too tired." I yawned again and we both laughed. He walked over and joined me on the bed, and I quickly put the piece of paper on the night table under my phone.

"What do you want to do tonight?" he asked as he laid down next to me and played with my hair.

"Let's play a board game." I sat up. "Something to get our minds off of everything."

"What about truth and dare?" He winked at me and I pinched him.

"No." I shook my head, trying to smile. "Do you have Monopoly?"

"I do." He smiled down at me and paused as he took in my face properly. "Are you okay, Lucky?" He frowned as he studied the pink

hue of my cheeks and the red in my eyes.
"You're sad?" He sat up and pulled me up next to him so he could look at me clearly. "What's wrong?"
"Nothing." I bit my lip and turned away from him. There was no way I was going to tell him that I had just spoken to his mother and that she was a coldhearted bitch.
"Is it about Leo?" He took a deep breath. "I promise it's not forever, just until I know Braydon is in jail. I don't want to risk him going off the deep-end if he finds out about the case. I wouldn't put it past him to do something to you."
"I don't think he would hurt me," I said softly. "But no, I wasn't thinking about him."
"Is it the baby?" Zane clenched his fist. "Are you worried about what will happen if you're pregnant?"
"I …" I tried to speak up but my voice cracked.
"Lucky, I will do everything in my power to make sure that this doesn't interrupt anything in your life. If you want to move back to Miami and go back to school, we'll go. If you want to move to Tanzania or Sydney, I will move with you. Wherever you want to go, whatever grad school you get into, I will support you. I promise."

"Oh, Zane." I reached over and hugged him. "It's not about the baby. Or the possible baby. We're being kind of ridiculous, you know." I touched his face. "We only had unprotected sex once. It's highly unlikely that I'm pregnant."
"I know." He looked down into my eyes with a smoldering look. "Trust me, I know. The chances are slim to none, but a part of me hopes that you are. I know that sounds wrong. But I think I'd quite like to have a baby with you."
"Really, Mr. Big Tipper?"
"Don't get me wrong. This is nothing that I would have planned for myself, but with you, well, it feels right."
"Yeah?"
"Yeah." He nodded and looked at me thoughtfully. "I'm not always a good guy. I don't think I'll ever be a perfect boyfriend. But, I think I'll be a good father. I think that I can make sure I'm a good father. The best father."
"I know you will be one." I kissed him lightly. "You'll be the best."
"I'm excited for the appointment." His eyes shone. "And scared as well."
"Same here." My stomach curdled and I listened to his heartbeat through his t-shirt. I

wrapped my arms around him and held him close to me. "You're so different from the man I first met, Zane Beaumont. I thought you were this stuck up, rich playboy. And I just knew you were an arrogant jerk. But you're not. You're a big old sweetie inside."
"Don't you dare tell anyone that!" I felt his hands creep up the back of my t-shirt and he rubbed my back. I sighed and closed my eyes at the warm feeling that was spreading through my body.
"Hmm, that feels good." His fingers started massaging my shoulders, and he pushed me down on the bed, stomach first, and straddled me.
"Put your arms up," he commanded, and pulled my t-shirt off. "I like it, no bra." His words were smooth as silk as he kneaded into the knots in my back. He ran his fingers up and down my back, squeezing my tender points and helping to rid me of my stress. After a few minutes I heard him humming and I listened as he sang me a song.
"She was the girl from the diner, she was the girl I knew would be mine, she was the one who stole my heart."
"Who was?" I giggled and looked up at him, happy that he was serenading me.

"Shh." He continued with his song. "She was the girl with the curls, the big frizzy curls, the curls that melted my heart. She was the one in my arms who made me sing, she was the one in my bed who made me come."

"Zane!" I squealed and turned over. "That's gross."

"It's not gross to orgasm, Lucky." He licked his lips and I felt his hands creep up to my breasts. "Have you ever come from someone playing with your breasts?"

"No." I shook my head and looked up at him with teasing eyes. "I don't think that's possible."

"Really? Is that a challenge?" His fingertips pinched my nipples and I squirmed underneath him.

"No." My breath caught as he leaned down and suckled on my left breast as he continued playing with my right one. "Oh, Zane."

"Oh, Lucky." He winked at me and his bites became harder and harder as he tugged away. I closed my eyes and let myself just experience the feelings. I felt myself growing wet and I eagerly ran my hands down his back and up his shirt. Zane's hand worked its way into my shorts and inside my panties, and he found my pleasure spot. He began rubbing it eagerly as he continued sucking. I moaned as

his fingers explored me further and pushed their way inside of me.
"Oh," I cried out in ecstasy as he brought me to the brink of an orgasm. He increased the speed of his fingers and bit down on my breast as I came underneath him. I screamed at the intense feeling of pleasure and pain and he removed his fingers from my shorts and grinned up at me.
"I told you I could make you come from playing with your breasts."
"But that's not all you did," I protested, laughing at the pleased look on his face. "You're a goof."
"You see the secret side of me," he said, only half-joking.
"I'm glad." I reached my hand down into his pants and realized that he was hard and ready to go. "I suppose you want to see the secret side of me as well?"
"Well, I won't say no." He closed his eyes as my hands grasped his erection and slid up and down the length of him. "Don't stop," he whispered with a deep voice.
"Hold on." I quickly removed my hand from him and he groaned as I pulled his shorts down. "I want to do something."
"Oh?" He looked up at me and his eyes glinted. "Backdoor already?"

“Zane, shut up, no.” I pushed him back down. “This is kind of embarrassing,” I began and my voice drifted off.

“Oh.” He sat up again and his eyes looked really interested. “Now, this I have to hear.”

“I want to give you a lap dance,” I mumbled slowly.

“A lap dance?” He looked up at me in confusion. “Like a stripper?”

“Yes.” I blushed and looked down and he jumped up and grabbed my hands.

“Well, what are we waiting for then? Let’s go downstairs.”

“Downstairs?” I was puzzled by his words, but all I could do was stare at his manhood. It was sticking out right at me and he was long and hard. I swallowed hard as I took him in. He was such a gorgeous, magnificent man, and he was all mine.

“I have a chair that would suit a lap dance perfectly.”

“Oh?” I wondered if he knew that from prior experience, but dismissed my jealous thoughts. *Don’t go there, Lucky. Not now.* I commanded myself. I knew that if anything, Zane would be honest and there was a likely chance that I wouldn’t be happy with the answer.

"Yes." He pulled me with him and stopped quickly, letting go of my hand and walking to the nightstand. "Condom." He showed me what he had gone back to retrieve, and I laughed.
"Well, aren't you the thoughtful one?"
"Now, let's go. I'm excited for my first dirty lap dance."
"Who said it's going to be dirty?" I raised an eyebrow at him.
"There is no way you're going to rub up and down on my cock and not have it be dirty." He laughed and we ran down the stairs.
He walked over to his iPhone dock and put on some music and I heard Usher crooning to me through the surround-sound speakers.
"You're gross."
"You don't want to be a tease, do you?"
"I don't know. Maybe I do."
"Come here, you." Zane pulled me down onto the chair with him and I found myself sitting atop of his lap with my breasts crushed against his chest. I leaned forward and crushed his lips against mine and started moving my hips in time to the music, loving the feel of him in between my legs.
"You're going to kill me, Lucky," he groaned as I rocked back and forth. I bit his bottom lip

before slowly licking down to his chest and lightly sucking his nipples.
“Oh,” Zane groaned.
I felt a sense of power fill me as I continued kissing down his stomach, until I had inched my way off of his lap and had his manhood in front of my face. Zane looked down at me with surprise in his eyes and I winked up at him.
“It’s a reward for being a good boy.” I chuckled at the delight on his face and then slowly took him into my mouth.

Chapter 7
Zane

"Do you think mom is looking for us?" Noah barged into my room without knocking and sat down on the bed next to me. "Maybe she's looking for us and can't find us."
"Don't be stupid. We still live in the same house." I looked at him with derision and anger. "If she wanted to find us she knows where to look—the same place she left us."
"Don't you ever hate being right?" Noah's eyes looked bleak and I felt sorry for being so mean. He was only 14 and still had hope that our mother would show up again. At 16, I knew that our mother was never showing up again. She was probably living it up on a Caribbean island, somewhere, with all our father's money.
"No." I looked away from him. "Can I finish my book, please?"
"What are you reading?"
"The Grapes of Wrath."
"Sounds boring." He yawned and stood up.
"Well, you'll have to read it for class one day as well." I laughed at him. "What are you going to do?"
"I thought I'd go play some drums." He looked at me, eagerly. "Want to join?"

I looked at my book and then back at his face and laid the book on the bed and sighed. The report could wait. "Okay, but I get to choose the songs. No more Rolling Stones, please."

"But I want to be like Charlie Watts."

"Can you be more like Ringo Starr?"

"What's your obsession with the Beatles?" Noah shook his head.

"I'm not obsessed with the Beatles," I protested.

"I thought you would hate them." Noah hesitated. "I'm just surprised."

"Why would I hate them?" My breath caught.

"You know." He paused.

"No, I don't. Why?" Did he remember? My body was burning up as I looked at him.

"Mom used to love them, she used to sing that lonely people song all the time."

"Eleanor Rigby." My voice was low and I looked away from him.

"Yeah." Noah rubbed my arm. "I love you, Zane."

"You're too young to be such a sap, bro."

"You know you love me, too."

"Okay, let's go play some Rolling Stones."

"It worked." He ran down to the basement and I followed him with a smile. I was glad he hadn't pushed the issue. I didn't like to think about my obsession with the Beatles. I didn't

like to think about it being one of the only connections I had to my mother. She left us; she didn't deserve to be remembered.
"Let's play 'Satisfaction.'" Noah grinned up at me as I entered the garage and he started drumming.

I felt my eyes open quickly and I looked around the room looking for Noah and his drums. I heard the music in my head as clearly as I had that day. Disappointment flooded through me as the silent darkness reflected back at me. Noah was gone. I laid looking at the ceiling, listening to the sound of Lucky sleeping next to me. I tried to concentrate on her light snores and not the sounds of music still echoing in my ears. I needed to think about something else. I was going to drive myself crazy if I kept dreaming about Noah and our mom.
My heart pounded as I thought about dinner with Angelique. I had to make sure that she had no idea about my relationship with Lucky. All though Braydon may have told her something, he probably thought that it was just about sex with Lucky, and Angelique wouldn't mind that. She knew what the deal was—what the deal used to be with me. My biggest worry now was Lucky. I felt my

stomach dip in fear and worry. My biggest fear was her finding out about Angelique and the dinner. I wasn't sure how she would react to finding out about the evening I had planned, and I couldn't risk her not accepting it. She had made some jealous comments about Angelique already, and I knew that it was a sore spot. I took a deep breath and rubbed my brow. I jumped out of bed and walked down the stairs. I couldn't stay in the bed and just lay there, knowing that I was living a lie.

I walked into the backyard and sat on one of the recliners, and looked up at the sky. The sun was about to rise, and it was quiet. I loved the stillness of early morning. The only sounds I could hear were the birds chirping and the sounds of a few cars passing by. I laid back and thought about everything that was going on. I had to change. This was going to be the last time that I lied to Lucky. She deserved better than this. Our relationship deserved better. Our baby (oh God, I hoped there was a baby), deserved better.

I must have fallen asleep because I woke up to Lucky standing in front of me, crying her eyes out. My heart froze as I thought to myself, *She knows*. She knows about the

dinner with Angelique and she's breaking up with me.
"What's wrong?" My voice was brusque. I was going to deny it. It hadn't happened, yet. She couldn't prove anything.
"I got my period," she cried and looked into my eyes with sadness.
"Okay." I looked at her for a moment, wondering if she had lost it. Why was she crying just because she had her period?
"I woke up and I had my period," she cried.
I gave her a smile. "It's okay. I don't mind if you ruined the sheets."
"I got my period!" she exclaimed louder, and then it hit me.
She got her period.
"You can cancel the doctor's appointment."
I felt my heart lurch at the words, but I pulled her into my arms to comfort her. "It's okay," I whispered. I kissed her hair, and then all over her face. "It's okay, Lucky. Maybe right now wasn't the right time to have a baby."
"I wanted to have a baby," she cried into my shoulders. "I wanted us to have a baby."
"And we still can. You just have more time to finish school and do all those other things you wanted to do."
I tried not to think about her going back to school and meeting all those other guys, guys

without issues, guys who didn't hold back certain information. She'd leave me. She'd meet a better guy, a man whose mother hadn't left him, a guy who wasn't fucked up.
"Are you okay?" This time it was her turn to ask me the question. I guessed that she heard the dejection in my voice.
"Yes, yes." I nodded and held her close. I didn't want to let go of her. I didn't want to be without her warmth and love. Lucky was healing my broken heart, piece by piece, and I was scared that it would shatter into a million pieces if she ever decided to leave me for good. "Don't leave me, Lucky."
"Leave you?" She frowned. "Why would I leave you?"
"There's nothing holding you here, now."
"Is that why you wanted me to be pregnant?" She sat back. "Because you thought I'd leave you if I wasn't?"
"No," my voice was firm and I stood up. "Let's go inside." I was done talking about emotions. I needed my head to be in the right place.
"Okay." She followed me into the house. "Oh, I can't believe I forgot to tell you, but Leeza is coming to Los Angeles."
"Okay."

"Today." Her voice was low and she wiped her eyes.
"Today?" That was all I needed, her busybody friend in my business.
"Is that okay?"
"It's fine. I can't cancel my meeting tonight, I'm afraid, but I'm sure Leo won't mind if she joins you both for dinner."
"Yeah, maybe they'll even hit it off." She grinned, her mood lightening as we walked up the stairs.
"Unlikely. Leo is picky."
"What's that supposed to mean?"
"Nothing, nothing." I looked at her upset eyes and brought her in close to me. "I'm sure they'll get on like a house on fire." I stroked her hair and kissed her cheek, suddenly happy that Leeza was going to be there.
I knew that Leo went for girls like Lucky - girls who were spunky and beautiful, with hearts of gold. He was like me, in that any girl was okay for a night in the sack, but for the long-term, he wanted a gem. And Lucky was the most sparkling gem out there. I trusted him and I trusted her, but I didn't want to put anything to chance. Maybe it wouldn't be so bad if her friend Leeza was there, even if I didn't trust her one iota.

"Yeah," she sniffled. "Don't worry, I don't want her rushing into a relationship with Leo after being with Evan."
"She dated Evan?" I frowned. "I thought they just knew each other."
"Well, they knew each other intimately, I guess."
"She gets around fast, doesn't she?"
"Hey." Lucky pinched me in the arm.
"Sorry, sorry."
"Uh huh." She pushed away from me and walked into her room. "I'm getting in the shower."
"In there?" I looked at her with a heavy heart. Was she mad at me again?
"Yeah, I'd rather bathe in here today." She nodded and blushed. "It's a girl thing."
"Oh okay." Understanding dawned in me and I grinned. "Sure thing."
I walked back into my bedroom and inspiration hit me. I grabbed a pen and paper and started writing, furiously. I grinned to myself as I read the words of the poem I had written for her. I had an idea and I wanted to make sure that everything was going to be perfect. I picked up the phone to call a friend, and went into the shower about 15 minutes later, a much happier man.

"One day people shall talk of this day, my love. One day birds shall sing of my joy, my love." I sang to myself as I changed and I paused as I heard my phone ringing. I answered it, immediately, and my heart stilled as I spoke.

"This is Zane."

"Zane. It's Special Agent Waldron."

"Hello."

"Is it clear?"

"All clear." My voice was tight. "Though we need to hurry. I have a guest who may come in the room soon."

"We're very close to linking Braydon to a cartel in Mexico. We think he's trafficking a lot more than we thought."

"Okay." My heart thudded in anticipation.

"We think he has a partner."

"Oh?" *Evan!*

"Someone who is brokering the deals, someone who has more connections."

"I see."

"We need both of them to make an arrest." The Agent's voice was firm. "We get both of them, and they implicate Sanchez for us, then we got him."

"Do you know who the partner is?"

"We have some ideas, but we aren't releasing any names yet."

"But I'm helping you—you can't tell me?" My voice was angry. "Look, I have a girlfriend now and I'm scared she may be targeted."

"Get her out of town."

"I can't do that." There was no way that I was sending Lucky anywhere, not when I couldn't be sure she was safe. "She's staying here with me."

"We can't guarantee her safety."

"I'm getting a bodyguard."

"Zane, I don't suggest you bring anyone else into this situation right now. It's very delicate."

"I know that!" I shouted. "And she's already involved. I didn't want it to happen, but it did. If you won't protect her, I will."

"You need to be careful, Beaumont. You cannot share any privileged information with her."

"She's not a spy."

"You don't know that. You can't trust anyone at this moment."

"I trust her with my life." I spoke the words and knew they were true.

"Zane, you cannot jeopardize this assignment. We have been working too long on bringing this cartel down. Do you want to bring

Braydon down? The man responsible for the ending of your relationship with Noah?"
"Do I want to bring down the guy who murdered my brother? Of course I do, you fucking asshole! Don't you ever question me again! I am helping you!"
"Calm down, Beaumont. We can't have you ruining this with your emotions."
"I'm calm." I wanted to throw the phone against the wall. "Does Braydon know you're on to him?"
"That cocky bastard has no idea." Special Agent Waldron laughed. "And he has no idea about you, so keep it that way."
"I'm not about to let him know now."
"Just let him think it's about the revenge. Mention nothing about drugs."
"I'm not dumb," I hissed angrily.
"We know that, Beaumont, but we're close to the end here. We just need to make sure we catch them both."
"What do you want me to do if you won't tell me who the other suspect is?"
"Just follow through with the plan we already have." The Agent's voice was rough. "Don't fuck it up."
"I won't," I sighed. Even if it fucked up my relationship with Lucky, I wasn't going to mess up this case.

"I'm sure you have an idea who Braydon's partner may be."
"Yes." I thought back to all those nights hanging out with Evan and I couldn't believe I had missed all the signs. He was such a kiss-ass with everyone, and now I knew why. My heart raced as I realized what Lucky had told me. Leeza was coming into town today - her best friend. Her best friend who had dated Evan. Oh shit! I had to make sure to tell Leo to keep an extra close eye on Lucky and Leeza. I didn't want her going anywhere with that girl.
"Beaumont, are you there?" The Agent's voice sounded tired. "Do what we asked and provide us with the information. That's all we want from you, okay?"
"Okay," I sighed.
"If all goes well, we may have enough evidence to make some arrests within the next week or so."
"I sure hope so."
"I gotta go, Beaumont." And with that, the agent hung up.
I stared at the phone in my hand, my heart pounding. We were close to the end. I couldn't believe it. I'd been a part of this case for so long and it was nearly over. I was close to seeing Braydon Eagle locked behind bars. I

grimaced as I thought about him. While seeing him in jail would make me happy, it wouldn't bring back Noah.

***

"So Leeza is your best friend?" I kept my voice light as we drove to the airport.

"Yeah, she's one of my best friends. She was really there for me when my parents died." Lucky looked out the window. "We've drifted apart recently, though."

"Oh yeah? Why?"

"After I adopted my rules and stopped partying with her so much, we kind of grew apart. She kept going out and meeting guys and bringing them home, and well, I just worked a lot."

"She's like your family, now, then?"

"Family's overrated." She pursed her lips and cleared her throat.

"I take that as a no."

"No, I don't mean that. She's a good friend of mine. Sometimes friends are better than family. Sometimes family lets you down and you just don't know why."

"You sound like me." I looked at her, worried. "Everything okay?"

"Yeah."

"You wouldn't lie to me, right? It's not the baby, right?" I reached over and squeezed her knee. "I know we're both disappointed, but it'll be okay. Everything happens for a reason."

"How did you get to be so wise?" She half-smiled. "But it will be nice to see Leeza. Maybe we can have a girls' day, and she can tell me what happened with Evan."

"Are you sure they broke up?" I kept my face looking forward.

"Yeah, that's what she said." She played around with the radio and I resisted the urge to keep questioning her. Leeza had tried to cause trouble for Lucky and me, before. Maybe she knew that I had never been stalking Lucky. Maybe she wasn't trying to be a good friend. Maybe she was just a bad friend, and Evan was using her to get to me.

"Remind me I need to talk to Leo before you all go to dinner tonight."

"We'll behave ourselves, Zane. I promise."

"You're always a bad girl, Lucky."

"I suppose you want to bend me over your knee, huh?"

"And give you a good spanking? Yes."

"I would not be surprised if you tell me you were a Dom in a previous life."

"You'd like that, huh?"

"Not really."
"What would you call me? Big daddy?"
"Oh my, Zane." She burst out laughing uncontrollably. "Please never say those words again."
"You don't want to call me big daddy?"
"Hell no, I don't. That sounds so pervy."
"I guess you can call me Big Zaney instead."
"I'll call you Crazy Zane, more like—or Pervy Zane."
"At least you'll be calling."
"You can't stop me from calling."
"Good." I reached over and squeezed her hand. "I started writing your song."
"Really?" She turned to me and grinned. "I want to hear it."
"Not yet." I laughed at her pout. "That won't work, baby."
"But, honey." She sidled up next to me and rested her head on my shoulder. "Please."
"Don't scare me." I glanced at her face on my shoulder. "You'll make me think you've become a Stepford Wife."
"I don't want to get your hopes up." She moved away from me again. "Well, whatever, I won't tell you the lyrics I wrote for you either."

"You did?" I was excited to hear that she had gone through with it. "Are you going to sing it to me?"
"I don't know," she said. "It depends on how drunk I am."
"Tell me the first line."
"And …?" She raised an eyebrow at me.
"I'll tell you a first line."
"Hmmm." She considered my offer. "I don't know."
"Okay, three lines then."
"Three lines? That's almost my whole song."
"Really?" I turned the radio down and cleared my throat and started to sing.

"One day, people shall talk of this day, my love
One day, birds shall sing of my joy, my love
One day, the wind shall scream the truth to the world, my love ..."

"Oh, Zane. I love it," she gasped. "Sing some more. Please."
"I'll think about it if you sing some of yours to me."
"You have to promise not to laugh."
"I promise I won't laugh."
"Liar." She wrinkled her cute little nose at me and I sighed as I saw we were approaching

the airport. I wasn't ready to share her with her friend. Especially because I had a bad feeling that Leeza wasn't here just to hang out.
"Okay, now I can't really sing, but here we go." She cleared her throat and I looked over and saw that her face was red. I felt bad for asking her to sing when she was obviously not into it, but before I could tell her it was okay, she started singing.

"Zane, there has never been a man like you
Who has taken my heart and swallowed it up
I want you to know that you never have to doubt ..."

She stopped and looked at me awkwardly. "I know it's not as good as yours. I'm not a writer like you."
"It was beautiful, just like you."
"Suck up, why don't you?" she teased me, but I could tell from the pink at the top of her ears that she was happy that I enjoyed it.
She certainly wasn't a songwriter, but the imperfection of her lyrics hit me hard. I had taken her heart and swallowed it up. The enormity of those lyrics hit me like a ton of bricks. Lucky really loved me. There was no rhyme or reason to it. I couldn't explain how I

knew, but I just knew. A sense of calm filled me. She was in it for the long haul. She was in it for me. She was obviously uncomfortable, but she had sung to make me happy. I wanted to turn the car around and go home. I wanted to forget Leeza and her hidden agenda, I wanted to give up on Angelique, I wanted to forget about bringing Braydon to his knees. I wanted to be able to let go. For a moment I slowed the car, but then I heard the song that was playing on the radio. It brought me back to reality with a swift kick.

"Yesterday." I looked at her, stating a fact and not asking for confirmation.

She nodded and smiled. "I love the Beatles. I hope it's okay."

"It's fine." I pressed my foot back down on the accelerator. I had come too far now. I had to do this for Noah's memory. I had to do this for the brother I had lost, the brother who had never given up hope. I had to do this for the boy inside of me that still loved to hate the Beatles.

***

"Lucky, this house is amazeballs." Leeza's mouth dropped as she stood in the entryway of our bedroom. I tried not to let my annoyance show on my face. She had been talking nonstop since we picked her up, and hadn't really asked Lucky how she was or what she was doing. Her favorite topic seemed to be herself, and I was mad that Lucky had such a selfish best friend. "And this room. Oh my gosh, could you see me in a room like this? Could you imagine the parties we could have here?"

I glanced at Lucky, who was sitting on the bed next to me, and I shook my head. There was no way in hell I was letting Leeza throw a party in my house. Even if I didn't think she was somehow working with Evan. She just wasn't trustworthy.

"Do you want to go downstairs and watch TV, Leeza?" Lucky jumped up and I watched as she walked towards her friend. She had the same swinging hips that she'd had in the diner, but now when I stared at her walking, I just felt a deep sense of contentment, as opposed to lust and wanting. I still felt the lust, but it was about more than that now.

"Not really." Leeza walked over to the bed and sat next to me, flinging her blond hair back in what I could only assume was meant to be a seductive move. "I want to get to know Zane a bit better." She smiled at me and

I noticed that the smile didn't quite reach her blue eyes.
"He has a business meeting tonight, Leeza. He needs to get ready."
"He doesn't have time for his guest?"
"What do you want to know Leeza?"
"Not much." She lay back on the bed and sighed, and I looked up at Lucky and she stared at us uncomfortably. I jumped up and walked over to her.
"Your friend is crazy," I whispered in her ear and she grinned at me before hitting me in the arm.
"Be nice," she whispered back. "Leeza, get off the bed and let's go downstairs."
"I'm coming, I'm coming." She jumped up and I noticed that she looked sad.
"Is everything okay, Leeza?" Lucky arched her eyebrows.
"Yeah. I'm just a bit down." She pouted her lips and I reluctantly decided to ask her why.
"What's wrong? Is there anything we can do?"
"I'm just sad 'cause Evan, you know, your friend Evan? Well, he dumped me." She batted her eyelashes at me. "I'm a little sad. I thought he was interested in me."
"Sex doesn't equal interest, Leeza," Lucky chided her friend and continued on. "You

didn't even really know him. And don't get me started on that crap you said about Zane and how he was a stalker."

"That's what Evan told me!" Leeza cried out. "He told me I should let you know." She pouted again as she looked at me. "How was I to know? I barely know him. You barely know him."

"I know him a lot better than you do. Do you think I'm an idiot?" Lucky's voice was taut.

"Well, you did just come here on a whim."

"I don't expect you to understand, Leeza, but I don't want you trying to sabotage my relationship. You're one of my best friends, and that won't change, but I'm not the same girl, anymore. I changed a long time ago."

"What did you do to her?" Leeza turned around and pointed at me. "Did you turn my best friend against me?"

"I don't know what you're talking about," I said, coldly, irritated and annoyed. The last thing I needed was for this to become a volatile situation. I didn't know what Evan was planning, but if he was as involved with this drug trafficking as I thought he was, and it went as deep as the FBI said it did, then Lucky was in some real danger with Leeza around.

“Leeza, let’s go downstairs.” Lucky grabbed her friend’s arm.
I put my hand up. “Wait.” I walked over to Leeza and gave her a big smile- a big, fake smile. I really wanted to interrogate her about what she knew, but I knew it wouldn’t be smart. “Maybe we got off to a bad start, Leeza. Hi, I’m Zane.” I offered her my hand. “I’m Lucky’s boyfriend.”
“Boyfriend?” Her jaw dropped open. “I thought you guys were just sleeping together.”
“Leeza!” Lucky’s voice was angry. “Let’s go get a drink.”
“Lucky, you go downstairs. I want a quick word with her.” I smiled gently and waited until I heard her going down the stairs to speak to her friend. “You listen, and you listen good. I don’t know what game you’re playing, and I don’t know if you realize just how much trouble Evan is and what sort of trouble you’re dragging Lucky into, but you better believe that I’m on to you and what you’re doing. If I find out you have betrayed Lucky in any way, I will make sure you never see her again.”
Leeza stood there with her mouth hanging open and I saw some saliva escape from her mouth. She looked at me in shock and I

thought my words really struck a chord. There was no way I was going to allow her to jeopardize Lucky's safety or the case against Braydon and Evan. I gave her one last, hard stare, and stood by the open door, ushering her out of the room.

As I got ready for my dinner date with Angelique, the nerves in my stomach threatened to bring me to my knees. Angelique and I had a connection, and I couldn't let it go. I had been excited about this night and this moment for a few months. Our relationship together hinged on this moment, and as much as I loved Lucky, I couldn't let this go. I couldn't let Angelique go. Not now when we had come this far.

Chapter 8
Lucky

"Take good care of them, Leo," Zane whispered urgently to his friend, and it was all I could do to not roll my eyes.
Zane had been acting weird ever since we picked Leeza up, and I wasn't sure why they had that near-fight in the bedroom earlier. Both of them were acting a bit weird, and I wondered if there was some history there that I didn't know about. I laughed to myself at my thoughts. There was no way Leeza would have slept with him and not told me, and I knew that Zane would have been honest with me about it, as well. We were a team now. We told each other everything.
"You never told me Leonardo was so gorgeous," Leeza gushed to me and played with her blonde hair. "Do you think I have a shot with him?" She flattened her short, black skirt and ogled Leo. Leeza's mood had improved since Leo had arrived, but I could tell she didn't like Zane at all. "He's a creep" had been her exact words to me.
"I think he may be seeing someone," I lied. I didn't know how to tell Leeza to slow down with the guys. It was a conversation we'd had before, but she had gotten mad at me and

called me a "Holier-than-thou, born-again nun." I had tried to tell her that her sentence didn't really make sense, and that I was only thinking about her best interests, but she had shot me down.

"If he ain't married, he's available." Leeza grinned at me and walked over to Leo and Zane. "Why, Leo, I'm happy to see that L.A. has some *good looking* men."

Zane looked up at me and rolled his eyes at her comment, and I stifled a laugh. I couldn't stop myself from staring at him in his dark, grey suit and tie. He looked so handsome and debonair, and his hair was shining and his eyes were sparkling. I wasn't sure exactly what business meeting he was going to, but it was obviously an important one.

I walked over to him and linked my arm through his. "You look very handsome tonight," I whispered into his ear while breathing in his delicious, manly scent.

"Thank you, my dear." He looked me over from the top of my head to the tips of my toes and licked his lips. "You look beautiful. I'm jealous that you've never gotten this dressed up for me."

"Well, you could come to dinner with us instead." I kissed him and he grabbed me around the waist and kissed me back.

"I wish." He took a deep breath. "I promise that, tomorrow, it will be you and me, and a nice dinner out, wherever you want."
"I'd like that."
"And we'll both get dressed up."
"Will you wear a tux?"
"A tux?" He groaned and caught me laughing. "I'll wear a tux if you wear a prom dress."
"Prom dress?" I shivered. "A big pink frilly mess?"
"It doesn't have to be pink; it can be a black frilly mess."
"Or a purple one, I suppose."
"What am I supposed to do when you guys go acting like high school kids?" Leeza's voice was sharp and I looked at her bitter face.
I wasn't sure what to say to my friend. I wasn't sure why she wasn't happy for me. Maybe it was because I was the girl that never had the best relationships. I was always the one that Leeza could look at and say well, "Lucky's relationship is worse than mine." We had bonded over our bad relationships the first two years of college, and she had understood my need to take a break from that scene after my parents had died. But she had never understood why I never went back to the partying scene. I suppose she didn't think it was fair that I now had a hunky boyfriend

and she still had no one. But that still wasn't an excuse to be a bitch.

"You can do whatever …" Zane started, and Leo interrupted him.

"You can come with me to a comedy show if you think you'd like that." Leo winked at me and I smiled at him, gratefully. I took in his appearance and I could see why Leeza was acting giddy around him. With his sun-kissed blond hair, and sky-blue eyes, he was as handsome as any movie star.

"Oh, that would be great. It's so nice that there are still some gentlemen left in the world." Leeza batted her eyelashes up at Leo and I could see her preening up at him.

I turned my face away as I saw her stick her chest out at Leo. Oh boy, this was going to be a long night.

"Thanks for that, Leo." Zane pat Leo on the shoulder. "I'm glad you're willing to take one for the team."

"Zane." I poked him in the stomach. "Be nice."

"I am." He looked at me with an innocent face.

"Don't you have a *business meeting,* Zane?" Leeza's voice was loud. "Shouldn't you be on your way? I'd hate for you to be late. Seeing as you're so dressed up and all."

“Leeza.” My voice was tight.
“Well, I don’t know anyone who has a business meeting at night and looks like he is on his way to the church to get married.”
“Leeza.” I bit my lip. “Stop it.” I looked over at Zane and I could see a murderous look in his eyes. I knew he was about to lose it.
“Can’t I voice what we’re all thinking?” She shook her head. “I’m not trying to say it behind his back. I think it’s rude and disrespectful that he is going out on my first night in town. What meeting is that important? Evan said you were a bit of a prick, and I understand why he said that.”
There was an awkward silence in the room after her words and I felt my blood boiling.
“Leeza, come with me.” I grabbed her arm and dragged her into the kitchen. “What is your problem? Why are you being so rude and obnoxious?”
“I just wanted to voice my opinion, Lucky. Don’t you think he’s a little too smooth? I don’t trust him.”
“Well I do trust him, and I won’t have you berating and accusing him like that, again. He’s my boyfriend, Leeza. You may not understand our relationship, but, frankly, it’s none of your business.”

"I'm your best friend, Lucky." Leeza looked at me with wide eyes. "It's always my business."
"What's going on?" I took hold of her hand. "What's wrong with you, Leeza?"
"I'm sorry, Lucky." Tears flooded her eyes. "I'm just really upset and hurt."
"About what?" I looked at her in confusion. "Because I'm with Zane?"
"No, no." She started crying. "I really liked Evan, and everything was going great. At least, I thought it was. Then, he just broke up with me. Like I meant nothing to him. Out of nowhere."
"He sounds like a jerk, Leeza. But that doesn't mean Zane is."
"He'll break your heart, Lucky. That's what those guys do. They aren't made for girls like us. They don't want a long-term relationship. They just want to screw us."
"Zane is different." My voice was soft, but firm. "I love him, Leeza, and he loves me. And yeah, he's not perfect. He has issues, and sometimes it's really hard, but I know, that at the end of the day, he loves me. He shows it in many different ways. And I know he trusts me and respects me. And maybe this won't be the last relationship I'm ever in. Maybe something will happen and we'll break up, but

that will be because that's life. Nothing's guaranteed. But as sure as I'm standing here in front of you, I'm sure of Zane. Don't you get it, Leeza? He's the one. He's my one. He's my soul mate."

"You don't know him well enough to know all that." She continued crying and looked at me with a worried expression. "Look, I'll admit that I'm slightly jealous, but something about him just seems off and I don't want you to get hurt. Not after last time. I was so worried, Lucky. Your parents had died and you were devastated by that, and then, well, you know. You were heartbroken. I don't want to see you like that ever again."

"Zane wouldn't do that to me." I hugged her to me. "I love you for being concerned, but Zane wouldn't do that to me."

"I've made a fool of myself, haven't I?" She wiped her eyes. "What's Leo going to think of me now?"

"Oh, Leeza," I laughed. "He's going to think you're a spirited woman and a concerned friend."

"I'd rather he think I was hot." She fingered through her hair. "I'm going to go back upstairs and redo my makeup, okay?"

"Okay." I followed her into the living room, and watched as she ran up the stairs, before I

spoke to Zane and Leo. "She's a bit emotional because her ex-boyfriend dumped her."
"I wouldn't exactly say Evan was her boyfriend." Zane's voice was dry.
I gave him a warning look. "Be nice."
"Your friend is a bitch."
"Zane!"
"Sorry. Your friend has issues."
"Zane," I admonished him, but couldn't stop the smile from spreading on my face. "She's had a hard time lately, and she was worried about me. Let's cut her some slack. I've asked her to be nicer."
"Good luck, Leo." Zane laughed as he patted his friend on the shoulder. "Better you than me."
"Thanks, Zane, you owe me," Leo drawled and I could see the laughter in his eyes.
"Don't forget to keep an eye out for Lucky. I want you to make sure she is protected at all times." Zane's voice turned serious.
"I'm right here, Zane." I glared at him. "And I can hear you."
"Take care of my girl, and no funny business."
"Zane." I blushed at his words and Leo shook his head.
"I love you, Lucky." Zane reached down and pulled me to him, kissing me hard. His hands

grabbed my ass, and as he brought me into him, I melted against his chest. "I'm sorry I can't be with you tonight, but I want you to have fun."
"Is there something you're not telling me?" I pulled away from him, slightly, and looked into his darkened eyes. "There's something going down with Braydon tonight, isn't there?"
Zane was silent for a moment as he studied my face. He kissed me lightly on the nose and shook his head. "Of course not. I just have some business partners from Japan who want to meet. I would have taken you, but it's customary, in Japanese culture, for business dinners to be just for the men."
"I see." My heart skipped a beat for reasons unknown, and I grabbed hold of his hand. "Just be home as quickly as possible."
"Of course, my dear. Of course." He kissed me again and looked back at Leo. "Thanks for doing this, man."
"No problem. Lucky and I will have fun tonight." Leo grinned at me. "We'll keep Leeza sane."
"I'll have to remind myself to think of you as a friend and not a bodyguard," I teased him and he laughed.
"Don't blame me, blame your man."

“I’ll take all the blame.” Zane held his hands up. “I just want to make sure my lady love is safe.”
“I’ll be safe!” I exclaimed.
Zane was really overprotective, and while it thrilled me that he obviously cared about me a lot, it was starting to get old. I didn’t really understand what he thought Braydon was going to do to me. But I understood that he needed to be in control, or to at least feel like he was. I had hoped to be able to make him realize that he couldn’t blame himself for Noah’s death, or his mother’s leaving. I had hoped that his mother would somehow come back into his life and help mend a piece of his heart that I would never be able to reach, but after that phone call, I didn’t think that was ever going to happen. My throat caught as I thought about the call with his mother. I couldn’t believe how uncaring she had been. I never wanted Zane to find out about the call. I didn’t want him to have to go through that pain and rejection again.
“Lucky, darling, I’m going out now.” Zane squeezed my hand and I looked up at him all flustered.
“Sorry, I spaced out.”
“Have a good night. Keep the bed warm for me.”

"I will."
"Maybe you can do another dance for me, tonight."
"Zane," I chided him, embarrassed that he was talking about my lap dance in front of Leo.
"What?" He grinned and gave me one long, hard kiss before walking to the door. "Have a great night, guys."

***

"Now *this* is a restaurant." Leeza sailed into Providence Restaurant in front of us with her eyes smiling in delight and anticipation. "So this is Hollywood?"
"Actually, we're on Melrose Place, and this is known as Mid-Wilshire," Leo interjected, and smiled at me.
"I love Hollywood, I want to move here." Leeza grinned at me, the tears from earlier firmly behind her.
"Uh huh." I prayed to God that she wasn't hoping to live with Zane and me.
"What do you think, Leo? Looking for a roommate?" She touched his arm and smiled into his eyes.
"I, uh," Leo mumbled, and I think that was the first time I'd seen him at a loss for words.

"Come on, Leeza." I grabbed her arm and we followed our hostess to our table. "Wow, look at the lights." I pointed to the sconce lights on the wall of the dining room and admired all the orchids. "Thanks for bringing us here, Leo, this place is amazing." I turned around to thank him and we shared a secret smile.

We sat at the table and my eyes nearly popped open when I saw the prices on the menu. The restaurant was expensive, a lot more than I had ever spent on food before. Maybe even more than I spend at the grocery store in a month.

"Don't worry about the prices, girls. Zane's taking care of it."

"He should be," Leeza said snidely. I could tell she was peeved that Zane had left before she had been able to come back downstairs and apologize.

"I hope you girls like seafood." Leo played diplomat and I nodded. I was overwhelmed with all the choices. "I suggest we all start with the 1978 Madeira, and I recommend the Kobe beef with bone marrow if you're not a huge fan of seafood. If you like seafood, you can't go wrong with any of the entrees."

"Sounds delicious." I placed the menu back on the table. "Will you excuse me while I go to the restroom to wash my hands, please?"

"Sure."
I got up from the table and tried not to gape when I saw Robin Williams sitting with someone in the corner of the restaurant. I walked into the bathroom and washed my hands, quickly, before heading back to the table.
"Lucky."
I heard his voice and froze. I looked over at the table I was walking past and saw Braydon Eagle sitting there with a cute redhead.
"Hi Braydon." I nodded and attempted a smile.
"I called you and texted you. I wanted to apologize."
"I saw."
"You didn't call me back."
"I had nothing to say to you." I looked at the redhead to see how she was reacting to the conversation, but she sat there with a smile plastered on her face.
"I didn't do anything to you, Lucky." He looked angry.
"Look, I have to get back to my table." I made to walk away.
"I'm not the bad guy here, Lucky." He stood up. "I don't know what Zane has told you, but I'm not the bad guy."

"Leave Zane out of it." I glared at him. "I just don't like you."
"You think Zane is so perfect, don't you?" Braydon chortled. "Do you think he's some lost boy you need to protect and rescue? Don't be an idiot, Lucky. Zane's not some lost boy. He's a calculating snake, and he's only using you to make Angelique jealous."
"Angelique was Noah's ex." The words tripped out of my mouth, hurriedly.
"Yeah, but did you also know she hooked up with Zane?" Braydon's eyes were hard and he leaned forward as he pushed the dagger further into my heart. "That's one of the reasons Noah stopped speaking to Zane. He found out that Zane had fucked her."
"You're lying." The blood left my face and my hands felt clammy. "Zane would have told me."
"He's not the perfect guy you think he is, Lucky. He's not the perfect guy you think he is at all."
"You're a liar." I turned around and walked away from him, quickly. I plastered a smile on my face as I got back to the table. "Hey, guys. Sorry about that."
"No problem," Leeza giggled. "This wine is so good. Have some."

"Thanks." I took a glass and drank quickly, trying to forget the poison Braydon had tried to put in my mind. There was no way Zane had slept with Angelique. He couldn't have. He would have told me. We were being honest with each other now. I trusted him.

***

It was 2 a.m. and I laid in Zane's bed alone with my cell phone. I had tried calling and texting him several times since we had gotten back to the house, but he hadn't responded, and he wasn't home. I had no idea where he was or who he was with. And I very much doubted he was still at a business dinner with the Japanese businessmen. If there had ever really been a dinner. A single, solitary tear fell and I closed my eyes. I was too tired and distressed to stay up any longer. I didn't know what to think anymore. All I knew was that Zane and I had to have a very serious conversation.

Chapter 9
Zane

I opened the front door, slowly, and peeked inside before stepping in. I half expected to see Lucky and Leeza sitting there, waiting for me. Lucky would be in tears and Leeza would have a smug look on her face. I was surprised to see that the living room was empty. I half-hoped that Lucky had fallen asleep early, and didn't realize that I had been gone the whole night. I took a deep breath and closed the door before leaning back and closing my eyes. I hadn't intended on spending the night with Angelique, but I hadn't been able to leave. I just wanted to go to my bed and think, I needed to process everything that had happened. It just didn't seem real.

"Why, good morning stranger." Leeza walked towards me from the kitchen. "Good night at your business meeting?" She smirked and flung her hair over her shoulders. Even though I knew she wasn't involved in anything shady, I still thought she was a big bitch.

"Where's Lucky?" I didn't even acknowledge her question. I knew now that she wasn't working with Evan to bring me down, but I

still couldn't stand talking to her. It made me wonder what Lucky's other friends were like.
"In the kitchen." She paused. "I'd go say your goodbyes if I were you." She laughed and the sound was as close to a cackle as I had ever heard.
"Goodbye?" I stared at her in disdain, but my stomach was flip-flopping with worry.
"You don't think she's going to stay here with you after last night, do you?" She looked at me like I was an idiot.
"You have no idea what you're talking about." My voice was cold and I wanted very much to tell her to go back to Miami.
"I knew you were a sleaze ball. All you care about is sex. You aren't made for commitment. Guys like you and Evan just use nice girls like me and Lucky."
"I'm sorry you feel that way, Leeza. But I have no idea what you're talking about." My voice was low and I walked past her, quickly, my heart thumping fast. The last thing I needed was to get into it with Lucky's best friend. I was in enough trouble as it was.
"You're a player Zane. I don't care what excuses or issues you have. Lucky's a smart girl. I'm sure she sees through you, now."
I ignored her and walked into the kitchen. Lucky was standing by the island with a glass

of orange juice in her hands. She was wearing the same outfit she had on the night before. I could tell from the tenseness in her body that she knew I was there and she was very upset with me.

"Morning, beautiful." I gave her a wide smile, trying to mask my worry. She looked up at me with red eyes and I could tell she had been crying. Shit! I should have known she would have been worried. I had been more concerned that she would be angry, but I knew in my heart that she must have been out of her mind with worry, too.

"I called you." The words were coarse in her mouth and her eyes looked at me unflinchingly. "I called you about ten times and you didn't answer."

"Sorry. My phone battery died." I walked closer to her. "I'm sorry I wasn't able to call you back last night." I reached over to take her into my arms. "I didn't mean to make you worry."

"That's not good enough." She walked backwards and away from me. My stomach dropped as she looked at me with cold, hard eyes. "Where were you?"

"I told you." I sighed and saw her face crumple. I knew that it was time to come out with the truth. "Okay, I'm sorry. I told you a

lie last night." I continued after taking a deep breath. "I'm sorry. I really am."
"You lied to me. It's like you can't help yourself. You just keep on lying to me." She nodded, as if she were confirming something to herself. "Zane, have you had sex with Angelique?" Her voice was loud and my heart stopped at her words. How did she know?
"What?" I took a deep breath, hoping that she was grasping at straws. This was not a conversation I wanted to have.
"I saw Braydon last night and he told me that you slept with Angelique. I didn't believe him, but now, I think he was right." Her voice broke and her shoulders trembled. "You slept with her, didn't you?"
"You spoke to Braydon last night?" My voice was murderous and I was furious. "Where the fuck was Leo?" I clenched my fist in anger. How had Braydon gotten to Lucky? What if he had done something to her? Oh my God, what if he had seen her just a few hours after everything had gone down with Angelique and me? He would have harmed her or even tried to kidnap her. I knew what he was capable of and I was furious. What had Leo been thinking?
"Don't change the subject." Lucky shouted at me and I stared at her, in shock. "I'm fed up

of your bullshit, Zane. All your lies and suspicions. This has nothing to do with Leo."
"He was supposed to be your bodyguard, Lucky. He was supposed to be looking after you. Anything could have happened."
"What could have happened, Zane? What?" Lucky came forward and pushed me. "I'm so tired of your bullshit. Braydon's not the one who hurt me, Zane. You are. You're the one who hurts me every day you lie to me. I can't take this, Zane." She started crying and my heart broke. I didn't know how to respond.
"Say something."
"I'm sorry." My voice was low and I reached my hands out to her. She recoiled from me, and I felt as if someone had just sucked away all the oxygen from my body.
"I want more than an apology." She came towards me and pushed. "Where were you last night?"
"I was with Angelique." My voice was bleak and I watched as the light died in her eyes. "It's not what you think."
"So you're still sleeping with her?"
"No." I grabbed her hands. "Please believe me." I begged her. "Please, just listen."
"You knew when you were leaving last night that you were going to spend the evening with her, didn't you?"

I nodded. How could I deny her the truth?
"So it was all a lie, the bullshit about the Japanese businessmen?"
I nodded again, willing her to understand why I had to lie. "Please let me explain, Lucky."
"Have you had sex with Angelique?"
"I did not have sex with Angelique last night." I pleaded with her to understand.
"But you have before?" Her breath caught. "Have you fucked her?"
"Lucky, please." I grabbed hold of her. "Let's not talk about her."
"Why didn't you tell me?" She cried and my heart broke at her tears. She looked so small and tired. Her bright smile and happy eyes were dimmed and I was responsible for making her miserable. My heart dropped as I realized that it hadn't been worth it. The events of the night before hadn't been worth it. Not if it meant I was going to lose Lucky.
"It was a long time ago. It was one night, before she and Noah started dating. It meant nothing, Lucky."
"Not to her," she gasped through tears, daring me to refute her claim.
"I'm sorry." I reached my hands to my forehead and closed my eyes. It was true; I knew Angelique still had a crush on me. It had been my in with her. I had been her

weakness. But now, now that I was standing here with Lucky, crying and upset with me, it wasn't worth it. None of it was worth it. Noah wouldn't have wanted me to ruin the relationship with the one girl I had ever loved to get my revenge.

"I thought we were finally getting through to each other. I thought you were finally being honest with me. But you're never going to be truly honest, are you?"

"I am honest with you, Lucky. I couldn't tell you about Angelique." My voice was hoarse and I hoped she could see how sincere I was. "I couldn't tell you Lucky. Please believe me."

"You couldn't tell me or you didn't want to tell me?"

"Look, it's true that we slept together once, but that was a long time ago. Last night's dinner was something that had been planned for a long time, since before we even came to Los Angeles."

"I see." Her face paled and she looked down.

"It wasn't a romantic dinner, Lucky." I sighed and brought her face up to mine. "Look at me, please. I've been working with the FBI and the DEA to catch Braydon for selling drugs. Their investigations showed that Braydon was connected to some powerful drug lords in

Mexico and Braydon is one of the biggest traffickers in the city. They needed my help because he is an actor and he's well-protected. It has been hard for them to get any real dirt or concrete evidence on him. Angelique and he were good friends, and the FBI thought that, if I maintained my friendship with Angelique, I could get even closer to the real dirt in the group."

Lucky frowned and looked away, but I knew she was paying attention and really listening. My heart pounded as I continued my story, hoping that Lucky would understand everything and forgive me for leaving her in the dark.

"So I've been playing friendly with Angelique, hoping she would be able to provide me with some information."

"She knew you were trying to bring down Braydon?" Lucky's voice was hurt.

"No, no." I shook my head. "No one knew that Braydon was suspected of being a major drug trafficker. I couldn't tell anyone. But last night, Angelique let something slip. She told me she was leaving the country for a couple of months. I thought she meant because she was so upset over Noah, but she gave me an odd look. And then it all hit me at once."

“What hit you?” Lucky’s face was confused and I slowed down.
“I had a conversation with the Agent in charge of the case yesterday, I’m sorry I didn’t tell you. He told me that Braydon had a partner, someone who was actually running the show. I thought it was Evan and I suspected Leeza of being here to do something bad to you.”
“Oh Zane.” Lucky looked upset and then angry. “Why didn’t you tell me any of this? Shouldn’t I have been warned if you suspected that about my best friend?”
“I asked Leo to keep an eye on Leeza and all her movements.”
Lucky was silent and I could see her eyes becoming more distant. “I was wrong about Evan and Leeza. I owe her an apology, I suppose.” I made a face, but Lucky didn’t laugh, so I continued. “Angelique was the partner. She was the perfect foil. No one would ever suspect a beautiful supermodel of running a huge drug cartel.”
“Angelique is a drug trafficker?” Lucky’s mouth dropped open. “What?”
“I know.” I shook my head. “It turns out that she and Braydon have been working together for years, and she was the brains behind the whole thing.”

"She was the brains?" Lucky made such a funny face that I laughed and she scowled at me. "I'm not forgiving you that easily, Zane. Why were you out all night?"

"I wasn't in her bed, even though she wanted me to be." I cut myself off before I made the situation worse. "Look, Angelique came from a very poor family, and in all her life, all she has ever wanted was money. After our alliance, I blew her off and I guess I became a bit of a challenge to her. Men didn't reject her - she rejected them. I think she convinced herself, in her own sick way, that she loved me, or rather she was trying to do everything she could to get me, to prove something to herself. I have never wanted to be with her. And I've never really liked her. Last night, when I realized that Angelique was Braydon's partner, I called my contact at the FBI. He told me to stay until they could get over there. Well, let's just say they didn't get over until about 3 a.m."

"It's 10 a.m. now." She glared.

"I was taken in for questioning." I grabbed her hands. "I'm so sorry, Lucky. Please forgive me. I never thought this would happen."

"You thought I'd just continue being a fool in the dark, here? Waiting for you to get back

from your fake business meeting?" She cried out, but she didn't remove her hands from mine.
"No, Lucky, never that. I wanted to tell you but …" I paused at the look in her eyes.
"But you didn't trust me." She snapped.
"I do trust you."
"You don't trust me to look after myself or to be safe. You don't trust me, Zane. What do I have to do to show you that I love you and I'm here for you? I'm not a little kid or some fragile doll. I can handle the truth, Zane. Life has thrown some shit my way, as well, and I survived. I'm strong. I'm a strong woman. And I can't be in a relationship with someone who doesn't see that."
"Lucky…" My heart stopped once again at her words and I imagined my life without her in it. It would be bleak and uneventful. A life without Lucky in it would be no life at all.
"Please don't leave me. I do trust you. I swear to God. The FBI told me to keep it to myself for the sake of your safety and the case."
"You still should have told me." Her stare was obstinate and I caressed her face.
"Please be patient with me, Lucky. I'm trying my best to be the man that you want. But it's hard for me to give up that control. I'm scared you're going to walk out and leave me. I'm

scared I'm going to lose you. I've never felt these emotions before and I love them. They make me feel alive. They make me feel like I never have to worry, ever again. But sometimes, that old devil jumps on my shoulder and whispers in my ear, and I get worried, and angry, and afraid."

"There is nothing to be worried about, Zane." She held my hand next to her cheek. "I'm not your mom, I'm not going to leave you."

"I just want you to be safe, Lucky. Please know that I would never have done anything with Angelique last night. I can't even look at another girl. You're it for me, Lucky. You're the one."

"I need to see it." She rested her head on my shoulder and looked up at me. "Last night, I thought my heart was breaking. I was so scared and worried. I didn't know what happened to you. I even thought that, maybe there had been another car accident, and that something had happened to you."

"Oh no. I'm sorry I didn't even think about that." I held her in my arms as she cried, and I felt her body trembling against mine.

"I was so scared, Zane. I didn't know what had happened and you weren't returning my calls. And then after Braydon told me about Angelique, I didn't know what to think."

"Don't remind me of Braydon. I'm going to have a serious conversation with Leo."
"Please don't." She looked up at me. "He doesn't know I saw Braydon. Don't be mad at him."
"He should have known and seen everything. He was supposed to be your bodyguard."
"Oh please Zane, don't blame him. I don't want this to affect his payment."
"Payment?" I looked at her and laughed. "Leo's richer than I am."
"He is?" She looked surprised. "Then why is he a bodyguard?"
"He's not really." I shook my head. "It's a long story and it's not mine to tell."
"Oh." She looked disappointed and I took her hand and led her to the backyard. I wanted to go to the living room, but didn't want Leeza to be hiding somewhere, listening to our conversation.
"It's not that I don't want to tell you, but it's not really my place." I squeezed her hand as we sat down on the lounge chair. "But if you want me to, I will."
"No, that's okay." She smiled at me briefly. "I hope one day he'll tell me himself." I watched her face as she spoke and I was annoyed at the pleasant tone she had for Leo. "I like him a

lot." She continued. "I hope we become real friends."
"I see."
"Oh Zane, don't be stupid." She poked me in the ribs and I looked up to see her shaking her head. "I don't like Leo like that, okay? You don't need to get all pouty and jealous."
"I'm not pouty and jealous." I retorted.
"So, what happened to Angelique?"
"She's in custody. And so is Braydon. They arrested him a few hours later. It seems Angelique turned on him within hours."
"Wow." Lucky looked surprised. "Really?"
"Yeah. I think they will get lighter sentences if they are able to get Sanchez, the guy who's running half the drugs from Mexico to L.A., but they will still go away for a long time."
"Wow!" Lucky exclaimed again and held on to me tightly. "I'm just glad you're okay. I don't know what I would have done if you hadn't been okay."
"I'm sorry, Lucky. I wasn't thinking." I stroked her hair around my fingers. "Forgive me?"
"If you promise me you won't do anything like this again without telling me."
"I promise." I paused. "Let me clarify, I promise to be open and honest with you and

to trust that you can handle whatever comes up in my life."

"I hope no more drug trafficking cases come up." She made a face. "I mean, I'm glad you got Braydon and Angelique, but I'm not sure I could go through all of this again."

"I promise no more drug trafficking." I slid my hand to her knee. "I promise to focus all of my attention on you."

"Oh really?" She giggled and I was happy to see the light back in her eyes as she stared at me and swatted my hand away.

"Oh yes, I'll get out my copy of the *Kama Sutra* and I'll spend hours each night devoting myself to your body."

"Uh huh."

"It'll be tiring, but I promise to give it my all."

"That's one promise I think you'll be able to keep, all right."

"You forgive me?" I held my breath as I looked into her eyes, searchingly. "Say you forgive me."

Instead of answering, Lucky leaned in towards me and kissed my lips softly. I could taste the remnants of orange juice on her lips. I sucked on her lower lip before plunging my tongue into her mouth and she grabbed the back of my head. I felt her fingers running along my scalp and I pushed her onto her back so I could feel her breasts crushed against my chest.

"Really, guys?" Leeza's voice echoed through the backyard and I groaned as I sat up and pulled away from Lucky. "Lucky, I don't know how you were able to forgive him so easily."

"Leeza…" Lucky's voice held a warning.

"I'm just saying." Leeza whined. "Are we going to go and do something today, or am I expected to sit at home and watch *Maury* and *Days of Our Lives*?"

"We can drive you around Los Angeles." Lucky jumped up. "Is there anywhere you want to go specifically?"

"Beverly Hills, 90210." Leeza's voice was excited and I rolled my eyes.

"Leeza, can you give Lucky and me a moment please? I need to ask her something," I said.

"Whatever." She twirled around and walked back into the house.

"I know she's your friend, Lucky, but she really annoys me." I muttered as I watched her friend leave. Even though I knew Leeza wasn't planning something with Evan, I still couldn't stand her. I was hoping in my head that she was on her way back to Florida very soon.

"What did you want to ask me, Zane?" Lucky looked at me with a worried expression and my heart went out to her. I felt ashamed of myself for making her feel that way. I made a vow to myself that I wasn't ever going to give her a heavy heart again.

"So, remember when I asked you about going to London?" I took her hands in mine and used my fingers to trace the lines in her palm.

"You mean the other day?"

"Yeah." I nodded and watched her face, carefully. "So, I was thinking, what about it? We could go for the weekend - just you and me. We could just take a break away from everything and relax."

"But, London?" She half-smiled, considering my proposition. "It just seems so far away."

"I just want to take a trip away, you and me. Somewhere romantic." A light bulb flashed in my head and I exclaimed. "Or we could go to Paris. See the Eiffel Tower and the Arc de Triomphe. We could eat French pastries in bed and shop along the Champs-Elysees."

"Well, I don't have money to shop, but I do love croissants." She smiled at me. "And I've always wanted to go to Paris."

"See? It was made to be. You, me, and Paris." I kissed the tip of her nose and we walked back inside the house. "This is going to be the trip of a lifetime. I love the French. They are such a romantic and passionate people."
"Oh, really?"
"Yes." I laughed. "We could learn a thing or two from them." I winked at her and she blushed. I felt a secret thrill that I could still make Lucky's cheeks redden with embarrassment.
"I don't really know much about the French, aside from the fact that they love French fries and that they got rid of their monarchy during the French revolution."
"I can't say I know much more than you, but Noah was obsessed with all things French. One of his favorite movies was called *Jules et Jim* and he would make us watch it every few years."
"Oh really?" Lucky gave me a peculiar look. "Was there a reason why Noah liked France so much?"
"Not that I know of." I shrugged. "Noah was a man with eclectic tastes, not that you would have known that by the look of him."
"Oh?"

"Most people looked at him and thought he was just a playboy." I laughed. "I suppose that's how you thought of me as well."
"Well, I…I didn't really know you well," Lucky stuttered.
"It's okay." I stretched my arms and turned to her. "So are we down for Paris?"
"This weekend?" Her voice was hesitant, but I could sense the excitement in her tone.
"No time like the present." I grinned.
She laughed. "I guess so."
"Is that a yes?"
"Yes." Her voice was small and I lifted her up and swung her around. We were both laughing, but as I set her down, she gave me a worried look. "Don't ever lie to me again, Zane. I don't think I can go through what I went through last night."
"I am so …" I started, but she held her hand up to stop me.
"I know how important Noah was to you, and I know you have been after Braydon for the last year, but I hope this is the end of it, Zane. I'm not sure my heart, or my sanity, can continue on like this. And I don't know if our relationship could get through one more hurricane."
"For you, I'd weather any storm, my love." I traced the lines around her eyes and it

saddened me that I had made my Lucky cry. She was the woman who had snuck into my heart without me even knowing it. She was the woman that had made me believe in love and she had broken down my walls. She was the last person that I wanted to make sad. Seeing her cry for me made my heart break. I wanted to see her with a smile on her face. She was the one I should be making happy. She was the one I should be lifting up to the heavens. I vowed to myself that I was going to make sure that no more tears would be shed on my behalf.

Chapter 10
Lucky

My head was spinning like a yo-yo. The last few days had gone by in a blur and I still wasn't sure how I felt about everything. I put on a good face for Zane because I knew he worried easily, but I still felt tense and worried. When I thought about what could have happened to him that night, I wanted to scream. I couldn't believe he hadn't told me what he was doing. It wasn't even sure about Angelique, though I knew I would hate her for the rest of my life. I could get over the fact that he had slept with her, though I didn't like it. It had been before we had got together and it wasn't as if I didn't have a past. But for him to have gone behind my back and been part of some big drug sting and not even think to give me the details—well that made my blood boil. I knew that Zane thought he was trying to protect me, but I wanted this to be a partnership, a real twenty-first century partnership. I didn't want to be stuck in the 1950s and in a relationship where Zane thought he was Ward Cleaver. I certainly didn't want to be in a relationship where Zane was the provider and I spent all day cooking

his meals. I had other plans and I didn't want to give up my other dreams just because he was my dream man.
"This is our second plane ride together." Zane beamed at me from his seat and winked. I knew he was trying his best to get things back to normal with me, so I tried my best to put on a good face.
"And my second time in first class." I beamed back at him from the comfort of my chair. "You shouldn't keep spoiling me like this. It might go to my head."
"Uh oh, you'll have me shopping for you at Cartier and Tiffany's soon."
"Don't forget Chanel and Louis Vuitton." I laughed.
He wrinkled his nose at me. "I knew you were only after my money."
"Your money and your loving."
"You mean my good loving." He leaned over and stuck his tongue in my ear and I pulled away, shaking my head.
"Eww, that was all slobbery and gross."
"Don't pretend you didn't love it." He winked at me and licked his lips.
"You're disgusting, Zane Beaumont."
"That's not what you said last night."
"How old are you, Zane? Fifteen or twenty-five?" I shook my head, but was happy at his

teasing tone. The last few days had been slightly tense in the house. Leeza had been upset that we were leaving the country, so Zane had gotten her a first class ticket back to Miami and given her a check for $5000 to make up for her vacation being cut short. She had loved him then, told him she had always known he was a great guy. I'd been embarrassed at her transparent nature, but had still felt sad when she left.

I had given Zane a bit of a cold shoulder as he had gone back and forth to the police station to give more and more statements about Angelique and Braydon. I still couldn't wrap my head around the whole ordeal.

We hadn't made love in days and I knew he was sexually frustrated. But I wanted to make sure he knew that he couldn't just do what he wanted and keep things from me anymore. If we were going to be in a relationship, then he had to learn to fully trust me and show me that trust with his actions as well as his words. I wasn't going to let him think he could do what he wanted, say sorry and then weaken my resolve with sex. Our relationship was about more than sex. It was true that when we slept together, it was like the most magical moment of my night, but I knew that feeling alone could not sustain our relationship.

"Do you want to join the mile high club?" He whispered in my ear and I decided to have a little fun with him.
"I don't have any panties on." I whispered back and took hold of his hand. "I'm ready and waiting for you, big boy."
Zane's eyes widened and he looked down at my lap. My skirt was pretty conservative and fell just below my knees. He reached his hand down to my leg and inched it up inside my skirt and over my knee. I stopped his hand as it reached mid-thigh and shook my head.
"Not now, Zane." I licked my lips and brought his hand up to my mouth. I took his index finger and put it into my mouth and sucked it while staring into his eyes.
"Holy shit, Batman, is this for real?" Zane's eyes sparkled with excitement. "I was just joking, Lucky, but I think you're about to become the best girlfriend ever."
"I think so too." I winked and stopped sucking on his finger. I reached my hand down to his crotch and ran my fingers lightly over the thick package in his pants. I turned my face away quickly as I felt how excited he already was. I wanted to burst out laughing at his gullibility, but felt a bit ashamed at my little joke.

"Shall we go now?" He made to get up out of his seat. "I think we have time before the flight takes off."
"Uh." I bit my lip at his eager expression and I burst out laughing when I saw him loosening his belt. "Zane. Stop." I reached over and placed my hand on top of his. "I was joking. I have on panties and I have no intention of joining the mile high club with you on this flight."
"What?" He looked up at me with a look of dismay and then he started laughing. "You little minx," he growled as he leaned forward and kissed me hard. "I'll get you for that."
"Uh huh." I laughed, relishing in the feel of his warm lips against mine. He kissed me passionately as if his sole goal was to turn me on as much as possible. He nibbled on my lower lip and sucked on my tongue while running his hands through my hair. I felt his left hand slowly creep down my shoulder and graze my breast. My body tingled as he caressed me and I wondered if I shouldn't change my mind after all. It had only been a few days since we had been intimate, but my body was already missing and craving his touch.
"Hi, guys, are your seatbelts both on and tightened?" The flight attendant stopped by

our seats and smiled. "We're about to take off."

"Yes, ma'am." Zane pulled away from me and sat upright as I nodded and blushed. Zane grinned at me as the flight attendant walked on to the next seats and he reached over and squeezed my hand. "I'm so glad you're here with me, Lucky. I'm so excited to show you Paris."

"I'm excited as well." I smiled back at him and tried to ignore the anxious feeling in my stomach. I was extremely excited for the trip and to be spending time with Zane away from all the craziness, but I was also a little worried. I had Zane's mother's phone number and address in my handbag and I was seriously thinking about getting in contact with her once we got there. It seemed to be as if this trip was fate's way of saying, "go for it and see what happens." I knew Zane needed closure. I knew that if he were ever able to start the healing process from his mother leaving, he needed to understand why she had left. In my heart of hearts, I was also hoping that his mother would have a change of heart and they would reconcile and develop a new relationship. Maybe she just needed to see him. I mean, what mother could just give up her son and walk away from him like that? I didn't see how she could walk away again if she actually saw him in the flesh. I wanted to give this to Zane. I wanted to be able to help make his heart whole again.

"Are there any places you really want to see?" He looked over at me curiously. "Sorry I haven't really asked you that before."

"I think we already have a lot planned for five days." I laughed and shook my head. "I'm not sure we could fit in any more even if I wanted to."

"Good. I'm going to take you to all of Noah's favorite places."

My heart raced at his words and the smile on his face. This was the first time he had brought up Noah's name in a positive and lighthearted context. "Oh yeah?"

"Yeah, he loved France. I wouldn't have been surprised if he had moved there. He went every few years at least."

"Oh." I looked at him cautiously. "Did he ever say why he went there so many times?"

"No, but I never really asked. I just assumed he had a thing for French girls or just really loved the food." He chortled and turned to face me. "My brother was a bit of a player in his time."

"Really?" I looked at him in surprise. "I thought he was really in love with, you-know-who."
"Are we not saying her name now?" He grimaced. "Not that I want us to go down that road again." He half laughed and half sighed. "Actually, to be honest, I was shocked when he became serious with Angelique. I mean, I knew he liked her, who wouldn't? She's a looker." I frowned at him and he grinned at me mischievously. "My bad. Anyway, I meant that she wasn't really the sort of girl I could see him falling for like that." His expression turned serious. "That's why I wanted to get Braydon. I honestly don't think it was feelings that made Noah jump. I think it was the drugs. I think it was all the drugs." He shook his head. "Noah was one of those guys who was open to love, but I certainly didn't think he found the real deal with that bitch."
"Oh." I pursed my lips at his words, but inside I was happy that he was calling Angelique the word I called her in my mind. "Did Braydon ever say why Noah jumped? Like what happened exactly?" I spoke softly, not wanting to push the conversation if Zane wasn't ready.
"You know what's funny?" Zane looked at me with a confused expression. "When I was

at the police station, the FBI office, Agent Waldron let me listen to some of Braydon's interrogation. And Braydon kept shouting something about how he never actually witnessed Noah jumping. He said he wasn't actually on the roof with him when he jumped. He was shouting that they weren't going to pin Noah's death on him. He said that Noah was talking all crazy, took the drugs from him and made some comments about flying, but supposedly Braydon then went to go and get some more weed from his car. He said when he went back to the roof, Noah had already jumped and before he knew it, the police were there and so was an ambulance. He said he saw Noah on a stretcher and before he could say anything, the ambulance was gone and he was pulled in for questioning." Zane paused. "It was just weird."
"Why was that weird?" I reached over and held his hand in mine and squeezed his fingers. Hearing about his brother's death always made me feel so sad.
"I don't know." He cocked his head. "It's just that the story was so much different from what I'd heard before."
"Oh?" I looked at him with questioning eyes.

"Yeah." He sighed. "I always thought that Braydon was there when Noah jumped. The police made me think that Braydon was on the roof just standing there when Noah ran and jumped." His voice cracked and my heart went out to him. "I guess it doesn't really matter."

"Maybe Braydon is just lying now." I reached over and stroked his chin. "We both know how shady he is."

"Yeah." He sighed. "I asked to talk to him. I wanted to know exactly what happened, but Agent Waldron told me it wouldn't be possible."

"What? After everything you did to help them?" My voice rose in disgust. "They should be ashamed of themselves. Why couldn't they let you get some answers?"

"I guess they don't want to compromise the case." Zane's eyes looked thoughtful as he stared at me. "I just thought it was strange."

"They should understand your need for closure." I was angry for him. "They basically used you to bring Braydon and Angelique down and now they can't even let you find out exactly what happened the night that he died? It's not fair."

"It's okay, Lucky." Zane issued me a crumpled smile. "I loved my brother and I will always honor his memory, but I need to live in the here and now. I nearly lost you with my focus on revenge. I'm not going to let it all control my mind anymore. I want to focus on us now, and making our relationship stronger."

"Oh, Zane." My eyes filled with tears at his words. He sounded so sincere and they were like music to my ears. "You don't know how much that means to me to hear you say that."

"I've noticed how distant you've been these last few days Lucky, and it has killed me. There is nothing I wouldn't do to make this relationship work. Nothing I wouldn't give to make this a forever love. I want to prove my love to you. I want the birds in the sky to chirp of my love for you. I want the pygmies in Africa to talk of my love for you. I want the fish in the bottom of the ocean to feel the depths of my love for you."

"You're going to make me cry." I bit my lip and looked at the sincere expression in his eyes. "I don't know what to say."

"I finished my song for you." He laughed. "But it's more like a poem. I'd like to say it to you, if you don't mind."

I groaned at his words. "Does that mean I'll have to say mine as well?"

"If you want." He laughed. "But you don't have to."
"I will, but you first." My stomach turned over with nerves. "The genius has to go first."
"Well, I'm glad you've finally admitted that I'm a genius."
"Yeah, I'm sure you are."
"Okay, here we go." Zane turned around to face me and his blue eyes were full of emotion as he started to talk. I focused on his pink lips and the slight stubble on his chin as he spoke, because I was scared that if I looked into his eyes as he spoke, I would be a blubbering mess.

One day, people shall talk of this day, my love

One day, birds shall sing of my joy, my love

One day, the wind shall scream the truth to the world, my love

Ten years of our love is not enough, my love

Eternity is just a drop in time for our love, my love

You have the key to my heart and soul, my

love

I don't want to walk a foot without you besides me, my love

I don't want to talk without seeing your smile, my love

I live for the moments when it's just us, my love

Give me forever to love you, my love

Give me your trust and your life, my love

I'll protect you and love you all my life, my love

One day will come when the whole world will talk of our love, my love

Be my love, feel my love, live my love, for today my love, is one day, my love

"Oh Zane," I couldn't stop the tears of joy from rolling out of my eyes. "That was so beautiful. I can't believe you wrote that for me."

"Well, believe it, my dear. And believe me when I say, I'm putting my all into being the man you deserve."
"I don't deserve or want anyone other than you, Zane."
"Then how's about we go into the bathroom for five minutes and you …" His eyes sparkled as he talked and he burst out laughing as I shook my head at his words.
"You're incorrigible, Zane." I growled at hm. "Sex, sex, sex." I laughed and gasped as his hand crept up to my breast and squeezed me through my top. "Stop it." I hissed.
"I couldn't resist." He winked. "You know us sex addicts."
"I wouldn't be surprised if you were a sex addict."
"Agent Waldron did give me a pair of handcuffs." He winked at me. "They're in my suitcase. Maybe I'll have to use them tonight and show you just how much of a sex addict I am."
"Who says we're going to have sex tonight?" I smiled at him demurely. "I may not have fully forgiven you yet."
"Lucky," he groaned, "don't tease me. I can't go another night without feeling myself inside of you. It's torture having you lying next to

me, feeling you against me and not being able to have my wicked way with you."
"Well, I guess you'll have to learn to deal with it." I giggled thinking about the feel of him pressed up against me each morning. He didn't know it, but it had been very hard for me every time I pushed his hand away as well. There was nothing I enjoyed more than feeling him inside of me. When we made love, I felt like we were one. Our bodies were fused together and when we moved, I felt like we were literally joining our souls together. I had never had that physical and almost spiritual moment with any other man and I think that was one of the reasons why our sex life was even more special to me. It wasn't just that he was the best sex I had ever had, he was also the man who made me feel more alive than I had ever felt in my life.
"We'll see." He growled at me and we both laughed as the flight attendant walked past us and gave us a knowing look.

***

"*Bonjour, alle le Hotel Opera Pelris*." Zane spoke slowly to the taxi driver and he looked at us blankly.
"*Pardon*?"

"*Nous allons le hotel Opera Pelris?*" Zane tried again and this time his voice was firmer, as if that was going to make the taxi driver understand what he was saying.
"*Pardon?*"
"*Je alle le hotel Opera Pelris tout rapidemente.*" Zane's voice was brusquer now and I stifled a giggle.
"I take it you never took French in school?" I raised an eyebrow at him as the taxi driver stared at us with a blank expression. "You do realize that he has no idea what you just said. Was that even in French?"
"No. Well, I don't know," Zane grinned at me. "Do you know how to tell him to take us to the hotel?"
"No, not really." I laughed. "And I did take French."
"Are you two ready?" The taxi driver raised an eyebrow at us. "The meter's running already."
"You speak English?" Zane looked annoyed and the taxi driver shrugged. "We're going to the Hotel Opera Pelris *sil vous plait.*"
"*Oui, monsieur.*"
And with that, we sped off. I stared out of the window in excitement, unable to believe that I was actually here in Paris. It didn't seem quite real. Everything about the city was amazing to

me so far. The tall older buildings all looked majestic to me and there were bakeries on every corner.

"I can't wait to get some croissants." I looked over at Zane and smiled. "And some hot chocolate."

"Or you could get a *pain au chocolat*." He grinned.

"What's that?" My stomach grumbled and we both laughed.

"I think it's a croissant with chocolate in the middle." He licked his lower lip and frowned. "But I could be wrong."

"Just as long as it's not snails." I made a face. "Or *foie gras*. Yuck."

"How can you not like *foie gras*?" He shook his head. "It's so delicious."

"I guess that's what happens when you're a country bumpkin."

"Do you like pâté?"

"Ewww. Gross." I shook my head.

"And you consider yourself the next Julia Child? For shame. I'll have to teach you to enjoy world class food."

"Ha. That's okay. I'm good with a juicy steak and a baked potato."

"Aren't we all?" He rubbed his stomach and leaned over and bit my lower lip lightly. "Thank God, we're both meat eaters. I'm not

sure what I would have done if you were a vegetarian."
"That would have been a deal-breaker?" I looked at him curiously.
"No." He laughed loudly. "But it would have made me feel guilty any time I wanted to eat meat."
"You, feel guilty? Yeah right." I scoffed.
He reached over to tickle me. "Shh you." His hands tickled under my arms and I giggled and pulled away. "I tell you that I do feel guilty sometimes. Not often, but sometimes."
"Uh huh."
"You better be nice to me or I won't take you to *le Louvre*."
"The museum?" I made a face.
"Don't you want to see the Mona Lisa?"
"Not really," I laughed. "I'd much rather go to Versailles."
"You are a girl, aren't you? You want to see the glitz and glamour."
"Actually, I want to see it because it was the center of Louis XIV political power before the beginning of the French Revolution. Versailles is the symbol of absolute monarchy in the old regime of France. All that opulence and all those riches are what helped to bring about the demise of the monarchy in France."

"I forgot I was dating a historian." He laughed. "I guess you'll be my guide."
"I don't know if I know enough to be anyone's guide. But I'm super excited to see the gardens and the Hall of Mirrors."
"Hall of Mirrors?"
"It's the most famous room in Versailles." I laughed. "It's one of the most renowned rooms in the world."
"A room with a bunch of mirrors?" Zane looked surprised. "Okay." He rolled his eyes and I saw the taxi driver shaking his head in disgust and stifled another laugh.
"It's not just some cheap ten dollar mirror you get at Walmart or Target, Zane."
"I don't shop at Walmart or Target." He scoffed.
I pinched him for being a snob. "Zane, that's not important." I rolled my eyes. "The point is, it's not just a room full of crappy cheap mirrors. These are opulent, gold-framed and gilded mirrors. And the hallway is huge and it overlooks the gardens. It's beautiful."
"You've seen them?"
"No, but one of my ex-boyfriends went with his family and he showed me some photos."
"Oh." Zane pursed his lips and frowned. "What ex-boyfriend?"

"My first boyfriend, actually. He was my high school love."

"I see." His voice turned cold. "Why did you break up if you guys were in love?"

"Oh Zane." I shook my head at his obvious jealousy though it made me feel warm inside. "We broke up because I got pregnant and he didn't want to help me look after the baby."

"What?" He looked furious.

"Sorry, that was a bad joke." I touched his shoulder. "He went to Princeton in New Jersey and I went to UM. Geography made it hard for us to keep dating."

"You could have tried long distance."

"We could have, but we didn't."

"I guess the love wasn't that strong then." He looked into my eyes searchingly.

"He was my high school boyfriend, Zane. Our love was juvenile and nothing more than a crush. I mean I was devastated when we broke up and I cried for a week straight but as soon as I got to Miami and starting make new friends and hanging out I forgot about him." I laughed. "And now, I can barely even picture his face."

"I guess it's easy for you to get over guys huh?" Zane's face was cold and I sighed. He really was a big baby sometimes.

"Zane Beaumont, are you really going to give me a hard time about my high school boyfriend? Especially after I forgave you for not telling me that you slept with Angelique."

"I didn't love Angelique; that was just sex." He frowned at me and his voice was matter-of-fact.

"That doesn't make it better." I glared at him. "In fact, that's worse."

"How is it worse?" He glared back at me.

I rolled my eyes. "Are you kidding me? It is …"

"We are here. Hotel Opera Pelris." The taxi-driver interrupted our conversation as he parked. "That will be 60 Euros please."

"Here we go." Zane opened his wallet and handed the man some notes. "Keep the change."

"*Merci.*" The taxi driver gave us his first smile of the day as he glanced at the notes and hopped out of the car in order to open the door for us.

"I guess money talks everywhere." I whispered to Zane and he laughed.

We walked into the hotel and I looked around in surprise at how normal it seemed. I had expected Zane was going to go all out and take us to some 5-star glittery hotel, but this was far from 5-star.

Zane walked up to the front desk and a man jumped up. "*Bonjour* and welcome to Opera Pelris."
"This is Opera Pelris?" Zane's voice was gruff and the man's face paled a little as he nodded. "This is the Opera Pelris where all the biggest stars in Europe stay?" Zane's voice rose. "This is the hotel of choice of all the aristocracy?"
"Yes, *monsieur*, this is Opera Pelris, one of the finest hotels in Paris." The man gulped and looked down at the desk in front of him. It seemed to me that even he had a problem saying that mistruth.
"Is this a joke?" Zane's voice grew louder and the man looked like he was about to faint. "This doesn't look like the photos on your website."
"Non, monsieur. Checking in?" The man averted his gaze and looked down.
"Where is the Seine?" Zane frowned and his voice was spiky. "Where are the crystal chandeliers in the lobby? In fact, where is the grand lobby with the doorman?"
"I, uh, I'm not sure I understand you, sir. My English is not that good." The thin man swallowed and looked at me with a wide smile. "Madam, welcome to Paris."

"Thanks." I nodded and smiled back weakly. I felt bad for the man; Zane looked like he was about to blow a gasket. I laughed at the analogy I had made and bit my lip as Zane turned around and glared at me.
"I want to see your manager." Zane glared at the man. "This was a case of fraud. I am not staying here."
"Come on Zane. It'll be okay." I touched his shoulder. "I just want to go lie down for a bit."
"Oh?" His eyes darkened as he stared and me and sighed. "We'll take the room for now. But we may be checking out tomorrow." He turned back around and glared at the man. "You better give us your best room."
"We only have one room left *monsieur*." The man swallowed, but smiled at me gratefully.
"Well, then you better hope that it meets my satisfaction." Zane looked around the drab entryway we were in and sighed. "Sorry." He mouthed at me.
"It's okay." I squeezed his arm and smiled. We were in Paris, that was all I needed. It didn't have to be perfect. We didn't have to have a room at the Ritz. We didn't have to hobnob with the stars. I kept my mouth shut but I was a little worried we would be sleeping with the rats instead.

"I love you." He leaned over and kissed my cheek. "You're such a sweetheart."
"Hey, I like hotels with character." I put my arm around my waist. "I'm just happy to be here with you."
"Madam, you will love it here." The man smiled at me again. "We also have breakfast in the restaurant from 7 a.m. - 10 a.m."
"Is room service open before and after then?" Zane interrupted.
"Well, we don't have room service."
"Are you joking?" Zane's voice rose and I pinched him.
"Be nice." My face flushed in embarrassment. "He's just the front desk clerk Zane."
"Just give me my keys." Zane muttered and the man quickly gave us a key attached to a piece of wood.
"This is the key for your door. You're on the second floor. A wonderful room. The elevator is just up the stairs and to the right." The man beamed. "Have a nice stay."
"Who helps us with our bags?" Zane looked around and sighed as he picked up our suitcases. "I guess that was a lie as well." He muttered to no one in particular.
"I can help." I reached over to take my case and he shook his head.

"No, I've got them." I watched as he struggled with both cases and just sighed. Let him be the big macho man, I wasn't going to fight him just so I could give him some help. I walked up the red-carpeted stairs and to the elevator. It was an old-fashioned elevator and I had to manually open the door. As I looked inside I realized there was no way that Zane, myself and the suitcases were going to fit in. In fact there was no way that anyone would fit in with either case. I took a deep breath before stepping back and allowing Zane to see inside the interior of the elevator. I was scared that he was going to completely lose it but he just muttered something under his breath when he realized that it was too small to be of any use.
"So, I guess I'll just carry these up the stairs." He sighed and I gave him a wide smile.
"You can do it, Superman."
"Not helping, Lucky."
"Sorry."
"You can make it up to me." He gave me a lascivious stare and then started up the stairs with the suitcases. I wanted to tell him to take one at a time, but I didn't think he was in the mood for any suggestions. Thankfully, the second floor wasn't too far of a hike and we made it there before Zane let go of the cases and called it a night.

"Let me get the door." I grabbed the key from him and fumbled with the lock.
Finally I opened the door and walked into the room. I looked around the room in dismay. It was small and cramped and the king-sized bed was made up of twin beds pushed together. I plastered a smile on my face so Zane wouldn't see how disappointed I was. I walked over to the windows and opened them widely, hoping to catch a glance of the Eiffel Tower, but all I saw was some scaffolding on the building directly across from us. I turned back around to check out the bathroom, maybe there would be an old antique claw-footed bathtub that I could soak in and relax. I opened the door to the bathroom and there was no bathtub at all, just a shower and a sink.
"What the fuck is this shithole?" Zane dropped the suitcases on the floor and cursed under his breath. "I'm sorry, Lucky."
"It's okay." I stood in the bathroom wondering how I was going to tell him that there was no toilet. "Let's just relax, yeah?" I turned around quickly and grabbed the remote control and turned the TV on. I smiled when I saw Sheldon from *Big Bang Theory* on the screen. "Yay, they have American TV." I grinned at him, but my smile became frozen as they started speaking in another language. I

kept the smile plastered on my face and sat on the hard bed while flicking through the channels. I got all the way through 105 channels before realizing that there was nothing in English. I looked up and saw Zane staring at me and the TV screen with a smirk on his face.
"What's so funny?"
"Your look of disappointment when you realized that there was nothing for you to watch on TV."
"Oh, oops, sorry." I stood up and walked over to give him a hug. "I'm just glad to be here with you."
"At least we have that." He kissed my forehead. "Now excuse me a second, I just need to go to the bathroom."
"Um, about that." I grabbed ahold of him. "I think we have to use a public toilet."
"What?" He shouted, his face growing angry again. "I am not paying $400 a night to use a public restroom."
"This place is $400 a night?" My eyes almost popped out of their sockets. There was no way this place was worth even $40 a night.
"Are you sure about the toilet?" Zane walked to the bathroom, opened a door and cursed.
"Okay, let's see if it is somewhere else." I tried not to look at him like he was crazy, but

the room was so dreadfully small, there wasn't even a place to hide a toilet.
Zane walked to the corner of the room and opened a door to what I thought I thought was the closet. "What the fuck?" Zane cursed again as he looked in front of the open door.
I walked over to him to see what had gotten him so worked up. My face paled as I stared at the toilet. It was a normal looking toilet, but it took up the whole "room." There was no way someone could sit on the toilet and close the door; it was literally impossible.
"Oh, that's a tight space."
We both stood there staring at each other for a couple of seconds before we both started laughing. Our laughter was so loud that I thought someone would think we were dying of a laughing attack. I doubled over from laughing so hard and Zane grabbed hold of me to keep me from falling over. "My stomach hurts." I took a breath and clutched onto his arm.
"I'm about to piss my pants." Zane gave me a wry smile. "Literally."
"Well then you better go to the toilet." I pointed to the door and he shuddered.
"Okay." He took two steps and I heard him unzip his pants, and then I heard the sound of his wee as it hit the toilet bowl.

I cringed when I realized that every noise someone made while on the toilet would be heard by everyone in the room. I quickly walked back to the bed and laid flat on my back, deep in thought. What was I going to do when I needed to go to the bathroom? There was no way I wanted him to hear me on the toilet, not for number 1 or 2. Number 1 was bad enough, but I knew I would die of shame if he heard me go number 2. There were some things that should just never be shared.

"That's better." Zane plopped down on the bed next to me and I frowned.

"You didn't wash your hands."

"What?" He looked confused.

"You didn't wash your hands and you were just holding your Johnson."

"My Johnson?" He jumped up and walked to the bathroom. "I'd rather we call him Zane Jr."

"I'd rather we didn't call him anything at all, actually." I stared at Zane as he made his way back to the bed. His hair was growing longer and I could see the facial hair growing on his neck and face. He looked handsome, and manly. I wanted to feel the rough of his stubble against the softness of my skin.

“Are you sure about that?” He laid down flat on his stomach and leaned on his arms while staring at me.
“Sure about what?” His eyes and lips had mesmerized me and I wasn’t sure what he was talking about.
“You know what.” He laughed and all of a sudden I was taken back to the first day I saw him come into the diner. It had been a Friday about 7 p.m. It had been pretty slow and Maria and I’d been dancing around behind the counter. She had been trying to teach me the basic salsa steps and I had been concentrating so hard that I hadn’t even noticed some customers had entered the restaurant.
“Sorry to bother you two dancing queens, but do you think we can get a table?” His voice had been deep and firm, but his tone had been full of laughter.
I looked up, ready to apologize, but the words had stuck in my throat as I gazed into his deep blue eyes. He had stared back at me, and we had what I had thought was an instant connection. I had given him a sweet smile and was about to lead him to a table when I noticed the gorgeous blonde behind him. She stood there snarling at me and then studied her fingernails, and I had felt about six inches tall.

"I'm sorry, sir. This way." I had grabbed the menus and berated myself mentally for thinking that we had had a connection. There was no way a man like him would be interested in a waitress like me.
"I thought I had walked into a dance class and not a diner." His eyes teased me as he took the menus and I blushed.
"Sorry about that." I muttered again and he winked at me.
"Do you guys only have burgers?" The blonde had looked at me in disgust. "What is this place, Zane? I thought we were going to Ruth's Chris."
"They didn't have any reservations, Emily." He had reached over and caressed her hand. "A burger won't kill you just this once."
"I guess so, Zane." She had tinkled and tightened her fingers in his. I had stood there staring at them for a moment when Zane had looked up at me and smiled. A real, wide, genuine smile, and I had been captivated by him. It wasn't just that he had been the most gorgeous man I had ever seen but there was a glint in his eyes that had lit a part of me on fire.
"Are you okay, Lucky?" Zane's expression was worried as he looked at me searchingly.

I nodded slowly. “I was just thinking about the first time we met.”
“Oh?”
“Yeah, your expression just now reminded me of that day.” I smiled gently and ran my fingers along his jaw line. “You were so arrogant and hot, I didn’t know what to think about you.”
“I’m just glad you thought about me period.” He stared into my eyes. “To think we may never have met if I had never gone in that diner that night.”
“We would have met.” I leaned forward and kissed him. “We’re soul mates. Soul mates always meet up at some point in their lives.”
“You’re just a regular old romantic sap aren’t you Lucky?” He kissed me back gently. “Can I hear your song for me now?”
“It’s bad.” I shook my head. “I don’t want to say it now.”
“Why not?”
“Yours was so beautiful and mine…well, mine is just really bad and goofy.”
“Nothing about you is goofy.”
“Have you seen me at the gym?” I giggled. “Trust me, if you saw me try to use some of those weight machines, you would think I was the goofiest person that you ever met.”

"Stop trying to change the subject." He licked my lips with the tip of his tongue. "Let me hear it."
"If you promise not to laugh."
"Of course I won't laugh."
"Okay." I groaned. "Don't say I didn't warn you, but it's really goofy."
"I'm waiting."
"Argh. Okay. Here we go." I cleared my throat and sat up a little bit so that we were eye to eye. I coughed and then recited the poem I had written for him.

Zane, there has never been a man like you
Who has taken my heart and swallowed it up
I want you to know that you never have to doubt
That you have my love forever
I'll never leave you, never stop loving you, never stop wanting to be with you
You are me, I am you, we are one

The room was silent as I finished speaking and I was scared that Zane was trying to hold his laughter in. I looked into his eyes and I realized that they looked wet.
"I told you it sucked." I mumbled, embarrassed.

“That was amazing, Lucky. Thank you.” He reached over and squeezed my hand. “Now, what do you want to go and do?”
“Wait, we’re going out?” I was surprised and disappointed that he had changed the topic so quickly but I didn’t want to ask him why. I knew he was a newbie to emotions and I was pretty confident that he was most probably feeling overwhelmed with everything that was going on.
He jumped up off of the bed and stared down at me. “Want to see the Eiffel Tower by night?”
“Sure, I suppose so.” I sat up and rubbed my eyes before getting off of the bed. “I didn’t know we were going to go out right away.”
“There’s no time like the present right?” He laughed forcefully and looked away. He walked over to his suitcase and started fiddling around with it and I stood there watching him unsure of what to say.
“Did I do something to make you mad, Zane?” I asked softly. “Was it my poem? I’m sorry if you didn’t like it.”
He turned around slowly and looked at me with a clouded expression. “I liked the poem, Lucky.”
“So why are you acting so funny?”
“You really love me, don’t you?”

"You know I do."
"It just suddenly felt real. I know that sounds dumb, but I think it just hit me like a ton of bricks. You really really love me and you are in this whatever happens." He paused. "I'm not an easy man to love and I know that I've already put you through a lot. I guess I'm just wondering how much you can put up with. There are going to be so many more ups and downs with me." He grimaced. "If you haven't noticed, I get jealous, angry, and annoyed, and it hit me that at some point you're no longer going to be thinking we are one. At some point you're going to regret that you said you would never leave me or stop wanting to be with me. I know you love me. But sometimes love isn't enough. Sometimes people can push you away so hard that it doesn't matter how much you love them."
"I'm not going to leave you, Zane."
"But you don't know that. You can't guarantee it." He took a deep breath. "I'm sorry, this is something I'm trying to be rational about. It's just hard."
"Don't freeze me out, Zane." I took a deep breath. "I need to tell you something."
"What?" His eyes narrowed and his body stilled. "What is it Lucky?"

"Noah found your mom." I began and when I saw the confused, but excited expression in his eyes, I suddenly felt scared to tell him more. "I guess he was looking for her online. That's what Sidney told me."
"I wondered what the two of you were whispering about."
"Noah gave him a file before he died and in the file was the contact information for your mom." Zane's expression was obstinate, but I could see the hope in his eyes and it killed me.
"I see. So what next?" He ran his hands through his hair. "I don't know what to say. Am I supposed to call her? Did Noah call her?"
"I, uh, I don't know." I bit my lip, unsure of how to tell him about my conversation with his mother without breaking his heart.
"I guess I'll call her when we get back?" He shrugged to pretend that he didn't care but I knew differently. "I'll have to tell her Noah died."
"The thing is… she's in Paris," I blurted out.
"What?" His head stilled. "She's here?"
"Yes." I took a big gulp. "I called her."
"You told her we were coming here?" His voice was low and angry. "I don't want to see her, Lucky."

"I …" My voice choked up and I wasn't sure how to finish my sentence. "I spoke to her and …."

"She's expecting to see me now, isn't she? She thinks she can just come back in my life after everything that happened? She thinks that after 19 years I'm going to greet her back into my life with open arms. Or did she run out of money? Did she ask you if I have money?"

"No." My voice was low.

"I can't believe you told her I would go and see her." Zane was fuming. "I'm done with her. I do not care about her. I do not care to see her. She left me, Lucky. She left me and never looked back."

"I'm sorry." Tears brimmed in my eyes at the anger in Zane's voice. I wasn't sad because he was shouting at me though. I was sad because I knew beyond a doubt that all he wanted was for his mom to have a good reason for leaving him. I didn't correct his misapprehension of our conversation because I didn't want him to know the truth. I'd rather he think she wanted to get back into his life than what had really been said.

"Lucky, I'm not mad at you." He stepped back and picked up his wallet. "I'm just not in that place. I didn't have a happy family like

you. She left and she can't expect to just come back into my life."
"I understand."
"What did she say?" His eyes looked at me intensely. "Anything important?" The words slipped out of his mouth casually, but I knew that what I said next would weigh on his heart and in his mind for the rest of his life. And so I did the only thing I thought I could do, I lied.
"She was upset." I tried to avoid his eyes. "She said it was the hardest thing she ever had to do. And every day, she thinks about you and Noah, and wonders what sort of men you turned into."
"I bet she wants to know if we ended up looking like her or our dad."
"Yeah."
"She was sad, huh?" Zane played with his fingers as he spoke and I started plaiting my hair.
"Yeah, she was really sad. I think she really regrets what she did." *And if she didn't, she should*, I thought to myself.
"That's not enough." Zane's voice was gruff. "You don't get your sons back because you realize you made a mistake."
"Yeah. I think she'll regret it for the rest of her life."

“Well,” Zane turned off the TV. “She should. Are you ready?”
“Yeah.” I nodded and picked up my bag and we left the hotel room. My heart was heavy at the lies I had told, but I’d rather have a guilty conscience than have Zane have another broken heart.

Chapter 11
Zane

"What shall we do today, boys?" She sat at her vanity table and brushed her hair. "Do you want to go to the beach?"

"Yes, please." I sat on the floor playing Legos with Noah.

"No, not the beach." Noah made a face. "I want to go wrestling."

"We can't go wrestling." I rolled my eyes and looked at her for approval. "Right?"

"Right, Zane, we can't go wrestling, Noah. Just think about what your dad would say."

I stuck my tongue out at Noah and jumped up. "Can I brush your hair?" I reached my hand out for the brush.

"Not today, Zane." She shook her head. "You take too long."

I stood behind her, awkwardly wanting to reach over and hug her, but I was too scared, so I walked away slowly.

"Come, Zane, it's your turn." Noah called out to me.

"I'm tired of playing Legos." I made to leave the room.

"You're just jealous because my army is beating your army." Noah picked up his toy

car and it came crashing down on the tower I had been building.
"What are you doing?" I cried out angrily. "You ruined it."
"I told you to come."
"He ruined it, he ruined it." I shouted and stood there with my hands clenched.
"Noah, say sorry to your brother and Zane please quiet down. It's not a big deal." She continued brushing her hair and spoke without turning around.
"You're such a baby, Zane." Noah jumped up and grinned, sticking his tongue out, back at me.
"Sally, Noah just stuck his tongue out at me."
"Zane did it first, Sally. He did it first." Noah ran over to our nanny and hugged her. She lifted him into her lap and patted his head. Noah leaned his head into her shoulder and I walked out of the room upset and jealous as she held him close to her heart.

"Zane, wake up." Lucky shook my shoulder and I opened my eyes slowly.
"Huh?" I looked up at her through sleep-filled eyes. "What happened?"
"You kept shouting, 'I want a hug too, I want a hug too!'" She looked at me with worried eyes. "Is everything ok?"

"Yeah." I nodded and sat up. My throat was dry and I cleared it. "It was just a dream."
"About your mom again?" Her eyes were sad and she reached over to hold my hand. It felt light and soft next to mine and I squeezed it gratefully. I liked having her in the bed next to me. I didn't know how I had gotten through the dreams without her by my side before.
"No, this dream was about one of my old nannies." I shook my head. "Weird, I haven't thought about Sally in years."
"Was she nice to you?"
"She was our first nanny after my mom left. She stayed for a few years and then left when she got married to a guy who owned his own car dealership."
"Were you close?"
"She was closer to Noah. I found it hard to reach out."
"But you were only six when your mother left. You never tried to get close to anyone?"
"No, you're the first person I've really let in. I guess you can say you're special." I gave her a weak smile and she sighed. "Though I suppose that makes me sounds like a bit of a loser. A 25-year-old man who never got over his mother leaving him."
"That's not something that many people can get over, Zane."

"They're not going to stop, are they?" I muttered without waiting for answer. "The dreams aren't going to stop, are they?"
"Do you want them to stop?" Her voice sounded as sweet as an angel and I wanted to just be able to focus on that. I wanted to be consumed by her love for me and only her love for me. I wanted to banish the pain and hurt from my life. And the first step to getting rid of the pain would be to know why my mom had left.
"I want them to stop. I don't want to be haunted by the past anymore. I want to focus on you. On us." I pulled Lucky into my arms and held her close. "I want to be able to wake up and only think about your warm body against mine. I want my only worry to be how many times I can make love to you before I go to work."
"Zane," she giggled and I felt her kissing my shoulder.
"I want to call my mom." I blurted out. "I'm going to call her and find out why." I felt Lucky's body still next to mine and I knew she must have been shocked at my change of heart. "You were right, Lucky, I need to talk to her to try and get closure. I can't be scared or bitter anymore. I need to move past those emotions."

"Are you sure, Zane?" Her voice was low and I could barely hear her. "Maybe she can't give you the closure you need."
"I just need some answers. I just want to understand why, and how she could leave us."
"What if she asks about Noah?"
"Then she'll have to know that her youngest son is dead." My words were harsh and my stomach was full of nerves. As much as I knew that I didn't want to see her and have that conversation, I knew that I needed to. I didn't come all the way to France to find out she was here to leave. I knew Noah would have wanted to know, he would have wanted me to call. "I have to call for Noah."
"No, Zane, you have to call for you. You have to call because it's what you want and need." Lucky pulled away from me and looked into my eyes. "You have to be honest with yourself, Zane."
"Maybe she misses me." I looked away from her as I uttered the words that I had never voiced before. In fact, I had never even allowed myself to think those thoughts. "Maybe we can make this right. Maybe she really does regret everything that happened. Maybe, and I don't mean right away, but in a few months or even a few years, maybe we can even have a relationship again."

"You'd like that, wouldn't you?" Lucky held me tight and I breathed in her scent.
"I'd like a mother who loves me. I'd like to know that she loves me. I'd like to understand why she left."
"So then I guess you should call her." Lucky sighed and I frowned. I had expected her to be happy for me, excited even.
"Is it too early to call her now?"
"It's 5 a.m.," Lucky whispered. "I'd say it's definitely too early."
"I'm nervous." I laughed. "Man, I sound like a sissy."
"No, you don't."
"I do," I muttered. "Let's go back to sleep."

***

"No answer." I tried the number one more time, disappointment coursing through my veins. "Maybe she moved?"
"Maybe." Lucky looked down at her plate.
"Wait, you said you had her address right?" An idea popped into my mind. "Maybe we can go visit her?" The more I thought about it, the better the idea sounded. "I mean a phone call is all good and well, but what I really want is to look into her eyes and ask us how she could have left us."

"Do you think that is a good idea, Zane?" Lucky chewed on her fingernails and looked worried. "What if she's not here?"
"That's a chance we would have to take." I called the waiter over so I could get the bill. "*La cuenta, por favor*."
"That's Spanish, Zane." Lucky giggled and I smiled at her vacantly. My mind was already thinking about what was going to happen when I saw my mom. It didn't seem real and I wasn't sure I was making the right decision. But I kept hearing Noah's voice in the back of my mind asking me where I thought mom was and if mom missed us. I knew that I had to find out, if not for me, then for Noah.
"I'm ready, Zane." Lucky grabbed my arm and I stood up. We walked to the corner and as the taxi pulled over, I realized that I wasn't ready. I didn't want to go, but I knew there likely wouldn't be another opportunity like this coming up again.
"It's a beautiful house." Lucky stared at the garden in front of us. We were in the outskirts of Paris now and there was green grass all around us as opposed to buildings.
"With the money she took she should have a nice house." I muttered, staring at the smallish farmhouse it front of us. It didn't fit my image

of my mother; I couldn't see her in a farmhouse or on a farm.
"Zane, please."
"I won't bring it up." I took a deep breath and walked up the pathway and to the front door. I could hear some noises from inside the house and I felt like I was going to throw up. This was it then, I was about to come face to face with my mother. Lucky stood next to me and slid her hand into mine. I looked down at her gratefully and gave her a quick smile. With my heart pounding, I lifted the knocker on the door and waited.
"*Allo, allo.*" A little boy answered the door and looked at us. "*Bonjour.*" He smiled widely at me and then at Lucky. He looked to be about seven and had a huge gap in his front teeth.
"*Bonjour.*" I smiled back at him with my heart in my mouth. "We, *uh Nous visite Mrs. Beaumont."*
"*Pardon*?" He looked up at me with oblivious eyes. He had no idea that my whole world was about to change in about five minutes.
"*Bonjour mon amie*," Lucky smiled at the little boy. "*Ca va*?"
"*Bien.*" He grinned.

"I didn't know you spoke any French?" I looked at Lucky in surprise. Why hadn't she helped in the taxi if she was fluent?
"That's all I know." She laughed and the three of us stood there at the door looking at each other.
"Jean-Pierre." I heard a lady's voice calling to the little boy.
"*Oui mama*."
"Jean-Pierre." The voice came closer to the door and as the lady opened the door, the little boy made a face and ran back inside.
"*Bonjour*." The lady stuck her head out the door and she had a contemplative look on her face.
As I stared into her blue eyes, I felt my heart still. She stared back at me, and her face paled. We looked at each other for what seemed like an eternity and I felt my brain asking a million questions that my mouth didn't seem to want to say.
"Hi." Lucky finally broke the silence. "Is Mrs. Beaumont here?"
"You." The lady broke eye contact with me and looked at Lucky, her eyes shooting daggers.
"Mrs. Beaumont?" Lucky's voice was hopeful and soft and I watched her talking to my mom

in silence. I felt like I was in one of my dreams, only someone had frozen me in place.

"I'm afraid you've come to the wrong address." Her voice was heavily accented. She sounded like a native French speaker. I was surprised at how easily her American accent had changed.

"Mom." I looked at her and said the words awkwardly. They almost choked me, but a part of me felt somehow lighter at being able to say the words to her face.

"Sorry, I can't help you." Her face looked upset and she looked away from me. "You should go."

"Mom, it's me, Zane." I spoke again, a little louder this time. "It's me, your son, Zane Beaumont."

"I don't know who you are." She clutched the door handle tightly, and I could see the palms of her hands turning red. "I have to ask you to leave."

I stood there staring at her not really understanding what was going on. Why was she pretending she didn't know me? I knew her face as well as I knew my own. I had dreamt of her almost every night for years; her eyes were ingrained in my mind.

"I just wanted to ask you a few questions." I frowned. "I didn't come for any money, and I won't tell dad where you are. I just want to know why you left. Please."

She looked up at me then and I could see tears in the corners of her eyes as she stared at me. She stepped forward and touched my face, staring at me in wonder. She then touched my arm and stepped back. "You're a handsome boy." She smiled. "But I'm sorry, I do not know who your mother is."

"*Mama, mama, viens ici*." The little boy ran back through the door and pulled on her top. He stood there holding onto her and stared up at me with a curious expression, as if to say, 'oh you're still here'.

"I have to go inside now." She looked away from me. "Good luck with your search."

"Wait." My voice was firm. "I know you're lying. I don't want anything from you. I just want to understand."

"I'm sorry, but I have to go. *Au Revoir*." And with that, she turned away and quickly closed the door. I stared at her face as she closed the door and I saw a small tear rolling from her eyes. At that moment, I felt as if my world had ended. My heart felt empty and a deep chill filled my body. I saw Lucky looking at me with a worried expression, but I was unable to even look at her and give her a reassuring look.

I picked up a rock and squeezed it tightly, hoping I could crush it in my bare hands. When I realized I couldn't, I threw it as far as I could and walked quickly away from the door.

My mind felt numb and I started running. I didn't stop to think about where I was going or to worry if Lucky could keep up with me, I just ran. I ran so fast and so hard that I tripped over a bunch of rocks and scratched up my hands and arms. The scrapes burned me and I saw traces of blood on my palms, but I jumped up and kept running. I welcomed the pain, it helped to take my mind off of my mother's rejection. A rejection that was worse than any I could have ever imagined. She had seen me, had me right there in front of her and denied me. There was never going to be any closure. I was never going to hear the words that she loved me and wanted to make it up to me. We were never going to bond. She was never going to be a grandmother to my children. She just didn't care. She didn't love me. It was as simple as that. She wasn't in my life because she didn't want to be. She just didn't care. I was nothing to her. I meant nothing to her. My heart felt empty and I collapsed onto the ground by an old tree trunk. I lay back in the grass and stared at an ant that was walking along the ground. I watched it walking until it disappeared from sight and then I focused on another ant.

I sensed Lucky before I heard or saw her. I didn't look up. I didn't open my mouth to tell her I was okay. I just laid there watching the ant. I felt her sit next to me in the grass. She didn't say a word to me and I was grateful that she didn't try to tell me that it was all going to be okay. We lay in the grass in silence for what must have been 15 minutes before I picked a piece of grass and turned towards her. She was staring at me with bloodshot eyes and a worried expression. It hurt my heart that she had been crying for me. Even I wasn't crying for me, but I didn't know what to say.

"Have you ever eaten grass?" I passed her the blade of grass and picked another one. "You should try it." I put a piece of grass in my mouth and chewed on it. "If you think about it, we eat a lot of grass anyway."

"Because we eat steak." She smiled at me as she spoke and I nodded. *That's why she's perfect for you*, a voice inside me said. She knows what you're thinking. She's already a part of you.

"Yeah, cows eat grass all day and we eat steak. I have to admit I prefer to eat the steak than the grass."
"Me too." She inched towards me and I stared into her brown eyes.
"Did you know your eyes are hazel when the sun hits them at a certain light?"
"No." Her voice was small.
"And your hair has red highlights. Or copper. Your hair shines like spun copper in the sun." I laughed. "It's a pity it's not real copper, then you'd be really rich."
"I knew, Zane." Lucky burst out. "I knew and I'm sorry."
I frowned at her, not understanding what she was saying. "You knew what?"
"When I called your mom and spoke to her …" Her voice cracked and she started crying. "I knew she didn't want to see you. I'm sorry."
"You knew?" My voice was light; surprisingly her words didn't stir any emotions in me.
"Are you mad?" She bit her lip and I saw the concern in her eyes. "I'm so sorry, Zane. I can't believe that just happened."
"It's okay." I reached out and took her hand in mine. I felt my body warming as I touched her and she moved in closer to me.

"It's not okay. Oh, Zane, I'm so sorry. I hate her. I really hate her."
"It's not your fault, Lucky."
I could feel her heart beating next to mine and I pulled her in even closer to me. The closer she was, the more I felt myself relaxing and breathing, until all of a sudden, I felt like myself again. I closed my eyes and listened to our hearts beating together in harmony. It was as if her heart were breathing life back into mine. I held onto her and just breathed her in. She ran her hands through my hair and her mouth found mine. I kissed her back hard, wanting to feel and taste all of her in the most primal of ways. I pushed her flat on her back and rolled over on top of her. I reached down and pulled her t-shirt off and pulled her bra straps down so I could gain access to her breasts easily. I bent my head down and suckled on her nipples and I felt myself becoming even more aroused as she squirmed beneath me. She moaned as I bit down lightly on her and I kissed down her body, licking the inside of her belly button and pausing as I reached the top of her pants. I looked up at her before unbuttoning her jeans and she nodded slightly giving me the go-ahead. I unzipped her jeans and pulled them down her legs, until they crunched up against her

ankles. I quickly untied her shoes and pulled them off before pulling off her jeans completely. She sat up and pulled her bra off and I stared at her beautiful body as she lay in the grass with only her panties on. I pulled my t-shirt off, and quickly pulled off my shoes and pants so that I was only in my boxers.
"I don't have a condom," I muttered frustrated at myself.
"It's okay." She smiled up at me.
"Are you sure?"
"Yes." She reached up and pulled me down towards her. "I want to do this. Here. Now. With you."
I leaned forward and kissed her hard, running my hands down to her breasts and cupping and caressing them. She ran her hands down my back and into my boxer shorts until she was squeezing my ass and I pushed my erection into her panties. She wrapped her legs around my waist and reached up and pushed me over so I was on my back and she was on top of me. Leaning forward her breasts grazed my chest and she grinded herself back and forth on me. I closed my eyes and concentrated on the desire coursing through me. I reached up and slipped two fingers into her panties, and her wetness made me gasp with lust and desire, as I felt how

ready she was for me. Pushing her off of me and onto her back, I reached down and pulled her panties off. I buried my face in between her legs and her moans encouraged me as I explored her with my tongue. I grinned as she orgasmed on my tongue and I quickly kissed my way back up her body before entering her. She cried out and I moved slowly inside of her so that I could feel every delicate and sensitive part of her body against me. Every fiber of my being felt connected to Lucky. As our bodies became one, I felt the pleasure course through me, making me feel alive and free. I pushed into her deeper and harder wanting our two bodies to fuse together and melt into one. Lucky was a part of me, her very essence flowed through my veins. Her smile was part of my lips, her taste was a lingering sweetness on the tip of my tongue, her scent was in every inhale I took, and the tenderness of her voice was like music to my ears. My heart had felt like it had been broken and snatched away from my body this afternoon after my mother's rejection, but as I made love to Lucky, I realized it had only been a small fracture. And I knew I would get over it. I knew it as well as I knew the exact color of Lucky's eyes and the way she smiled and giggled when she was nervous. As long

as I had Lucky, I would never be or feel alone.
"Don't stop, Zane." Lucky's raspy voice turned me on even more and she scratched my back as I went faster and faster before collapsing to the side of her. We laid there staring at each other, grinning like idiots, and she reached over and ran her fingers down my chest.
"You are one good lover, Zane Beaumont."
"Finally," I grinned. "I finally got you to admit it."

***

"So, what did you think?" I looked at Lucky's face to see if she had enjoyed our trip to the top of the Eiffel Tower.
"Honestly, I was a little underwhelmed." She made a face. "That was a long wait to get up there and then we could barely see anything."
"It is a pretty nasty day." I grimaced up at the sky. "Rain and overcast doesn't do the city of Paris justice."
"I'm just glad I live in Los Angeles, I mean Miami." Lucky laughed. "You know what I mean."
"I do." I took hold of her hand and we walked together past all the other tourists. "Thanks

for being you." I looked at her face, and all I could think about was how much unconditional love she had given me.
"Thanks for being you, too." She paused and stopped to look at a young boy who was painting the Eiffel Tower. "Hello." She smiled at him and he grinned up at us.
"Hello." He continued painting and we stood and watched him for a few minutes. "Are you American as well?"
"Yes, we are." She smiled down at him. "I love your painting."
"I'm painting the Eiffel Tower."
"It looks wonderful," Lucky beamed at him. "You're very talented."
"Thank you." He pointed to a lady sitting on a chair a few yards away. "That's my mom."
"She must be very proud of you." Lucky waved to his mom and the boy nodded.
"She's happy for me." He looked at us solemnly. "I got my wish granted."
"Your wish?" I looked at him curiously.
"From Make-A-Wish Foundation." He nodded. "I wanted to come to Paris to paint the Eiffel Tower and they granted me the wish."
"Oh, I see." I studied the little boy's face and I noticed that his hair looked very thin and his

eyes looked bigger than normal. “You must be very happy.”
“I had neuroblastoma.” He picked up two paint tubes. “Should I use the purple or the blue next?”
“I like the purple.” Lucky smiled at him and I looked away quickly at the sight of her crouched down next to the young boy. I wondered at how some people could give their heart so easily and freely.
“Me, too.” I sat crouched down on the other side of him. “Do you think you could paint one for me as well?” I smiled at the happy surprise in his eyes.
“You want one?” he asked eagerly and excitedly.
“Of course.” I grinned at him and rubbed my hands. “You’re going to be a famous painter one day, and I would love to have one of your original paintings.”
“I’d like to be a famous painter.” He looked worried. “As long as the cancer doesn’t come back.”
“Well, we should all pray for that.” I nodded and looked at him solemnly. “Cancer is a bad thing.”
“Yes.” He nodded. “What color do you want your painting to be?”

"Surprise me." I smiled at him. "Whatever you paint will look great on my walls."
"You're going to hang it on your wall?"
"Oh, yes. It will be front and center in my living room, and I will tell everyone I got it from a famous painter in France."
"Well, I'm not famous yet; it's not good to lie." He chewed on his lower lip and looked like he was thinking very hard. "But I don't mind if you tell them I'm going to be famous one day."
"Then those are the words I shall use." I smiled at him gently and was rewarded by a huge smile.
"I'm going to paint it now."
"Thank you." I stood up and saw a man selling some souvenirs. "I'll be right back, guys." I walked away quickly and looked through the key chains on the table. I grinned when I saw one in the shape of a key and the word 'Paris' on it. I was going to give it to Lucky that evening because Paris was the place she had unlocked my heart. I was still devastated from my mother's lies, but I knew that I would be okay. It was a weird feeling to know and accept that the pain would eventually dull. I saw another item that I thought Lucky would love and bought it as well, and then quickly returned back to them.

"Paul is nearly done." Lucky smiled up at me. "It's a beautiful painting."
I looked down at the paper and smiled at the colorful picture. Paul had painted the moon a sunshine yellow and stars of gold and silver.
"Who's that?" I asked, pointing at a little stick figure in the bottom left-hand corner of the picture.
"That's me." He gave Lucky and me a shy smile. "So you never forget me."
"Oh we will never forget you, Paul." Lucky reached over and gave him a big hug and the little boy flushed with pleasure. "We will treasure this picture forever." We stood there watching him finish the painting and then he handed it to us before turning back to his paints.
"I'm going to finish mine now." He grinned at us and I reached over and touched his shoulder lightly.
"Thanks, Paul."
"*Au revoir*." He smiled and Lucky held the picture carefully. I told her to wait with Paul while I walked over to his mother, who was beaming at me as I approached.
"Thanks for talking to Paul, so many people are scared to stop and talk to him." Her eyes glistened with tears and I saw the love and appreciation in her eyes for our simple deed.

"It was our pleasure." My heart went out to this woman. "I actually support St. Jude Children's Hospital and so I know some of what you're going through."
"It's been hard, but Paul is a trooper."
"I want to give you something." I took out my pocketbook and pulled out a check from the inner flap. I made it out for 100,000 dollars, signed it, and then folded it and handed it to her. "I want you to take this. Put your name on it or Paul's and use it for whatever bills you have or for a college fund. Whatever you want or need."
"Oh, no. I can't take your money." Her eyes almost popped out as she looked at the check and she shook her head with a shocked expression.
"Trust me when I say I can afford it." I smiled down at her. "Consider it payment for the wonderful painting your son made for me."
"God bless you, sir."
"No, God bless you for being so strong and raising a wonderful boy. God bless you for being a wonderful mother." I reached down and kissed her on the cheek. "Please cash the check and let me do this for you and your son. It would mean more to me than you will ever know."

"Thank you, Mr. Beaumont." There were tears in her eyes as she looked down at the check. "Thank you."

I smiled at her one more time and then walked away. My heart was full and heavy. Lucky walked towards me and I laughed as I started at the front of her head.

"What did you say to her?" Lucky inquired as we walked off arm and arm.

"I just gave her our best wishes."

"It must be hard raising a child with cancer." She sounded sad and I squeezed her hand.

"It is. But you do the best you can. As a parent, you just love your child and hope for the best."

"Yes." She nodded and looked up at me. "I'm really sorry about your mom, Zane."

"I know." I kissed her cheek. "I don't want to talk about it right now, but I know."

"What do you want to do now?"

"Let's go and get something to eat. I have some presents to give you."

"Oh, Zane," she giggled. "Not more presents."

"Yes, more presents."

"I have something for you as well." She looked up at me slyly and I looked down at her in shock.

"You do?"

"Uh huh." She grinned. "I got it yesterday."
"What is it?"
"You'll have to wait and see." Her eyes sparkled and I was intrigued. "Don't tell me you got lingerie."
"Okay, I won't tell you that."
"Oh, my God, you went and got some new lingerie, didn't you?" I asked excitedly.
"Zane, you wish." She shook her head and laughed. "I didn't get any lingerie."
"Oh darn. Well, I got you a cute keychain with an actual key on it because you unlocked my heart. I also got you a cute pink notebook with a little Eiffel Tower statue on it because I want you to be able to write me more wonderful love songs." I paused. "Okay, I didn't intend to just blurt that out like that, I had a whole conversation planned for dinner, but you're killing me here, Lucky. I want to know what you got me."
"My, my, aren't we impatient?"
"Did you get beads?" Dirty thoughts entered my mind and I hoped Lucky couldn't tell what I was thinking.
"Beads?"
"You know." I winked at her and she shook her head in confusion.
"You mean like a necklace?"

“No, I mean beads-beads.” I winked again and caressed her behind with my hands, and she shrieked as she realized what I was talking about.
“You’re so disgusting, Zane Beaumont.”
“What?” I faked a frown. “A guy can dream, right?”
“Argh. Let’s go eat.” She rolled her eyes at me and I watched her ass as she walked in front of me.
I tried to keep my thoughts clean, but all of a sudden, I was no longer hungry for food. I laughed at my dirty thoughts and then I thought back to Paul and his mother, and my heart started to crack. His mother loved him so much. She was the sort of woman that would do anything for her child. She would never give him up. She would never pretend she didn’t know him. I just didn’t understand why. In some ways, having seen my mother was worse than not having seen her. Before I was heartbroken and hateful due to the unknown, but now, now I was just heartbroken and devastated. I was literally devastated that my own mother could look into my eyes and not feel a thing. There was no doubt in my mind now that she didn’t love me. I didn’t know why she left, and frankly, I didn’t care. I hated her. I hated her with every

fiber in my being for making me feel like a nothing. Like I wasn't good enough. It was at moments like this when I witnessed the real love of a mother to her son, that I felt the weight of the world on my shoulders. I felt empty and alone, and as I walked, I felt like the pavement could swallow me up and that no one would care.
"I got some furry handcuffs." Lucky's voice interrupted my reverie and she grabbed my hand. I looked up at her blankly and she stared into my eyes with a searching look.
"What?" I tried to smile, but it didn't quite hit my eyes.
"I got furry handcuffs?"
"Really?" I tried to look interested, but every time I thought about my mother, I felt as if I was living in the pits of hell and that nothing would be okay again.
"No, not really." Her hands left mine and she reached up to my face. "Look at me, Zane." She pleaded and I focused on the look in her eyes because they were shining bright with love for me. My breath caught as I stared at her, and she smiled a wide, happy beautiful smile. "I got you a puzzle piece."
"Oh?"
"Well, two pieces. Two connected pieces." She reached into her handbag and pulled out a

small bag. “Look.” She handed me the bag and I looked at the two wooded jigsaw pieces that were joined together, one of the pieces said ‘Zane’ and the other side said ‘Lucky’ and there was a heart in the middle, joining the two pieces together.

“I don’t know what to say.” I stared into her eyes, unable to think of words to express how touched I was. “I’ve never received a gift that has meant this much to me.”

“Do you really like it?” She looked unsure as she spoke. “I know it’s not a Rolex watch or a gold chain or anything, but it represents my love for you. You’re a piece of me now, Zane. And I’m a piece of you. We’re connected by our love for each other. We complete each other, Zane. I know that more than I’ve known anything in my life. And I know that you’re hurting right now. I know that you’re hurting more than you’ll ever be able to express to me. But that’s okay. I love you. And I know how hard this is for you. I know how much you want to just curl up and scream and shout. I know that the pain in your heart sometimes feels greater than your love for me. But it’s okay, because I’m not letting go. I’m not leaving. You’re a good man. The best man I’ve ever met in my life.” She took a deep breath and continued. “Yes, there have been nights I have wanted to scream at you. There have been nights that I have questioned what I'm doing, and I've even wondered what I would have done if you had cheated on me with Angelique. But I know you, you would never hurt me. Everything you have done has been to protect me. You are my prince, Zane. You are my knight in shining armor. And I am here for you, forever. I'm not going anywhere. We'll get through the pain. I don't know how a mother can do that to her own child, but I know that there is no way that she will ever forgive herself for leaving you or for what transpired the other day. I could see it in her eyes."

"It's hard, Lucky." I choked out in response, overwhelmed by her love and devotion to me. "One moment, I'm fine, and then it hits me, and I just feel like nothing is worth anything."

"You're grieving." She hugged me tight. "You're grieving because the dream you had is dead and the hope you held in your heart is gone."

"Noah thought she was looking for us." I could hear the pain in my voice and I was angry at how pitiful I sounded. "I'm glad he wasn't there to witness what she said and did."

"Maybe he was a lot stronger than you thought, Zane." Lucky looked up at me. "Maybe he already knew."
"Perhaps." I took a deep breath and buried my face in the top of Lucky's head. "I love you, Lucky. I know that there are going to be hard days and easy days, and I know that I'm going to annoy the shit out of you, and you're going to make me worry like crazy, but I want you to know that I love every inch of you. Your love means the world to me. It is the only thing that is stopping me from going insane."
"We're puzzle pieces, Zane." She kissed me softly. "We were made to fit together. I'll never let you go insane."

Chapter 12
Lucky

I looked at the framed painting on the wall on the living room and smiled. It had been a little over a month since we had gotten back from Paris and it still feels like yesterday. As I walked into the kitchen, I smiled to myself at how close Zane and I had become. I knew he was still hurting from what had gone down with his mother, but I also knew that he was trying to accept that that was a part of his life that he couldn't change. He was more open now, and the dreams had stopped. I looked at the envelope in my hand and said a quick prayer before putting a stamp on it. I was mailing off an application to UCLA to transfer to their History Department for the next semester and I thought I had a fairly good chance at being accepted. I placed the letter on the counter and opened the fridge to get something to eat for lunch. I was supposed to go out with Zane, but he got caught up at the police station, finalizing all the details of his year working alongside the FBI.
I looked in the fridge and pulled out some pickles and cheese. I walked to the cupboard to go and grab some crackers, but all of a sudden I felt sick to my stomach.

"Oh man," I groaned out loud as I rested my head on the countertop. I was pretty sure I had caught a cold from the changing temperatures, and wanted to go and lie down. I literally felt sick to my stomach, and all I wanted to do was throw up. I left the food on the counter and walked to the living room to go lie down on the couch. As I was leaving, I heard my phone ringing, so I grabbed it and answered.
"Hello." My voice was weak and I hurried to go and sit down in the nearest chair.
"Lucky, is that you?" Sidney's voice was loud and vibrant and I smiled into the phone.
"Yes, Mr. Johnson. How was Chicago?"
"My dear, it was fabulous, just fabulous. Betty and I went to the Sears Tower. Do you know how high up that is? We thought we were going to die." Sidney laughed and I heard Betty muttering at him in the background. "But that's not why I called." His voice turned serious.
"Is everything okay?" My head slowed and I was scared he was going to tell me some bad news.
"Betty and I found some more papers in the file." Sidney's voice was slow and I heard him sighing. "I told Betty we should leave this alone, but she told me we needed to pass

it along, and so I did, well now I know we were wrong."

"What are you talking about, Sidney? What's wrong?" My face paled and I clutched my stomach as it churned.

"We shouldn't have given you Noah's paperwork." He sighed. "I don't think you should contact his mother."

"Why do you say that?" I turned onto my side and closed my eyes.

"Noah has some notes, in the file. I wasn't being nosey, but the file fell and I saw them," Sidney continued.

"I see." I was scared to talk because I was sure I was going to throw up.

"Zane's mom ain't good people, Lucky." He sighed. "There's a lot of shit in Denmark, excuse my language, dear, and let's just say she lives in the smelly part of Denmark."

"What does it say Sidney?" My heart stopped as I wondered what Noah had found out.

"I can't say, Lucky." Sidney's voice was firm. "Noah gave me this paperwork for safekeeping. He didn't want me to share."

"But Noah's dead now, Sidney." I sighed and took a deep breath. " And Zane's still here and he's hurting. His mom rejected him, Sidney. He needs to know why."

"What are you talking about, Lucky?"

"We were in Paris and we went to visit her and she turned us away. She turned her own son away, Sidney. Zane has a right to know why."

"I don't think Zane gonna want to know this." Sidney's tone was firm. "I don't want to be involved no more."

"You don't have to be involved. Please, can I just get the files, Sidney?"

"Noah gave them to me for safekeeping."

I heard Betty in the background hissing something that sounded like "tell her, tell her," and I felt myself growing angry.

"Sidney, I think you need to tell me what's going on."

"It's not my place. I gave my word." His voice was obstinate. "I don't break my word. No one will ever say that Sidney Johnson breaks his word."

"Zane needs this Sidney, please." I felt the bile rising up my throat and I wasn't sure what was going on. I felt so emotional and tense, yet I had never had this reaction before. I had never been so upset that I wanted to throw up.

"He's at the police station, right?" Sidney's voice sounded excited. "I heard that he helped catch Braydon and Angelique."

"Yeah, he ..." I paused. "Wait, how did you know about Braydon and Angelique?"
"Child, when you get to my age, you know everything."
"What's going on, Sidney?"
"All shall be revealed in due time." Sidney's voice sounded funny and rushed. "I guess now that the case is over, it doesn't really matter that you called his mom. He was bound to find out anyways."
"You're not making sense." My voice rose with frustration. "Please explain to me what you're talking about."
"Lucky, do you remember I told you that nothing is always as it seems? Well sometimes, even though everything in life points you in one direction and to one conclusion, that conclusion is not correct. Do you understand what I'm saying?"
"I have no idea what you're saying, Sidney." I frowned into the phone and my head started aching.
I rubbed my temples and I thought about his words for a moment. But as I was about to respond to him, I threw up. All over the leather couch. I groaned at the sight of my puke, but then I felt immediately better. As I stared at the bile on the leather couch and thought about his words, I realized that I

understood exactly what he meant. My feeling sick wasn't due to a cold or the change in temperature. The signs had all been there, but I had ignored them. "I think I understand."
"All will be revealed in good time, Lucky."
"He was so hurt, Sidney." I stood up slowly and cringed at my bile on the chair.
"But he has you, Lucky, and maybe now that the case is over, everything else in his life will come back together as well."
"Yeah." I wasn't really listening to him anymore, because I was feeling shocked at the realization I had just made.
"I promise it'll work out my dear. It's like my mother used to say, just when you think you're down to your last bag of rice, Jesus gon' come and make a miracle."
"Thanks Sidney. I'll talk to you later." I hung up the phone and buried my head in my hands, half-happy and half-shocked.
I made a mental checklist, I was feeling sickly, I had weird food cravings, my breasts felt swollen and tender. I had to be pregnant. But it didn't make sense. I got my period. *Just because you got your period doesn't mean you couldn't still be pregnant*, a little voice in me cried out. *You should have done a test.* I grabbed ahold of my stomach and I suddenly

knew. I just knew. I didn't even need to go to the doctor.
I heard the front door opening and I stilled. Zane was home and I wasn't sure how he was going to feel. With all the emotional turmoil he had been through recently, I wasn't sure if he was in a good place to be a father. I didn't want it all to be too much too soon. I stood there debating what to do when I heard a car pull up in the driveway. As I heard his footsteps, I looked up, ready to tell him that I thought we were going to have a baby, but no words came out of my mouth.
Zane was standing at the front door staring at me, but my eyes weren't on him, they were on the man standing next to him. The man who looked so much like Zane, only different. The man who looked like I imagined his brother would look. I rubbed my eyes, not knowing if I was hallucinating or what.
"Lucky," Zane walked towards me slowly. "I'd like you to meet my brother, Noah." His words tripped out of his mouth smoothly and innocently, and as I stared at the other man's familiar, wide smile, I felt myself feeling woozy and then fell to the ground.

***

"Shit, man, is she okay?" I heard a male voice say, but I was unable to open my eyes.
"I'm sure she just went into shock." Zane's voice was worried. "Help me pick her up."
"I would have thought you'd be the one to faint, not the girlfriend." The voice was silky and warm. "And bro, you never told me she was hot."
"Eyes off, Noah." Zane's voice held a warning.
"Come on now, bro." The guy laughed. "I've been back a day, I don't think I'm going to try and steal your girlfriend."
"You couldn't steal her even if you tried." Zane laughed. "And what do you mean a day? Why did I only find out today?"
"Paperwork." The guy sighed. "You know how it is."
I felt two sets of arms pick me up and carry me. "Shit bro, what's this on the couch?"
"I don't know." Zane's tone sounded worried again. "Fuck, maybe I should call the doctor. Maybe she's sick."
"Yeah. You don't want to take a chance." The other voice sounded worried as well. "Where should we take her? She's not exactly a feather."
"Upstairs." Zane's voice was firm and I slowly opened my eyes.

"Hi." I stared up and he was looking down at me with an extremely concerned expression. "Lucky, are you okay?" He continued staring at me as they walked up the stairs.
I nodded slowly. "I think I fainted." I looked towards my legs and saw the other voice smiling at me. "Are you, Noah?"
"Indeed, I am." He grinned at me and I saw that he had the same blue eyes as Zane, only his hair was darker and he was bigger built.
"But you're dead." My voice was accusing. "How can you be here?"
"Don't upset yourself, Lucky." Zane looked at me and pursed his lips as they set me down on the bed.
"So this is real?" I propped myself up on the pillows and looked at them standing together. "I'm not in some weird funky dream of yours."
"This is real." Zane nodded and came and sat down next to me on the bed. "This is my brother, Noah."
"But how?"
"I guess this is where I come in?" Noah walked towards the bed and looked down at me. "I was in witness protection."
"Huh?" My head was aching and I stared at him in confusion. "I thought you jumped off of a roof?"

“Have you met Angelique?” He grimaced and I nodded. “Do you think anyone would kill themselves over her?”
I laughed slightly, but saw Zane’s furious expression and I knew he didn’t think it was a joking matter. “But that’s what Braydon said, and the police and even Angelique believed that, and—and even Zane.”
“That’s what I needed everyone to believe.” Noah looked at his brother slightly and then back at me. “We needed everyone to believe I was dead.”
“You should have told me, Noah.” Zane’s tone was angry and he stared at his brother. “You should have fucking told me. Do you know what I’ve been through?”
“Dude, I couldn’t tell you.” Noah looked miserable. “It wouldn’t have worked if you had known.”
“I would have gotten the information.” Zane’s face was obstinate and he shook his head. “You fucking don’t pull that shit on me, Noah. You don’t make me think you’re dead.”
“It was the only way. It wasn’t my choice.” Noah pleaded with his brother and I held my hand up and waved it.

"Sorry to interrupt the love-fest, but I have no idea what you guys are talking about." I frowned. "And I very much want to know."
"Yes, Noah, why don't you tell Lucky your little story." Zane stood up and walked to the door. "I'm going to go and get myself a stiff drink. Anyone want anything?"
"I'll have some whiskey, on the rocks." Noah nodded and I shook my head.
"You sure, Lucky? No wine?" Zane studied my face and I shook my head.
"No thanks."
"Okay." He left the room and Noah looked at me awkwardly.
"Do you mind if I have a seat?" He patted the side of the bed and I shook my head, not believing that I was seeing Noah, alive in the flesh.
"I'm glad you don't take any nonsense from my brother." He grinned at me and I stared at him in astonishment, surprised at his words.
"Zane's always been a bit of a worrier, he won't admit it, but he is. He's overprotective and thinks he knows everything. He needs a strong woman like you."
"I don't know what to say." My mouth dropped open.

"Don't say anything." He laughed. "I just want you to know I'm glad my brother found you."
"I love him."
"I can see that." He looked around the room and sighed. "I couldn't tell him, you know? You can't fake heartache and pain, no matter how much you want to. And for him to bring down Braydon and Angelique, he had to be believable."
"You knew?" I frowned, not really understanding what was going on.
"Yeah." He ran his hand through his dark hair and he reminded me so much of his brother that it was uncanny. "I got caught up with Braydon and Angelique. Not doing any hard stuff, just smoking some weed, but I guess you could say I was in the wrong place at the wrong time. We went down to Mexico City one weekend, and let's just say I saw some things I shouldn't have seen."
"Oh yeah?"
"The guy in charge, Sanchez, ordered a hit on one of his dealers that had given the police some information on a shipment from Colombia."
"Oh, my God." My face paled at his words.

"I was sitting in the toilet in the next room as he ordered it." Noah shook his head. "I wasn't meant to overhear any of it."
"What did you do?"
"Well, as I sat there, I planned to tell Braydon that we needed to hightail it out of there, but then I heard his voice."
"Braydon's voice?" I gasped.
"Yeah, he was the one Sanchez was telling to order the hit! I nearly shit my pants. I thought we had just gone down for some good weed, I didn't think all that was going down."
"So what did you do?"
"I kept my mouth shut and pretended like I hadn't seen or heard anything. When I got back to L.A., I called a number I found online and ended up speaking to someone in the FBI who was investigating Sanchez and Braydon."
"Wow." I looked at him with shocked eyes. His story sounded like something from a movie, and it was all I could do to not make loud gasping sounds.
"Yeah, it was pretty crazy." He looked at me with direct eyes. "I didn't want to go away you know. I knew Zane would take it badly, but the Agent told me it was the only way to guarantee my safety and bring down the cartel."
"Why is that?"

"Braydon found out I went to the cops." Noah sighed. "I didn't realize Angelique was involved so deeply, I told her some things. She told Braydon, and when I told the agent at the FBI, he set it up so that everyone would think I died."

"By jumping off of a roof?"

"I didn't actually jump." His voice was irritated and he reminded me of Zane even more. "Braydon was an idiot for believing that. But he was fucking high, he had no clue what was going on. I made him think I was high and depressed, like they told me to do and when he left the roof to go get something, I ran down the emergency exit stairs. The ambulance and police were ready and waiting to go as soon as they saw me make it outside."

"So, it was a setup?"

"Yeah." He nodded. "They put me on a stretcher and made sure that Braydon saw me being escorted into the ambulance."

"But didn't he wonder who called 911?"

"They had a guy with his dog." He laughed. "They thought of everything. They had this guy pretending he had been walking his dog, and he was there screaming about how he saw me jump. So Braydon just assumed what the cops said was true."

"Wow." I paused and sat back thoughtfully. "So that's why Zane was never able to see your body, huh?"
Noah nodded and grinned. "I see you're a smart one."
"And that is why Braydon's story and the police report didn't really add up." I played with my curls as all the inconsistencies came to mind. "Braydon really didn't witness you jumping off the roof, so he wasn't lying in the interrogation. He couldn't have saved you because you never died."
"Crazy, right, Lucky?" Zane walked back into the room and handed Noah his drink.
"Thanks for telling me about the plan before it went down, Noah."
"We needed everyone to think that I was dead." Noah shook his head and sighed. "They told you that man. It wasn't my choice."
"You can't just disappear and make people think that you're dead, man. You were all I had. You fucking tore me apart."
"I'm sorry." Noah's voice was soft and I could tell he was devastated at Zane's obvious hurt. "But we did it, man, we got them."
"You risked my life, Noah, you risked Lucky's life. If anything had happened to her..." He took a deep breath and I saw his

face turning red. "Do you know she went on a date with Braydon?" Zane's voice rose with anger. "Who knows what he may have tried to do to her?"

"You dated Braydon?" Noah looked at me in surprise and I rolled my eyes.

"I did not date Braydon, we were friends and we went to dinner."

"He wanted more than dinner from you." Zane glared at me and downed his whiskey.

"Well, I didn't want more from him."

"You thought he was a nice guy." Zane's eyes narrowed. "You …"

"Bro, don't get mad at her when it's me you really want to punch."

"I do want to punch you, you jerk." Zane looked at his brother and then brought him in for a hug. "If you ever pull a stunt like that again, I will kill you myself."

"Well, it's a good thing I don't plan on doing that again then." They grinned at each other and something hit me. Something I wanted to ask but I didn't know if I should bring up.

"Did Sidney Johnson know?" My voice was quiet as I asked the question in my mind, a part of me didn't really want it to be heard, but I needed to know.

"What?" Noah turned towards me with a glint in his eyes and Zane froze still.

"She asked you if Sidney Johnson knew."
Zane looked at his brother and sighed. "You told Sidney Johnson and you didn't tell me?"
"I could trust him." Noah sighed and he looked at me. "How did you know he knew? I know he would never say a word."
"He didn't tell me exactly, but I think if I had really listened to some of the things he had told me, I wouldn't be as surprised as I am now."
"That Sidney." He laughed and then looked at me curiously. "How did you meet him anyway?"
"We've been working on the documentary."
"My documentary?" He looked shocked and turned to his brother. "You've been working on civil rights stuff now? Wow, you must really have missed me."
"While I did miss you bro, the documentary was for Lucky." Zane raised an eyebrow at me and I blushed. Noah looked back and forth between us and shook his head. "This is all too much for one day. I need to take a nap. I hope you feel better, Lucky. We'll talk later?" He smiled at me warmly before yawning and I nodded eagerly.
"I feel awful. I haven't even asked where you've been. Or how you were able to come back. Or if Braydon knows you're really

alive." I blurted out a bunch of questions. "Sorry, that was a bit much."
"No problem." Noah walked over to me and kissed me on the cheek. "I'm honored that you're interested. I'd love to tell you more."
"Back off, Noah." Zane teased his brother and winked at me. "You can sleep in the room two doors down. You okay to go by yourself? I want to make sure Lucky is okay."
I felt myself flush at his words. Oh shit, he still doesn't know that I may be pregnant. I bit my lip and I saw Noah frown as he saw the worry in my face. He gazed at me in concern for a moment before turning back to Zane.
"No problem bro, I can find it."
He reached over and gave Zane a pat on the back and Zane brought him close for another bear hug. They stood there for what seemed like five minutes just hugging and then they broke apart. I could see the love and happiness shining in Zane's eyes as he stared at his brother and I couldn't believe I was in this moment. It was truly one of the most beautiful things I had ever seen in my life.
"Sweet dreams, Noah." I smiled up at him and he winked before he left the room. Zane watched his brother walking away and then came back to the bed to join me. "Crazy day,

huh?" I grabbed his hand as he sat on the bed next to me.
"I don't think I even know the definition of crazy anymore." He shook his head in disbelief. "I don't know that I even know which way is up and which way is down right now."
"Are you okay?" I looked at him, worried that it had all been too much for him.
"I'm beyond okay." He shook his head. "Today has been the best day of my life. Lucky, when I saw Noah walking towards me, I thought I was going to pass out or that I had died and gone to heaven."
"I'm surprised that he got to leave the program? On TV, they always make it seem like once you go into witness protection, it's for life."
"It was slightly different for Noah." Zane explained. "The FBI was worried that Braydon would hire someone to take Noah out. They weren't worried so much that Braydon would do it, but they knew he had a partner that was a lot more coldhearted. The problem is, they didn't know who, so they didn't want to take any chances."
"Oh, my God, Braydon's partner was Angelique right?" My blood ran cold. "What

if something had happened to you that night? What if she got suspicious?"
"She didn't harm me, Lucky. Nothing happened." Zane leaned over and kissed me.
"But something could have happened." I closed my eyes. "And I never would have known. I would have just been sitting here waiting for you to come home and you would have been laying dead in a ditch somewhere."
"It didn't come to that Lucky." He pulled me towards him. "And I don't think she or Braydon had a clue that I was working with the FBI. Or about Noah. My grief and hatred was too real." He shook his head. "In a way, I understand why they didn't want to tell me that he wasn't dead. It was the best way for me to get into the group and to do everything I could to make sure I could get the evidence to prosecute Braydon."
"They used you." I frowned and we sat there in silence for a few minutes. "So what is going to happen to Braydon?" I was scared he was going to try and come and exact revenge on Zane and Noah now.
"Braydon and Angelique both took plea deals to testify against Sanchez." His eyes burned. "But they will likely still be in jail for 20 years at least."

"But what about Sanchez, will he come after us?" I trembled a little at the thought. I didn't want to be looking over my shoulder every time I went out, and I certainly didn't want Leo to become a full-time bodyguard.
"Sanchez was murdered last week." Zane shrugged. "What can I say? Drug lords don't play fair."
"That's really scary." I cuddled up next to him. "Please tell me we don't have to deal with this anymore. I don't want to even think about these things anymore."
"I promise, Lucky. It's over." His eyes gleamed as he looked down at me. "And I have Noah back."
"He looks a lot like you."
"Just a bit more handsome," he laughed and I ran my hands through his hair and down his face.
"No one's as handsome as you, my love."
"Well, I'm glad to hear that." He grinned and kissed me deeply. "I feel so happy Lucky, I don't know that I've ever felt happier in my life."
"I'm glad."
"Make it the best day of my life." He whispered while staring into my eyes. "Say you'll marry me."

"What?" My eyes popped open at his words and I thought my heart stopped beating for a moment. "What did you say?"
"Say you'll marry me, Lucky. I love you to the moon and back. Since you've been in my life, I have felt such contentment. You've been able to awaken my heart and make me whole again, I don't just want to be your last boyfriend; I want to be your husband."
"My husband?" I breathed the words back to him, still shocked to my core.
"Say I can be your last husband, Lucky." He winked at me. "Make me the happiest man in the world. Make this the happiest day in my life."
"Yes, Zane. Yes, I'll marry you. I love you, Zane. I love you more than life itself. I don't even want to think about a day without you in it."
"You will never have to know a day like that ever again, my dear."
"I have something to tell you." I took a deep breath. "Well, two things to tell you."
"What?" He looked worried for a second. "Please do not tell me you're already married."
"No, goofy." I laughed and he laughed back at me, stroking the hair away from my face. "I decided to apply to UCLA. I researched their

History program and it's great. I'm hoping to be able to transfer."
"Are you sure?" His face was full of concern. "Don't do that for me, Lucky, I'd be happy to go back to Miami with you so you can finish school there."
"No." I shook my head. "This is our home. I feel like this is my real home. I love it here. I don't want to leave."
"Then we will never leave, my love." I felt Zane's hand creep up to my breast and I pushed it away gently.
"I have something else to tell you, Zane." I grabbed both of his hands and stared into his eyes. "I think we're having a baby."
"What?" His jaw dropped open and he looked at me in shock. "How?"
"Well, one day we had sex and we didn't use a condom …" I started and giggled as he started to tickle me.
"I know how, you little …" His words drifted off as he kissed me and then he looked back up at me. "I thought you got your period."
"You can still be pregnant when you have your period. Plus remember that day in the field in Paris?"
"Oh yeah," he grinned.
"And the day at the beach."
"Oh, yeah." This time he licked his lips.

"We haven't exactly been the poster children for safe sex." I shook my head and we both made faces at each other.
"I guess that is what the puke was doing on the couch downstairs?" Zane made a face and I smacked my mouth across my face. "Oh shit, I forgot. Sorry. Let me go and wipe it up." I tried to get off the bed and he held me down. "Don't worry about it, Lucky. I'll go clean it up later." I smiled up at his caring face and felt so special to be loved by this man.
"So when will we know?" He looked serious all of a sudden. "We have to get a doctor's appointment so we can check and find out for real this time. What makes you think that …" All of a sudden his eyes popped open. "Oh shit, you've had morning sickness, haven't you?"
"I think so." I nodded my head.
"And that would explain why you have been eating so many pickles." He shook his head and laughed. "I thought you were trying to turn me on."
"What?" I laughed. "With a pickle?"
"Well, you know." He paused. "It's the way you eat it, all nibble, nibble and then gulp, gulp. It makes me think things."

"You're disgusting, you know that?" I wrapped my hand around his waist and pulled him closer to me. "But that's why I love you."
"You love me because I'm disgusting?" His hand found its way to my breast again and this time I didn't push it away.
"I love you because you look and act like this big macho guy, but you're really a big ol' softie inside."
"I am?"
"Well, maybe just a big old goof."
"I love you because you're the most beautiful woman in the world."
"I bet you say that to all the girls."
"There are no other girls. For me, there is only you."
"Unless we have a daughter," I spoke softly and he looked at me with shocked eyes.
"I never thought about that. We may have a daughter. I may be a dad."
"Are you okay with that?"
"I'll be the happiest father in the world." His words were light, but I could tell from the intensity of his eyes that he meant every word that he said. "I'd love to see a little Lucky with big curls and big brown eyes."
"I'd like to call her Ruby Lane, if we have a girl." I allowed him to run his fingers gently across my lips. "When I was young, my

mother used to read me this book about a little girl, who was the luckiest girl in the world. She had the best mother and father in the world, and she was the happiest girl in the world, and her name was Ruby Lane. I always told myself that if I had a little girl, I would call her that."

"Ruby Lane Beaumont," Zane said the words aloud. "I like that, I like it a lot."

"I love you, Zane Beaumont." I sat up and studied his face. "I'm so thankful you chose my diner to come into that day."

"It was fated, my love." He reached into his back pocket and took out a ring. "I bought this for you before we went to France. But I wanted to wait to ask you. I didn't want to ask you and have you say yes because you felt bad for me in Paris. I wanted to know that when you said yes, it was because it was something you wanted for you, and not because you felt bad for me."

"Oh, Zane, I would never do that." I stared at the large diamond as he slid the platinum band onto my finger. "I love it." I smiled shyly at him. "And yes, a million times over."

"Do you remember my song for you, my love?" He ran his hand along my cheek. "Today is our day, my love, today is our day."

"Do you remember mine? You are me, I am you, and we are one." I sang out in a reggae tone and we both laughed.
"That we are my dear, that we are." And with that Zane and I fell back into the bed and he held me close in his arms. I pressed my face against his chest and allowed myself to breathe all of him in, this man was mine. This handsome, wounded, strong and spectacular man was going to be my husband and I knew that without a doubt he would be the only one I'd have for the rest of my life.

Chapter 13
Zane

"I'll give you my watch," he handed me his watch with sticky fingers and a reluctant look on his face.
"I don't want your watch, Noah." I hit his hand away. "Just get out of my way."
"But I don't want you to go out." He pouted and his eyes bore into mine. "You said you'd stay home and hang out."
"I'm going to a sleepover," I looked at him with an annoyed expression. His whiney 10-year-old voice was irritating me and I just wanted him to leave me alone.
"I wanna come too." He pleaded.
"You can't come." I grabbed my bag and headed to the door.
"I'll give you my watch and all my coins." He looked at me as if he was going to cry. "And three Twix bars I have in my room."
"Noah, I don't want any of those things." I ran down the stairs and headed to the front door. My friend John and his mom were waiting in the driveway to take me to his house. I stopped at the front door and looked up the stairs. Noah was sitting there with a sad face, staring down at me. He looked so

alone and tiny, and in that moment, I knew I couldn't leave.
"Alright you win, I'll stay." I dropped my bag on the floor and shouted up at him. His face lit up and he came running down the stairs.
"Here's my watch Zane. It's yours now." He reluctantly held it out to me and I shook my head. I felt guilty that he was willing to give me the watch he had begged to receive for the last six months.
"Thanks, Zane. You're the best big brother ever." He hugged me close to him and I patted him on the back awkwardly.
"Don't ever forget it." I grinned at him and we both walked outside to tell John that I would no longer be attending the sleepover.

"Oh, what a beautiful morning." Lucky's singing woke me up and I saw her pulling on a pair of shorts. Her face was vibrant and happy, and she looked like she was going to workout.
"Where are you going?" I yawned, still slightly tired. The events of the last week had been exhausting and I was emotionally spent.
"I thought I'd go downstairs and cook Noah breakfast."
"Just Noah?" I pretended to pout, but I sat up and jumped out of bed eagerly. I had almost

forgotten that Noah was here and back in my life. It had all seemed like a dream—the best dream of my life, but a dream all the same.
"Don't tell me you're going to help?" She looked astonished and walked over to give me a kiss. "Good morning sleepyhead." She played with my hair and then stepped back and looked at my face.
"What's so funny?" I grumbled, grabbing her around the waist and pulling her towards me.
"I think you need the chia now." She mussed with my hair again and giggled.
"Are you telling me I look a mess?" I squeezed her ass and was about to lean down and kiss her when I heard someone clearing their throat.
"Sorry to interrupt you lovebirds, but I was wondering if one of you would let me know where the coffee is?" Noah grinned at us as he stood in the doorway and my heart thudded as I stared at my little brother. Though he wasn't so little now, he was buffer than me.
"Always preventing me from doing something, aren't you Noah?" I walked towards him and slapped him on the shoulder.
"Next time knock, yeah?"
"I didn't think I had anything to worry about." He stared at Lucky. "She's been singing for the last 30 minutes at least, and I know you

may be good in bed bro, but you're not that good."
"Noah." I chastised him and looked at Lucky. "You're in the presence of a lady."
"My bad, Lucky." He grinned at her. "You look beautiful by the way, I'm glad to see you're feeling better."
"Thank you, Noah." She walked over to join us and I stared at her legs. She looked sexy as hell, but I hadn't realized before just how short her shorts were. They seemed to be showing an awful lot of leg, more leg than I thought any other guy should be seeing, not even my own brother.
"Do you want to change, Lucky?" I looked at her pointedly and she stared at me with a blank expression.
"I have no idea what you're talking about, Zane. You just watched me get dressed." She shook her head and linked her arm through Noah's. "Now let's go and get you some breakfast." She smiled up at him as they walked to the stairs.
"So what am I then?" I called out to them. "Chopped liver? Doesn't anyone want to make sure I get some breakfast?"
"Stop being a crybaby." They both uttered at the same time and then they started laughing. I stood in my doorway, watching them walk

down the stairs arm in arm and I wondered at how lucky I was to be witnessing my brother bonding with my fiancé. It was a sight I'd never thought I would see happen. I had never planned on getting engaged. I hadn't believed in love and I certainly hadn't planned to give my heart to some lady to trample all over. But then Lucky had wormed her way in and drilled a hole so deep that even I couldn't ignore the way she made me feel. I smiled to myself at the feeling of complete and utter joy that I was experiencing. I don't think I could remember ever feeling this happy before in my life.
"Yo bro, you coming?" I heard Noah call up the stairs and I hurried down to join them before he ate all of Lucky's special home fries.

***

"You still mad?" Noah's voice was cautious as he helped me put away the dishes from the dishwasher.
"What do you think?" I shook my head and placed the last glasses in the cupboard before turning around to face him. "I thought you were dead, Noah, and you weren't. You didn't even call me." I glared at him and kept my

voice low. "The only reason I'm not shouting right now is because Lucky's upstairs in bed and not feeling well. I don't want her to see how mad I am at you, but trust me bro, I'm still really mad."

"I know you don't understand why I did what I did. And I'm sure you feel like—" he started and I held a hand up.

"You have no idea how I feel. I feel overwhelmed with happiness and love. I feel like I've been given my whole heart back. You're my best friend, Noah. All our life, it's just been you and me. I thought you respected and loved me enough to let me know what's up."

"I couldn't tell you." He looked into my eyes and I was reminded of the little boy who followed me around everywhere. "You know I would have told you man if I thought it would be okay." His eyes pleaded for my understanding.

"I don't understand why you told Sidney Johnson." The words sounded childish coming out of my mouth and I glared at him for making me sound like a jealous pansy.

"Sidney was the only person I told." Noah sighed. "I can't tell you why, but I trusted him."

"More secrets, Noah?" I shook my head. "Whatever."
"Trust me, Zane." He grabbed a hold of my arm. "Please just trust me."
"I missed you, man." I turned my face embarrassed at how my voice had broken. "You know I trust you, but I missed you."
"I missed you too, bro. Every day." He looked at me and made a face. "But I knew you'd get them, Zane. I knew it wouldn't be forever. You've always been there for me. I didn't doubt you'd come through for me this time as well."
"I was fucking going to get Braydon if it cost me my life." I croaked out a laugh. "I wasn't going to stop until his sorry ass was in jail."
"I knew you would do whatever it took. Even when we were children, you thought about me first." He looked up at me with admiration. "You were like a mom, and a dad, and a big brother to me, dude. You were always the one I went to, the one I could rely on, the one I pestered when I was bored."
"You were a pest all right."
"I knew you'd come through for me, Zane. I knew that it wasn't forever. I knew that I'd see you again."

"Just don't ever do that shit to me again." My voice was gruff and I turned away from him quickly. "This last year has been hell for me."
"But at least you got to meet Lucky." Noah's voice was soft. "If you hadn't been working the case you never would have met her."
"Yeah." I nodded and thought about everything for a moment. "I love her you know."
"She's good for you." There was a wistful look in his eyes. "You should be thanking me, man. If I hadn't gone away, you never would have met her. And right now, it would just be you and me here. You wouldn't have a beautiful girl upstairs in your bed, waiting for you."
"She's not exactly waiting for my loving, Noah, she's taking a nap." I laughed.
"Hey, she's in your bed right? If I hadn't gone away and if you didn't think I was dead, you would never have met her. In fact, you should be thanking me." Noah grinned at me.
"That's some twisted thinking, bro, but thank you." I laughed. "I'm thankful every day for meeting Lucky."
"She loves you bad, man." Noah laughed.
"I've never seen a girl so kooky over you, not even those girls in high school. What did you do to her? Drug her?"

"Very funny." I punched him in the shoulder, but I was pleased at his words. I knew that Lucky loved me, but it felt great to see that other people could tell as well. "I asked her to marry me."

"Well, I should hope so." Noah laughed.

"Oh?"

"She's the love of your life. She's gorgeous. She's kind. She's nice. She sings like an angel. You don't let a girl like that go." Noah smiled at me weakly. "When you meet a girl like that, you don't let her go."

"I won't ever let her go." I knew that I had never spoken any truer words. Lucky was my life, and as long as she was in it, I knew that everything was going to be okay. We may have gotten off to a bit of a rocky start, but I knew that I was going to be the best husband and father that I could be.

"I'm glad I'm home, bro." Noah reached his hand out to me. "I missed you like hell." I knew that was his way of apologizing to me. I knew that an awful lot must have gone on while he was away and I could tell that there were things he wasn't telling me, but I was patient. When Noah was ready to talk, I'd be here for him. No matter what. Because that was what family was really about: being patient, being loving, and being understanding.

“Me too, bro.” I gave him a hug. “You, me, and Lucky. We’re one big family now. And I’m not going to let either of you go again.”

Epilogue
Lucky

"So I guess we're going to be parents then?" I was dumbfounded as we walked out of the doctor's office.
"Looks like it." Zane's voice was nonchalant and I turned to him to make sure he wasn't overwhelmed. I looked at his face and tried to look into his eyes, but he was too busy fumbling around in his pocket.
"What are you doing?" I frowned.
"I'm getting my phone out." He grinned at me and his eyes were jumping for joy. "I'm calling Noah to tell him we're having twins."
"Zane," I shook my head and laughed at his excitement. "So, you're not mad?"
"Mad that I have super virile sperm?" He winked at me and I punched his arm. "Of course not, I'm probably more excited than a guy my age should be." He put his phone to his ear and almost shouted into the phone. "Bro, guess what? We're pregnant. We don't know the sex yet. But guess what? There were two heartbeats. We're having twins. I know, bro." Zane laughed and passed the phone to me. "Noah wants to talk to you."
"Hey Noah," I smiled into the phone, wondering what he was up to.

"Hey sis," his voice is warm. "So Zane tells me I'm about to become an uncle."
"Well, you know." I giggled. "I hope you're ready."
"I guess that means that there is no chance that we will ever be together now." He teased me and I giggled. I had only known Noah for a week, but I already loved him like a brother.
"Sorry about that." I laughed.
"You should be." He growled. "But fair is fair, Zane found you first. I guess I'll just be the bachelor uncle, babysitting every Friday night while you and Zane go out and party."
"You got it, I'm glad you'll be our on-call babysitter."
"Try and get rid of me." He laughed, but I knew that he was finding it hard being back in this world. He had hardly talked about where he had been while in the witness protection program and Zane and I were a little worried about him.
"We don't want you to leave ever." My voice was soft and earnest, I wanted him to know that he would never be an unwelcome guest in the house. I saw Zane staring down at me with tender eyes and I reached over and grabbed his hand.

"You'll make a great mom, Lucky." Noah's tone was serious. "I'm so glad you came into our lives."
"Thank you. I'm so glad I am in it as well."
"I gotta go, but I'll see you both soon." Noah's voice caught, and I hung up the phone and handed it back over to Zane as we walked to the car. "I can't believe we are having two babies, we have so much to do."
"Like getting married?" Zane raised an eyebrow at me. "I assume we're going to do that before the babies come."
"Well, yes." I laughed at the eagerness in his voice. "But that wasn't what I was talking about. I had an idea!"
"Oh?" Zane looked worried. "Please don't say you want to get all experimental in the bedroom now, I'm not sure I'm ready for that until the babies come."
"Zane." I shook my head at him in exasperation.
"Okay, okay." He laughed. "If you insist, I suppose I can show you some new moves."
"Zane, listen to me." I pulled at his shirtsleeve. "I want us to hook Noah up."
"What?" His eyes looked at me in amazement. "We just found out we're having twins and we have a wedding to plan, and now you want to hook Noah up?"

"It'll be good for him. I think he needs to get out there. I know he hasn't been back long, but I don't want him to get stuck in a rut and well, he never really talks about where he was. I think this would be good for him."
"Oh Lucky, I hope you know what you're doing." He groaned.
"I do." I leaned up and kissed him as he opened the door for me. "I just want him to be as happy as we are, because I love you, Zane."
"I love you more, Lucky."
"I love you to Timbuktu and back."
"I love you to Mars and back."
"I love you to Neptune and back."
"I love you to the sex shop and back." Zane burst out laughing at his joke and placed his hand on my belly. "In all seriousness Lucky, you've made me the happiest man alive, and if you think you can help Noah find what we have, I'm all for it."
I smiled up at him gratefully and got into the car. I had gotten my fairytale ending and I wanted to make sure that Noah got his as well.

Noah's story and Lucky's pregnancy and marriage to Zane will be continued in Noah's book titled, *The Other Side of Love*. *The*

Other Side of Love will be released in September 2013. The prequel Before Lucky will be released in July 2013 and one more book about Leo, Guarding His Heart will be released in December 2013. Join my mailing list so that you will be informed when I have new releases.

OTHER BOOKS

Are you interested in reading other books by J. S. Cooper? Then go here.

Scarred
Healed
The Last Boyfriend

Connect With J. S. Cooper

Hi, I hope you enjoyed this book. If you did, please think about leaving a review!

I love to hear from my readers so please feel free to:

Email me at jscooperauthor@gmail.com

Like me at Facebook

Join my mailing list

CPSIA information can be obtained at www.ICGtesting.com
Printed in the USA
LVOW08s0517191113

361876LV00001B/3/P